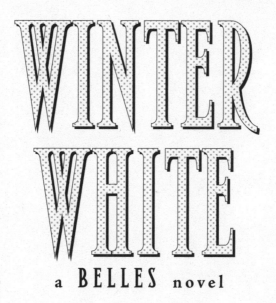

WINTER WHITE

a **BELLES** novel

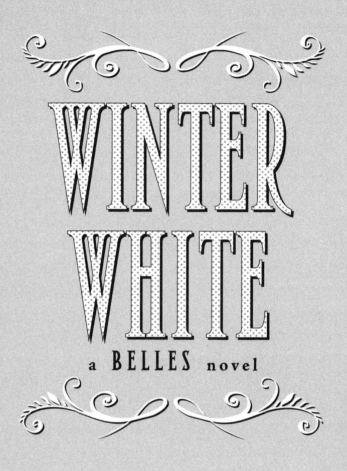

WINTER WHITE

a BELLES novel

by Jen Calonita

poppy

LITTLE, BROWN AND COMPANY
New York   Boston

Poppy

Hachette Book Group
237 Park Avenue, New York, NY 10017
Visit our website at www.lb-teens.com

Poppy is an imprint of Little, Brown and Company.
The Poppy name and logo are trademarks of Hachette Book Group, Inc.

The publisher is not responsible for websites (or their content) that are not owned by the publisher.

First Paperback Edition: October 2013
Originally published in hardcover in October 2012 by Little, Brown and Company

Library of Congress Cataloging-in-Publication Data

Calonita, Jen.
    Winter white / by Jen Calonita.—1st ed.
        p. cm.—(Belles ; 2)
    "Poppy."
    Summary: The daughters of a North Carolina senator, Isabelle and Mirabelle, who are still reeling from the knowledge that they are not cousins, but actually sisters, barely have time to process the news with cotillion season right around the corner.
    ISBN 978-0-316-09116-9 (hc) / ISBN 978-0-316-09118-3 (pb)
    [1. Balls (Parties)—Fiction.   2. Dating (Social customs)—Fiction.
3. Social classes—Fiction.   4. Preparatory schools—Fiction.   5. Schools—
Fiction.   6. Sisters—Fiction.   7. North Carolina—Fiction.]   I. Title.
    PZ7.C1364Wi 2012
    [Fic]—dc23

                                                            2012008414

10 9 8 7 6 5 4 3 2 1

RRD-C

Printed in the United States of America

For Mallory Calonita.
You may be my cousin, but I love you like a sister.

One

"How y'all doing this fine morning, North Carolina?"

Wendy Wallington's famous Southern twang ricocheted throughout the television studio, whipping her audience into a frenzy. The adulation increased as she strutted down the aisle in her signature four-inch sparkly heels and shook hands with excited viewers, like the woman wearing a *Waa-Waa Wendy* T-shirt. The nickname was one the legendary talk show host nabbed after it became apparent that she was a whiz at making her guests cry.

If there was ever a day Wendy wanted to work her tearduct mojo, it was this one. Bill Monroe, the charismatic state senator in the middle of a deliciously juicy scandal, was bringing his whole family on *The Wendy Wallington Show.* Wendy adored her old college buddy, but she couldn't help seeing the bigger green dollar-sign picture: If this episode with Bill and his family turned out to be the solid gold she thought it was, she might finally get that syndication offer she had been dreaming of for years.

Wendy turned to the camera with a sultry pout that likely nabbed her the Miss USA crown. "Let's settle down, y'all. We need all the time we can get today. My good friend North Carolina Senator Bill Monroe is here with his gorgeous family."

The cheering quickly died out, and whispers rippled through the crowd like the wave at a ball game.

Wendy adopted a serious tone. "Unless you've been living under a rock these last few weeks, then you already know this family's heart-wrenching saga," she told the cameras. "A few weeks ago, just as Senator Monroe was about to announce his run for the U.S. Senate seat up for grabs because of Senator Harmon's retirement, Bill revealed that his recently discovered niece, Isabelle, was, in fact, his daughter." More whispers. "They're here today to talk about how their family is dealing with his confession and what this revelation means for the senator's political future." Her effervescent smile returned. "And they've chosen to exclusively share their story with y'all! We are the only show you will see that has the *entire* Monroe family on to speak for themselves," she couldn't help but add. "So let's give them a huge Wendy Wallington welcome!"

As the Monroes walked onstage and took their seats on the floral couches sandwiched between Wendy's girlie armchair and the camera crew, they looked like an average family—if the average family were wealthy and gorgeous and played a major role in state politics. None of them had a hair out of place, a wrinkle in their expensive threads, or a frown on their beautiful faces. If they were worried about Wendy's notoriously prying questions, they didn't show it. Instead, the senator looked as relaxed as ever when he moved in to hug his old friend and said, "Thanks for letting us come on today."

"Honey, are you kidding?" Wendy looked at the audience in mock surprise. "Thank *you* for having the decency to come on and tell us the truth. We are dying to hear from this stunning family of yours." She looked at the Monroes' smiling faces. Bill, as usual, looked dignified and prepared to face the press. His wife, Maureen, always the proper Southern belle, was ready with a polished hairstyle and a picture-perfect dress that brought out her green eyes. It was the same twinkling shade of green she shared with her two sons, seventeen-year-old Hayden, the crush of almost every girl at his private school, and Connor, a precocious six-year-old who seemed slightly in awe of the lights, cameras, and studio audience.

But first impressions can be deceiving, can't they? If those in the audience were paying attention—instead of fishing under their chairs to peek at the show's daily giveaway—then they would have had their eyes on the Monroes' two most-talked-about members, Mirabelle Monroe and Isabelle Scott. The fifteen-year-old girls were stunning brunettes with hazel eyes so similar, some might wonder how they didn't catch on to their true relationship sooner. What Wendy picked up on that day were Mira's clenched fists and Izzie's nervous toe-tapping. A good talk show host—especially one who wanted a show that would tear up *The View* in the ratings—always noticed those kinds of things.

Wendy settled into her plush chair and leaned forward intimately. "I have known y'all forever. I was at the hospital when Mirabelle was born, for goodness' sake! So it breaks my heart for y'all to air your dirty laundry to the world."

"Thanks, Wendy," Bill said with a thin smile, running a hand through his slightly graying brown hair that people said reminded them of Patrick Dempsey's. "This has been two of the hardest weeks of my life. What we've been dealing with is so personal, and yet, living our lives in the public eye as we do, I know we owe it to the people of North Carolina to set the record straight."

"And what do you wish they knew, Bill?" Wendy asked. She looked at her studio audience. "I can call him Bill, y'all, because I knew him before he was a senator. We met when he was nothing but a fraternity boy." The audience laughed.

Bill smiled. "I want them to know the truth."

4

"I don't mean to be blunt," Wendy said, "but don't we already know the truth? You knew about your daughter Isabelle and kept it not only from the world but also from her."

"The story isn't as black and white as people make it out to be," Bill said, crossing his legs carefully so he wouldn't wrinkle his tan suit. "You're a mom, Wendy. You know how hard it is being a parent. If you learned something that would change your daughter's life, wouldn't you want to protect her till she was ready to face the truth?" He looked at Izzie. "I wanted Isabelle to have a chance to get to know me and our family before she knew her world was turning upside down again. It had already changed so much." His face creased slightly with worry, and his wife took his hand. "What I regret is how this story came to light. I feel terrible about the pain it caused Isabelle and our family, but I was trying to do what any father would—put the needs of my child first."

The audience applauded, the Monroe family smiled brightly, and Bill went on to tell the story most of them already knew from the nightly news.

Up until a few months ago, the Monroes had never heard of Isabelle Scott, and the only thing Izzie knew about them was that Bill Monroe was a state senator. Izzie was raised in the gritty neighborhood of Harborside by her grandmother after her mom died in a car crash right before Izzie's tenth birthday. Her grandmother looked for a guardian for Izzie when her health had started to go downhill last year, and a hidden diary revealed Bill to be Izzie's dad. Quicker than you can say *paternity test*, Izzie's grandmother was on the phone with the Monroes. But by the time the details were sorted out months later, Izzie's grandmother was a shell of her former self and Izzie was on the verge of entering foster care. The situation deteriorated so quickly that Izzie got only a few hours' notice about her move to her "cousins'." To hear Bill tell it, there had been no time to second-guess his decision—the right choice was to let Izzie settle into her new life first and drop the bombshell later. And boy, was it a bombshell. The only thing keeping the mess from truly becoming a full-blown scandal was the fact that Izzie wasn't born out of an affair—Bill didn't know Izzie's mom was pregnant when he was traded to the Atlanta Braves and got back together with Maureen, who was a widow with an infant son. The pair married almost immediately, and Mira was on the way soon after.

"I know you're a great father, Bill," Wendy told him, "and I think we can understand why you didn't want the world to know who Isabelle was till she was ready. But didn't you think about how Isabelle would feel when she found out the truth?" She turned her attention to Isabelle before Bill could answer. "In just a few short months, you've gone from living with your ailing grandmother in a humble home in Harborside to attending private school in privileged Emerald Cove. Then

6

you find out that your uncle is in fact your daddy." Wendy shook her head at the audience. "That is a TV movie waiting to happen, y'all." The audience murmured their agreement. "What was your first thought when you heard the news?"

"Shock?" Izzie questioned herself. She tucked a piece of her wavy, shoulder-skimming bob behind her ear. "Surprise?" She spoke slowly, trying to find her words. "They were already my family; now they were closer. For me, that was a good thing. I had so little family as it was."

"But you must have felt some sense of betrayal, no?" Wendy pried. "Did you wonder why your father would keep you from knowing the truth about yourself?"

Izzie's toe-tapping started again. "I'm not sure I could have handled hearing it all at once. Losing my grandmother, my home, moving, *and* learning my uncle was actually my dad?" She rolled her eyes. "Talk about a freak-out session waiting to happen." The audience laughed. "But I won't lie. This has definitely been an adjustment."

"What about the rest of you?" Wendy asked the other Monroe kids. "How does it feel to know your cousin is actually your sister?"

"I like her," Connor said. "Izzie plays with me, and sometimes she takes me to get ice cream when she tells Mom we're just going for a walk." Everyone laughed.

"I'm with Connor," Hayden agreed, his green eyes gazing at Wendy so piercingly that she would have swooned if he wasn't so young. "But not just because she likes ice cream. Izzie is awesome. I liked her before, so nothing's really changed."

"Hayden, you must be able to relate to Izzie the most," Wendy said. "Bill adopted you as a baby when he married your mom after your birth father, a Marine, was killed in the line of duty. Isn't that right?"

"Yes," Hayden said, shifting slightly. "I obviously don't remember my dad, but I know what it means to feel different in a family." He grinned at Izzie. "Izzie knows if she ever needs me, I'm here."

"They're all very close, Wendy," Maureen Monroe said, touching one of her heirloom pearl earrings that matched her necklace, bracelet, and even her cream pumps. "The kids were upset we kept the news from them, of course, but now we're all really coming together."

"What do you think, Mira?" Wendy asked. "Are you one big, happy family?"

"Yes," Mira said decisively, bobbing her head up and down so quickly her curls bounced. "I'm thrilled to finally have a sister."

"But you're always yelling at her when she locks you out of the bathroom and you have to get ready for school," Connor said, making the audience laugh.

Mira's hands clenched tightly, but then she relaxed. "That's different. Bathroom privileges are sacred, and Izzie doesn't seem to realize that yet." Mira shot Izzie a reproachful look.

"You take over an hour in there sometimes!" Izzie shot back playfully. "Can't I brush my teeth without you yapping to me?"

"See, Wendy? We act like sisters already," Mira said wryly.

Wendy laughed. "I have two sisters, and the fights we used to have over the bathroom weren't pretty." She shook her head and turned back to Bill. "I'm glad y'all are taking this in stride, but you can't deny that a man on the verge of a political run can't risk the sort of scandal this story has brought you." Wendy held up the *North Carolina Post*. The headline said, **Daddy's Not-So-Little Hidden Girl**, and there was a picture of Bill and Izzie from a recent charity event where the news had broken. "The timing on this couldn't be worse," Wendy said grimly. "You announced your run in the middle of this firestorm, and your Democratic primary is this May. Do you really think you can win that and move on to the race for the open seat when a story like this is out there?"

"North Carolinians are smart folk," Bill said. "They know how to differentiate between news and hearsay. I can understand why people are covering this story, but I want to remind the press that we're talking about a child who has been through so much. I've asked the press not to approach her at school. I'm a big boy, and I can take their punches, but she shouldn't have to." There was more applause. "This was a private family matter, and I don't believe it affects how I would work for the people of this great state," Bill said, looking at the audience and then at the cameras. "I let down the people I love, but my intention was never to hurt them. I wanted to cushion Izzie's blow to this new world she entered for as long as I could, and I think I did that." He smiled at her. "At least, I hope I did. And now I'm ready—we're all ready"—he took his wife's hand—"to be the family you need us to be to help represent North Carolina. If you vote for me during the primaries, you're voting for a man with heart, with resilience, and determination to do right by all."

The audience applauded again. Some stood up and cheered. All eyes were on the Monroes, including Wendy's. She'd gotten the interview she wanted, and she'd nailed it. That syndication offer was probably waiting on her desk already.

"Thank you, Bill," Wendy said, shaking each of their hands before turning back to the camera again with a winning smile. "When we come back, y'all, we'll meet Chef Allison Hyde and get her recipe for buffalo-style chicken chili!"

The camera panned out to show one last shot of the Monroes. This was their moment, and they stood together and waved to everyone in the studio. Bill was in the middle with his arms around Mira and Izzie, and then he broke free to shake hands with audience members. Anyone watching the episode was probably thinking, *What a nice story! This family weathered a perfect storm and won.* But Wendy knew better.

You can't believe everything you see on TV.

TWO

Aunt Maureen was the last one to get in the limo. When the door finally closed behind her, she removed her heavy pearl earrings, dropped them into her butter-colored leather bag, leaned her head against the seat, and sighed. "That wasn't so bad, was it?"

No one answered her.

The limo carrying the Monroes from *The Wendy Wallington Show* in Raleigh was eerily quiet, and it was making Izzie start to feel claustrophobic. She couldn't wait to get out of this car and back to the safety of Emerald Cove.

The safety of Emerald Cove.

She smiled to herself. Had she really just described EC as safe? She used to think of the wealthy community she now called home as a lion's den. But compared with being on a talk show with Wendy Wallington, EC was safe. Wendy was scary, mostly because she was live in the flesh and asked questions that made Izzie feel nauseated. Izzie couldn't wait to leave the studio. When those hot lights and all those cameras were on her, all she could think was, *What would happen if I puked on television?*

Some things had been easy to gush about, Izzie realized as she ditched the uncomfortable heels she seemed to wear for all Monroe outings and slid back into her reliable woven flip-flops. She loved her slightly fussy aunt, Connor was adorable, and she and Hayden were as tight as a pair of leggings. Even Mira and her over-the-top, high-society ways were growing to be amusing. The Monroes had given her a home when she had none, put Grams in an incredible nursing home, and given Izzie all the stuff a fifteen-year-old girl could possibly want (laptop and iPhone) and some of the stuff she didn't (a closet full of way-too-frilly dresses). But when Wendy had asked how she felt about Uncle Bill, or Bill, or Dad (exactly what was she supposed to call him now, anyway?), Izzie had no choice but to lie. Of course she hadn't forgiven the man she was suddenly supposed to call Daddy from keeping a secret this big! But she couldn't say that to Wendy. Thank God the senator's newly appointed image consultant trained her how to answer dicey questions.

Callista Foster was sitting across from Izzie in the limo, her BlackBerry and laptop never far from her fingertips. "I think you all did super!" she gushed. "Wendy lapped up everything you guys said. I told you the Q-and-A prep work would help, didn't I?" Hayden was sitting next to her, and she nudged him for an answer.

Hayden winked at Izzie. "The fake Q-and-A was a *super* idea." Aunt Maureen glared at him.

The Monroes' new PR guru, a twenty-five-year-old juggernaut who had reshaped the world's opinion of onetime pop bad girl Lyla Lowry was now on board Team Monroe. Callista was incredibly cool, except for one annoying habit. She used the word *super* way too much.

"Okay, maybe I'm selling it a bit," Callista admitted. She pushed her long reddish-blond hair behind her ears and adjusted the tortoiseshell glasses that served as a window to her sky-blue eyes. "This story is a hard sell, but the more we plug away at your side of the story, the more people will get to know the truth just like Wendy did. I just know they're going to love you as much as they did before." She gave an encouraging smile.

"Wendy was very complimentary," Aunt Maureen said. "And she went pretty easy on you, Bill, considering how upset she was when she first learned what you'd been hiding from Isabelle."

"At least she didn't run me over with a Mack truck," Bill said grimly. Izzie thought his hair got more gray with each passing article about the scandal.

"Kissing butt is a miserable job," Callista agreed. "I hate making you tell this story over and over till it sticks, but in today's media-hungry world, this is what we have to do." Callista smiled. "Now we can take a breather and let all your goodwill sink in. Even if Oprah's OWN network begs me to put you in one of their specials, I'll say no." She bit her lip. "Okay, no one says no to Oprah, but…"

Izzie might hate doing press, but she and Mira liked working with Callista. She talked to them before booking appearances, and even when they groaned about interviews, she didn't get ticked off. Instead, she took the time to listen to what was bothering them, like a friend would. Callista even gave them advice when their problems had nothing to do with press at all. She was the perfect buffer between them and Bill.

Callista's BlackBerry pinged. She glanced at the screen and frowned. "Okay, I take back the part about getting a breather." Mira, Izzie, and Hayden groaned. "This is the last thing, I promise! The *North Carolina Monthly* wants to come by tomorrow at three-thirty to take pictures of you guys playing flag football in the backyard."

Mira groaned the loudest, letting her displeasure for contact sports be known.

"Mira, don't tell me you've never tossed around a pigskin." Callista stopped herself, looking at Mira in her Elie Tahari dress and peep-toe pumps. "Okay, we'll have Hayden show you how."

Connor snorted. "One more thing," she added as she continued scrolling through her messages. She glanced at Bill, who had barely said a word since he got in the car. "I pitched the morning shows the idea of coming to your house to see you throw a barbecue for Izzie's community center. It was a long shot, which is why I never said anything, but I just got an e-mail from a producer at *Good Morning America* who might be interested."

"Seriously?" Izzie couldn't help being surprised.

Callista nodded. "Why not make you guys look good and get a plug for your community center at the same time? You said it could use some TLC, right?"

"Absolutely." She couldn't believe Callista remembered how much Harborside's community center meant to her. The thought of the center going under because of a lack of funding—which was the rumor, even after all the money she'd helped raise at Emerald Prep's recent fall festival—made Izzie sick to her stomach.

"That's a wonderful idea, Callista." Bill nodded approvingly.

"I love the idea of helping Izzie's community center, too. We'll just have to make sure there's enough time to hire caterers and a waitstaff and get more seating for the yard and…" Aunt Maureen fidgeted slightly.

"Don't panic." Callista's short pink nails flew across the BlackBerry keys. "I have people who can take care of every detail. You won't have to do a thing, Maureen."

Bill chuckled. "I'm not sure what panics my wife more: that this party could actually happen or that you're leaving her completely out of the planning."

"Want to shop for outfits for the family?" Callista suggested. She was speaking Aunt Maureen's language now. "How do you guys feel about matching shirts?"

Connor looked up from his Nintendo DS. "Cool! Can they be red like Iron Man?"

"Uh, I don't know, C. I think we would feel too matchy," said Hayden.

Bill jumped in. "Callista, if you think we need matching shirts, we'll wear matching shirts. You are Yoda till I get a new campaign manager in here to boss us all around."

Izzie knew he was joking, but his comment wasn't funny. His last campaign manager, Lucas Hale, had blackmailed her and was the reason why Bill had covered up his paternity in the first place. Just thinking about Lucas made her queasy. Wendy made her nauseated. Seeing her own picture in the paper all the time made her ill, too. Maybe what she needed right now was lunch. She was starving.

"I am not being caught dead in matching shirts," Mira declared. Izzie couldn't imagine Mira in anything other than high-end designer clothing, like the fitted beige dress she had on now. "I get enough grief at school without having videos on YouTube pop up of me looking like one of the Von Trapp kids."

"Do people even know who the Von Trapps are?" Hayden wondered aloud. "Not everyone was as annoyingly obsessed with *The Sound of Music* as you were." Hayden was the only one in the family who had regained his sense of humor after everything that had happened. He had even made peace with their dad. One golf outing together and the two were already back on good terms. Izzie couldn't imagine forgiving someone that easily. But then again, Bill hadn't lied to Hayden about being his father.

Mira's voice reached a feverish shrill when Hayden started singing "Do-Re-Mi."

"Okay, we'll forget about the matching shirts," Aunt Maureen said to keep the peace. "Is anyone up for a celebratory lunch?" Mira's mom pulled out her BlackBerry and began scrolling through restaurants in the surrounding area without waiting for a response. "That seafood place we've been dying to try, Wildfish, is right near here." Her eyes met Izzie's. "What do you say? We haven't had a decent meal out together as a family since..." She trailed off.

Since we all found out Bill lied, Izzie thought.

"Don't you guys want to start acting like a family again?" Aunt Maureen pressed. She was met with more silence. Mira appeared to be examining a chip in her nails, and Izzie stared at her shoes. "We need to stop ignoring each other when there isn't a camera around to capture every sound bite. We can't fix things unless we sit down and talk, and maybe a restaurant is just the neutral territory we need." Aunt Maureen sounded so desperate, Izzie felt bad.

"I'm with your mother," Bill agreed. "If Callista wouldn't mind, we could drop her off first." Callista nodded. His face was pensive. "There is so much I want to say—"

"I have to study for my Spanish midterm," Izzie interrupted. "I don't want my being out of school for a talk show taping to affect my grades, which are on their way up." She could feel the anger bubbling up inside her again. She might have liked being able to skip school for the day, but she was *not* sitting at a table and making small talk with Bill. It was hard enough being in the same car.

"I was great at Spanish," Bill said, his hazel eyes meeting hers. "I could help you when we get home later. *Podemos trabajar en su tarea juntos.*"

"*No, gracias. Que puedo hacer yo mismo la tarea. Estoy bien,*" Izzie said, hoping that proved she could handle studying on her own.

"Very good," Bill said softly. He turned to Mira. "Pea, what about you?"

"Please don't call me that," she said quietly, playing with her Pandora bracelet.

"Mira"—her mom sounded exasperated—"that's been your nickname since birth."

"I have a landscape scene I have to finish for my painting

class since I was out today, too." Mira's eyes met Izzie's. Maybe their dad was ready to make peace, but they weren't.

"What if we ate somewhere in EC?" Aunt Maureen suggested. "Somewhere close so you girls could—"

"No," Izzie and Mira said in unison. They both smiled slightly. They were a lot of things at the moment, but mad at each other was not one of them.

"Hayden? Connor?" Bill asked, trying not to look hurt.

"I don't have plans," Hayden told him as he tried to steal the DS from Connor.

Connor clung to his DS. "Somewhere with fries?" Their dad nodded. "I'm in!"

"Girls, are you sure you can't get away and . . ." Aunt Maureen's voice trailed off. Izzie had tuned out again, and she assumed Mira had done the same. She watched the open farmland roll by her window. The car grew quiet again. "Well, if you really can't come," Aunt Maureen said reluctantly, "we'll drop you guys off first."

Izzie breathed a sigh of relief. She wasn't in the mood for another fight or a family feeling session. Forget studying for Spanish. All she wanted to do was clear her head and hit the waves. And that's exactly what she planned on doing.

Three

"Bye! Have a super time at lunch!" Callista waved as the limo backed out of the Monroes' driveway. Mira watched the car go, her hair billowing in the light breeze and getting caught in her lip gloss. She still felt deflated. She wondered if Izzie felt as guilty as she did for bailing on the post–*Wendy "Big Mouth" Wallington Show* celebratory lunch. Her mom had looked disappointed, but Mira still couldn't force herself to break bread with her dad. Even though it had been more than two weeks since he told them the truth about Izzie, every time Mira thought about what he did, she wanted to scream. She had a sister. A *sister*. And she was standing right next to her with a pout on her face that was probably an exact duplicate of Mira's own.

Callista waved till the car disappeared from sight, then

turned to the girls with a sad smile that was partially masked by the breeze whipping her hair around. "You can breathe, ladies. They're gone. You've got at least two hours to bash your dad all you want."

"Is it that obvious?" Izzie asked, scuffing the brick driveway with her flip-flops. The heels she had been forced to wear for the taping hung from her right hand by the straps.

"A little bit," Callista admitted. "But probably only to me because I know what you guys have been through. You guys were rock stars on Wendy's show. You made my job much easier, but I'm sure it wasn't much fun for either of you."

Mira bit her lip. "Do you think the audience could tell?"

Callista shook her head. "No. Just me. I know your quirks already." She pointed to Mira. "You make a fist every time someone asks you something that makes you nervous, and Izzie taps her feet like drumsticks." Callista studied them curiously. "Things aren't getting any better with your dad?"

Izzie and Mira shook their heads.

"I know he's trying, but I don't forgive him," Mira said.

"Don't look at me," Izzie said. "I get angry just being in the same room as him."

"Me, too," Mira agreed, happy to have an ally. She and Izzie were so in sync lately, it was scary. This fight with their dad might be rough, but it had brought her and Izzie closer. "Last night at dinner, he said, 'Mira, pass the peas?' and I wanted to throw the whole bowl at him." She bit her lip. "That's wrong, isn't it?"

21

Izzie laughed. "It could have been worse. You didn't actually pelt him with peas." She grinned mischievously. "I, on the other hand, think I spent half of dinner dreaming about dumping the bowl of mashed potatoes on his head!"

"I probably wouldn't forgive my dad yet, either," Callista agreed. "I think it's practically law in the teen handbook to fight with your parents. I know I did. Just don't do it in public," she added as an afterthought. Callista reached into an oversize Gucci bag and fumbled for her keys. "Now, do you guys really have places to be and tests to cram for, or can I take you somewhere for lunch that your family will never find you? You have the day off from school! You should do something fun."

Mira smiled to herself. This was why she liked Callista so much. The public-image guru might work for her dad, but she seemed to know exactly how it felt to be a frustrated fifteen-year-old girl. Every interview or press request she gave to the girls came with an apology ("Diane Sawyer doesn't deserve to know what you think about half siblings, but it would help your family a ton if you answered the question anyway."). When they finished an event, Callista let them complain ("Maria Menounos really asked you that? How tacky. I'm going to give her a piece of my mind."). Callista acted like their big sister. Their dad had done one thing right by hiring her.

Izzie looked up from texting. "While I could use something other than the celery sticks Wendy had in her green-room, I have to pass. Brayden has off last period, so he is skipping out early and meeting me to surf."

"In this weather?" Mira asked. The breeze sent leaves tumbling down the driveway almost like they were trying to say they agreed with her. Callista's cell rang loudly to put in its two cents, too. Callista stepped away to take the call.

"It's not *that* cold," Izzie said. She headed for the front door to go get her wet suit and board. Once Izzie had her mind set on something, there was no talking her out of it.

At Emerald Prep, everyone thought Izzie and Brayden were doomed, and they weren't even officially going out yet. No one took Savannah Ingram's boyfriend and lived to tell the tale. But Mira couldn't help being impressed with Izzie anyway. She always seemed to know what she wanted, and she went after it with gusto. Maybe it was time she tried that. She couldn't stop thinking about Kellen Harper. He had been kind of weird at the fall dance, but Mira still thought— okay, hoped—he might be into her. Maybe it was time she found out for sure. She got out her phone and texted him.

MIRA'S CELL: Hey, do I smell french fries?

Kellen always had food on his mind, so she wasn't surprised when he texted her back.

KELLEN'S CELL: Smothered w/cheese & bacon? I'm there.

MIRA'S CELL: Corky's. Meet you there in a bit?

KELLEN'S CELL: Yep! Need time to digest first. Just had lunch.

MIRA'S CELL: LOL. Deal!

Callista ended her call and walked back over to Mira, who was now grinning from ear to ear. "What about you?" Callista asked. "I know you're not putting on a wet suit."

"I've never worn a wet suit, and I don't intend to start now," Mira said. "They're too clingy. They show everything." She shivered at the thought.

"I agree," Callista said. "So, want to drown your daddy sorrows in a milk shake at Corky's? I keep hearing how good that place is, but I feel too lame to go alone."

Were publicists also psychic? "I'm actually meeting someone there a little later," Mira said sheepishly. She wanted to add, "You can join us," but hanging with both Kellen and Callista seemed strange. "Corky's is great, though. Want to go tomorrow instead?"

"Nah. This is the universe's way of telling me I don't need a milk shake," Callista told her. Mira doubted that. Callista was probably a size two. She'd said she had a scary-fast metabolism, and her pants were always falling down on her. "Are you sure you don't want to talk about anything that happened at the taping?" she asked one last time. "I felt bad when Connor caught you off guard with that bathroom comment."

24

Mira winced. Why did Connor have to call out her bathroom habits? He was six, but still. "That's not your fault. You can't know everything Wendy was going to ask me."

Callista laughed. "I should. That's my job! You bounced back quickly, though."

When Wendy "Big Mouth" Wallington—her dad's supposed good friend from college—had asked Mira whether they were one big, happy family, Mira had smiled, of course. She had been raised to be a proper Southern belle, and that's how she always behaved. She had grown up in front of cameras, thanks to her dad's professional ball-playing and political careers, but that morning she wished she could have thrown some punches. Not just at Wendy for her invasive questions, but at her darling dad, the one she had always held up on a pedestal. Maybe she and Izzie wouldn't have had such friction if they had known the truth. They were still polar opposites—if their two hometowns were jewels, Emerald Cove would be emeralds, of course, and Izzie's Harborside would be the plastic stuff you got in Piggly Wiggly vending machines—but they were trying to get along now. They had been through too much not to.

Callista unlocked her Prius, which was sitting at the curb. "Want a ride to Corky's?"

"Oh, I'm not going to Corky's yet," Mira said with a grin. "First I'm going to de-stress."

"How do you plan on doing that?" Callista asked.

"By doing what I always do when I'm stressed. Shop."

Four

Two and a half hours later, Izzie and Brayden collapsed in a booth at Scoops, their favorite Harborside Pier haunt. Between the frigid water and the chill in the air, they were still trying to catch their breath.

"Let's promise each other right now," said Brayden, holding out his pinkie. Izzie hooked her finger with his. "We will *not* go back in the water till May."

Izzie pouted, her lips still blue. Being able to go from her front door to the ocean in less than ten minutes flat used to be her favorite thing about living in Harborside. Now that she lived in Emerald Cove, she had to make actual plans to go to the beach. She hated the idea of not getting back in the ocean till May, but she kept her finger linked with Brayden's anyway. She liked when their hands touched.

Brayden kept his blue-green eyes on her, almost as if he knew she still needed persuading. "Iz, today it was only sixty degrees! That means the water temperature was only..."

"I know, I know." Izzie tried to run her free hand through her sticky hair. The *Wendy* show hairstylist had put so much lacquer in her normally product-free tresses that her locks were practically one big knot now that they'd been tangled up by the waves. "You think it's too cold to swim, even with a wet suit on." She didn't want to admit it, but she knew he was right. When they dove in today, her body practically screamed in protest at the icy intrusion.

"*I* think?" Brayden repeated. "Everyone thinks so!"

"Everyone?" Izzie gave him a skeptical look. "No one else was out there."

"Exactly!" Brayden said. "Other people are smart! They don't go in the freezing cold water just because the girl they like wants to and they don't want to seem like a jerk for saying no." She bit her lip and blushed. "The only fools in the water today were us and the pelicans, and they thought we were crazy, too." Izzie tried not to laugh. "Oh yeah, I totally speak pelican," he said seriously. "It is one of my hidden talents."

Brayden looked so cute, it was hard for her to keep a straight face. His light brown hair was still wet from the frothy surf, and he had changed out of his wet suit in the back room of Scoops and into jeans, a long-sleeve T, and his rope

27

necklace with the pirate medallion. This is how she liked seeing Brayden, not in his stuffy private school uniform. Here, he was relaxed, funny, and all hers, without the drama of Emerald Cove breathing down their necks.

Brayden was still ranting. "If we had seen any dolphins, I'm sure they would have thought we were deranged as well. Even the penguins..."

Izzie started to laugh and squeezed his finger tighter. "I get it! You're the animal whisperer! Every sea creature and bird you've encountered agrees that it is too cold for us to be in the water, and they're right. I admit defeat." Satisfied, Brayden unhooked their fingers.

Izzie tried not to appear disappointed when he let go. She glanced around the nearly deserted ice-cream shop. The pier was still officially open for another few weeks, but most of the seasonal T-shirt, arcade, boardwalk fries, and custard stands would close that weekend. After the annual Halloween parade, no one really visited the wind-whipped boardwalk unless they were skateboarding or taking a shortcut to the community center.

"I'm going to miss being here," Izzie admitted. "If we're not surfing, I really have no excuse to come around as much as I do." Her aunt and Bill didn't even know she was in Harborside at the moment. She was supposed to be home studying.

"That's not true," Brayden disagreed. "You've still got to

single-handedly save the community center and mentor the younger kids on your old swim team, and you can't do either of those things from a remote location. You tell the Monroes I said that if they give you a hard time." He winked.

Sometimes Izzie still couldn't believe one of the most popular guys at Emerald Prep was into her. She wanted to be with him, but things were complicated, and that complication had a name: Savannah, Brayden's utterly awful former girlfriend.

"Here comes one more reason you can't ditch Harborside this winter," Brayden added, gesturing to the girl walking toward them. "This pain in the neck right here."

Izzie's best friend, Kylie, grinned mischievously. "Hello, lovebirds."

No matter how many times Izzie begged Kylie not to tease her about Brayden, she wouldn't listen. Kylie followed her own rules, which was pretty much how most of her friends in Harborside were.

Kylie wiped her hands on her ice-cream-covered apron. "What are you two talking about? How much you love me?"

"Yes," Brayden said solemnly. "That's all I talk about all day long. Kylie, Kylie, Kylie." Izzie tried not to laugh.

Kylie gave a satisfied smile. "That's what I like to hear, surfer boy. So, what are you two having today? I won't even make you go up to the counter to order." Her smile turned to a scowl. "And don't say nothing, because you owe me for

29

letting you change here. Andy would have my head if he knew I let you in the back even if it is the last week of the season." She pushed her long blond hair away from her paling face. None of them had summer tans anymore. It was sort of depressing.

"Relax," Izzie told Kylie. "We're starved."

"Good," Kylie said. "I don't want you to turn into one of those toothpick prisses from Emerald Cove who come in here and order a cup of sprinkles, hold the ice cream."

"Not in a million years," Izzie promised. "In fact, today I was thinking of a three-scooper with mint chocolate chip, caramel, and Reese's Pieces." She gave her a look. "Non-toothpick-priss enough?" Kylie nodded.

"Make that two," Brayden told Kylie. "But make mine five scoops."

"I knew I liked you, Prep School," Kylie said. She went back to the ice-cream counter and turned up the rock radio station full blast. No customers meant she could pretty much run the shop however she liked. That was the freedom that came with being a kid in Harborside. Most times, you were pretty much on your own. For some reason, Izzie thought of her own family. Or what was left of it.

"What's wrong? Mad I outscooped you?" Brayden teased. When Izzie didn't answer him, he tried again. "Are you thinking about Grams again?"

"I really miss her," Izzie admitted. "I know she's better off at the nursing home, and I'm better off in EC." She hesitated. "Living with the Monroes makes sense. He is my…" She stopped and looked down at her lap. "Sorry, I still can't say the *D* word."

"Yeah, I wouldn't be able to say that yet, either." Brayden tapped his fingers lightly on the table. If he moved them slightly to the left, his hands would be on hers. "He screwed up big-time. He seems to feel bad about it, though." He raised his eyebrows. "At least when he's talking to Waa-Waa Wendy."

"I think he does feel bad," Izzie admitted, then sighed. "But it doesn't make it okay. I don't know." She drummed her fingers, too. "It's like when I walk by the potpourri Aunt Maureen has in bowls all over the house. One minute I like the scent, the next I get a whiff of something in there and I feel sick." She shrugged, trying not to move her arms so their fingers would still be grazing. "I can't get over being lied to."

"Order up!" Kylie slid their sundaes across the table, and Brayden caught them.

He didn't waste any time before scooping up a chunk of ice cream drizzled in caramel sauce. "No matter how bad things are right now, you can still tell that the Monroes care about you." His face clouded over. "You're lucky. Your family is not just about appearances."

"I'm sure your family is the same way," Izzie said, because it sounded like the right thing to say. She had a feeling the

31

Townsends weren't as warm and fuzzy as the Monroes. From the way Brayden talked about his mom's society commitments and his dad having a Bluetooth glued to his ear twenty-four-seven, she didn't get a parental vibe.

"My family is...calculated," Brayden said carefully. "Sometimes I feel like I have a part to play, and if I screw up..." He jammed his spoon into his sundae and pushed it away as if the very mention of his family was enough to ruin his appetite. "But I don't want to talk about them." He looked at her. "I want to talk about us, Iz."

At the word *us*, Izzie's spoon stopped midway to her mouth, and a drop of mint chocolate chip plopped onto her shirt. She quickly wiped it away with a napkin. Why did everything in life have to be so messy? She put down her spoon and placed her hands nervously on the table so she could focus on what he was saying. Brayden placed his hands right on top of hers, and she felt a tingle go right through her.

"There never seems to be a good time to talk at school, and you've had so much going on, but I want you to know I can't stop thinking about you."

"Really?" Izzie smiled. Brayden *did* want to be with her. She felt so full—even with half a sundae still in front of her—that she wanted to burst. But as soon as Brayden took her hands in his, Savannah's face flashed in her mind. What if Savannah walked in right now? What if anyone from EP walked in right now? "But..."

"No buts," Brayden insisted, reading her mind again. "Savannah and I are over. I want to be with you, and I don't care if it's weird for anyone else or whose parents know," he added strangely. "I want us to be together."

The words hung in the air as they looked at each other and grinned. Then Brayden's phone rang, and he frowned. "It's my mom. I didn't tell her where I was going."

"Go ahead," Izzie said, and squeezed his hands.

He winked at her. "Don't go anywhere, okay?" He looked over at Kylie. "Hey, can I take this in the back?"

Kylie nodded. As soon as Brayden was out of view, she scooted over to the table. "Did I just see you two holding hands? Does this mean you're finally going to date him for real?" She stopped jabbering only when the little bell on the door signaled a customer. When Kylie saw who it was, she lost her focus.

"What are you doing here?" Kylie asked, rushing toward a tall, pretty girl Izzie vaguely recognized. She knew she had met her once or twice when she had come to visit Kylie, but it had been right after she moved to EC and, needless to say, she had been a little distracted. She couldn't even remember the girl's name. All she could remember was liking the girl's kicks. She wore the same black Chuck Taylors as Izzie's, but this girl had covered all the white spaces on hers with ballpoint-pen doodles and quotes.

"I came to see you, obviously!" said the girl, hugging

Kylie. "Your brother said you were on, and I'm craving the Marshmallow Devil's Food Cake Delight. The model wannabees at my school do not eat." She pulled her blond hair away from her face, and Kylie squealed again. Izzie saw a small tattoo right where her hairline ended at her neck. It was a red-and-black star surrounded by waves.

"I can't believe you got it! I'm so jealous," Kylie said, sounding bummed. "My mom won't let me get a third tattoo until I'm sixteen."

"That's the nautical star, isn't it?" Izzie asked.

"Yeah," said the girl, sounding impressed. She stared at Izzie with blue-green eyes that seemed very familiar. "How'd you know that?"

Izzie shrugged. "I've always liked that symbol." If she ever got a tattoo, the nautical star was the one she would want. It stood for the ocean, something she loved, but it also meant something bigger—finding your way in life, which was something she was constantly trying to do. Izzie stared at the tattoo wistfully. It looked so cool. She quickly made herself play the game she usually did when she got an itch for a tattoo: She asked herself how the tattoo would look when she was eighty. It did the trick.

"It also stands for good luck," said the girl, holding her long hair back so both girls could look. "And if you met my family, you'd know I need all the luck I can get."

"Dylan?" Brayden had walked back in without anyone noticing.

When the girl saw Brayden, she ran over and hugged him.

Kylie and Izzie stared at each other in confusion.

"What are you doing here?" she asked. "Don't tell me. I told you you would like Harborside if you gave it a shot. It's nice to get out of EC and take a breather, isn't it? That place is such a lion's den."

Lion's den. That's exactly *what I've called EC*, Izzie thought.

"How do you two know each other?" Kylie asked.

"She's my sister," Brayden said, staring at Dylan as if he were seeing a ghost.

His sister. That was a relief. Izzie had assumed Dylan was an extremely stunning ex-girlfriend. With her height, almost olive skin, and long blond hair, she easily could have been EP's homecoming queen, or Miss North Carolina, but Izzie didn't have to look hard to see that she fought hard against that stereotype. Her outfit (black shirt, jacket, and skinny jeans), her graffitied sneakers, and everything from her nautical star tattoo to the way she described EC told Izzie that Dylan Townsend bucked the Emerald Cove class system. Izzie already liked her.

"How do you two know each other?" Brayden asked Kylie and Dylan.

"Dylan hung out with my brother and his friends all

summer," Kylie explained. "Which meant she basically watched him sleep for a while and then we would go hang." They both laughed, and Izzie felt a little left out. It was all coming back to her now. Kylie had mentioned hanging out with Dylan several times, but with taking care of Grams all summer and then having a new school and an army of mean girls to contend with, she hadn't paid much attention. What else had she missed?

Dylan turned back to Brayden. "So, rebel, what finally brings you to Harborside?" He didn't answer her, and she grabbed a lock of his hair. "Wait, why are you wet? Don't tell me you are surfing. Oh my God, they're going to kill you!" She laughed, and he colored slightly. "No wonder you come down here where no one knows you. Wait"—she turned to Izzie—"are you a Harborside townie, too?"

"She was," Kylie said. "This is my best friend, Izzie. I told you about her. She's the one who fell into the champagne-and-caviar lifestyle. She's the senator's daughter."

Dylan slapped her own face, and Izzie noticed the evil eye pendant ring. She was wearing the same one. She and Mira had bought them together a few weeks ago. "You're Isabelle Scott! How did I not know that? I read about you in *People*."

Izzie unconsciously started tapping her foot. *Here it comes*, she thought. *The classic Emerald-Cove-princess-bashes-the-Harborside-townie exchange.* "That's me. Live in the flesh." *Let me hear it.*

Instead, Dylan pulled her into a hug. "Get over here. I want to thank the girl who saved my brother from that she-wolf, Savannah Ingram. It's about time somebody did!"

Izzie was so taken aback, she didn't know what to say.

"I cannot stand her or her social-climbing minions," Dylan said, releasing Izzie and taking a seat at their booth. "Is this yours?" She asked Brayden, pointing to the half-eaten sundae and then digging in before he could stop her. "I hated growing up in EC," she said between bites. "Every girl I went to school with thought a black Amex equaled power. They do all these fund-raisers and charity events, but do you think any of them even stop for two seconds to think about who they're raising money for? No, they just care about writing an oversize check and getting their pictures in the town paper."

Izzie was flabbergasted. She had said basically the same thing to Kylie on more than one occasion. She felt disgusted every time she sat in on a Social Butterflies meeting at school and heard the other girls talk about charities as if they existed just to look good on their college applications. Izzie may have joined the club reluctantly, but she actually believed in its mission. She was constantly thinking of new ways they could raise money. She just hadn't raised her hand and brought any of them up yet.

"I can't wait till those girls leave EC and see how little people care about their summer homes and two-thousand-dollar bags in the real world," Izzie chimed in, then blushed.

She was talking about Brayden's hometown, and he was standing right there. Maybe that was taking things a bit too far.

"Finally, someone who speaks my language," said Dylan appreciatively. "Glad to see EC hasn't suffocated you yet." She pushed her hair behind her ear. Izzie noticed that Dylan had several earrings, and instinctively reached for her own multipierced ear. "Being shipped off to boarding school my final year of high school turned out to be a good thing. I couldn't wait to get out of town, but some of those girls will never leave EC. They're lifers. Like my mother." She stared at Izzie curiously and smiled. "I like you."

"Iz, you've got to come back to Harborside more and hang with us," Kylie insisted. "Dylan is a riot. She's the one who streaked on the boardwalk on a dare so we didn't have to pay for dinner at the diner. I told you about that, right?"

"Sounds like my sister," Brayden said, but it didn't sound like a compliment.

The story was hazy, but there was no denying the cool factor attached to a girl who could pull off something like that. Dylan Townsend seemed to be as unaffected by her EC upbringing as a girl could get. Izzie was about to say something to Brayden about how cool his sister was when she noticed that he was squirming.

"So what are you back to pull off this time, Dylan?" Brayden asked quietly.

"Nothing really. Just here to give Mom and Dad a slight heart attack." Dylan stretched her legs out in front of her. "I just came from the house. God, B, I wish you could have seen their faces when I told them I dropped out of college."

"You dropped out of Vanderbilt?" Brayden's jaw dropped. "You've only been there for two months!"'

"I don't know what I was thinking going there," she said to Izzie and Kylie. "It's *so* stuffy, and the girls are all buttoned-up, headband-loving beauty queens in training."

"Who would want to deal with that every day?" Kylie agreed.

Dylan rubbed her temples just thinking about the travesty. "I'm transferring to the University of South Carolina next semester. I was originally wait-listed, but a spot opened up, so I'm in come January. My friend Lila goes there, and that place is a lot more fun." She squeezed Brayden tightly. "Till then, I'm all yours."

"For two months?" Brayden reminded her. "You'll never survive."

"Of course I will. I've been craving home," Dylan told him. "I haven't been home for more than a weekend since boarding school."

Brayden didn't look convinced. "What are you not telling me?"

Dylan glanced at Izzie. "Is he always this paranoid? I swear, sometime in the last two years, we switched roles. When did you become the older sibling?"

"When you left me to fend for myself with Mom and Dad," Brayden said pointedly, and Dylan stopped laughing. Izzie could sense some tension, but she pretended to stare at her nails. It was a Mira technique that always seemed to work.

"I should probably get going," Dylan said, and for some reason, that disappointed Izzie. She liked this girl, and the truth was, she hadn't liked a lot of people from Emerald Cove she'd met so far. She watched as Dylan threw a twenty down on the table. "This should cover their sundaes."

"Nice tip," Kylie said appraisingly. "Will I see you this weekend?"

"Absolutely," Dylan told her, and looked at Izzie. "You should join us, Izzie. We can hang out and compare EC notes."

Brayden's face was strained, but Izzie was too busy staring at Dylan to notice. Trading EC war stories with Dylan sounded like a better way to spend an afternoon than shopping for yet another dress with Aunt Maureen. "I'm in."

"Great." Dylan slung her bag over her shoulder. "Want to hang tomorrow, too?"

"I have school," Izzie said.

"So?" Dylan winked and headed for the door. "As far as I know, missing fourth period never killed anybody."

Five

100% CASHMERE. Mira stared at the sweater tag in her hand and smiled. Just the words *100% cashmere* were enough to put her in a good mood.

The pale pink sweater with a ballet-scoop neckline was so soft that she could have slept on it. Prepsters, Emerald Cove's popular high-end clothing boutique (so named for girls like her who went to Emerald Prep and could afford three-hundred-dollar riding boots) must have just gotten a shipment because the cashmere sweater was available in every size and color. The only decision Mira had to make now was pink or taupe. She was going to try on both along with a pair of those new jeans she saw on the table at the front of the store. While she was here, she might as well look for some casual dresses, too, to wear to a few of her dad's fund-raisers she was dreading. There was so much to choose from at Prepsters, she wished she could stay all day.

Shopping really was retail therapy. Maybe that was why Mira had been doing so much of it in the last few weeks. When her dad apologized to the family for the first time, Mira ran out afterward and bought expensive white flip-flops with interchangeable bands. When her mom cried over a blog that said she was crazy for standing by her dad, Mira bought luxurious lavender 900-thread-count sheets for her bed. And when Savannah, her friends, and pretty much the whole tenth grade blacklisted her, Mira bought her and Izzie matching sterling-silver evil eye rings so she would have something to look at in class when her former friends were talking about her.

Today's TV interview with Waa-Waa Wendy had shot Mira's nerves so badly that she headed to Prepsters in search of new sweaters. It was getting colder—well, cold for North Carolina—and she needed something to warm her up, especially now that she was single and didn't have a boyfriend's arms to wrap around her.

Not that she was that upset about the boyfriend part. Taylor Covington, EP's own version of the Ken doll, had been nice to look at, but he wasn't really boyfriend material. Mira knew she was better off without him; she just wished she had a few more shoulders to cry on. But Savannah had taken those away, too. Losing friends had definitely turned out to be worse than losing a boyfriend.

Mira piled a few pairs of jeans on top of the cashmere sweaters she was carrying and headed to the fitting room. She made it only a few feet when she spotted a wine-colored sweater dress with a turtleneck collar that would look adorable with her new riding boots. She stopped to check it out, and that's when she heard talking.

"Sarah Collins, daughter of Myra and Peter Collins, was escorted by Todd Selzner, at the White Ball in Birmingham, Alabama...."

Hearing the voice made Mira freeze with her hand on the dress tag.

"Miss Collins is a proud cotillion participant who hopes to someday study special education at her mother's alma mater, Ole Miss."

"What does she look like? Stop hogging the magazine, Lea!"

"Would you two stop? Give it to me. I paid for it. Which one is she? Oh, *her*. Talk about bad lighting. She looks like she should play a vamp on *The Vampire Diaries*." The others laughed. "What a waste of a gorgeous gown. See what I mean, girls? My mother is right. One bad photographer can ruin your whole cotillion."

Cotillion! How could Mira have forgotten about her favorite tradition in Emerald Cove? Making her formal debut into society was something she had dreamed about since she was in pre-K. She'd spent the last three years preparing for the sophomore girl tradition—taking etiquette classes, going to Saturday morning dance lessons, and doing approved Junior League charity work—and somehow she had let all this drama with her dad make her completely forget the most important event of the year!

"It says here Sarah Collins made her debut with forty-five girls. That's not a debut; that's a cattle call. Maybe that explains why half these girls look like cows." The girls' laughter increased, and so did the snorting.

Mira prayed they couldn't see her behind the rack of sweater dresses. When she peeked through the rack, she saw exactly what she'd suspected. Savannah, her former best friend, and her two—make that three—sidekicks, Lea Price, Lauren Salbrook, and their protégé, Millie Lennon, were huddled around the latest issue of *Town & Country*, reading the magazine's debutante announcements. It's something Mira had done with Savannah many times before. She used to love picking up the latest issue, getting iced coffee, going for pedicures, and then ripping apart each girl's announcement sentence by sentence. It wasn't till Izzie showed up that Mira realized words, however nicely said, could still cut so deep that they made people bleed.

"Miss, can I help you find something?"

Mira looked up. *Dang.* A saleswoman had spotted her. She could only imagine how this looked. She was crouched down, her right hand clutching a dress like a towel and her left arm holding the cashmere sweaters and now-crumpled jeans. The saleswoman did not look pleased.

Mira shook her head, hoping that would be enough to send the woman away. If she opened her mouth, Savannah might realize she was there.

"Should I put that dress in a fitting room for you?" The woman attempted to pry the wrinkled dress from Mira's hands, but she wouldn't let go. "Or wrap it up?"

That would work. "Yes," Mira whispered, and reached into her bag for her credit card. "Wrap it. Please. Quickly. I, uh, have a doctor's appointment to get to."

The woman glanced at the name on the credit card, and her expression changed. "Are you Senator Monroe's daughter?" she asked, her voice going up an octave. "You look just like your father!"

This was Mira's cue to get out of there. She left the dress on the counter and snatched her credit card back before the saleswoman had the chance to react. "I'll come back for this later," she said, and headed for the exit. She'd made it to the accessories table when Savannah and the other girls stepped into the aisle and blocked her path. They looked like the fashion mafia in their color-coordinated designer outfits.

"Hi, Mira," Savannah said pleasantly, looking like she had just come from a modeling shoot. Her long pale blond hair was as glossy as ever, held back in a plaid headband, and she had on the same fitted navy sweater as the mannequin

45

behind her that always modeled Prepsters' latest must-have outfit. Savannah gave Mira a brief once-over. "What are you doing here?" she asked with a thick drawl. "I hear you were on TV. *The Wendy Wallington Show* is so"—she hesitated, trying to find the right word to make Mira flinch—"quaint. I don't think anyone outside the state even sees that show."

"Probably not." Mira glanced helplessly at the door feet away.

Savannah smiled. "I haven't seen the show because I was at school, but my mom said you managed okay."

Savannah was like a python. Mira had learned to watch her closely because she was never quite sure when she would strike. Even her compliments were venomous. Mira ignored the comment and looked at the others. "Hi, guys." The girls responded by glancing at their shoes or the items on the accessories table. Millie seemed particularly interested in a thick headband that was clearly last season.

"You're not here alone, are you?" Savannah's eyes widened innocently. She knew the answer without Mira even saying it. Who would Mira hang out with? Savannah had claimed all their mutual friends after their nasty friendship breakup, and she'd probably destroy any girl stupid enough to befriend Mira now.

"I was just leaving," Mira said.

Savannah and the others didn't move out of her way. "I never understood how anyone could go clothes shopping alone," Savannah said, leaning on Lea. "I could not make a single decision on dresses for cotillion events without backup. You *are* still going to do cotillion, aren't you?"

"Of course," Mira said, feeling drained. "Why wouldn't I?"

"Oh, I…never mind." Savannah broke into another one of her patented plastic smiles. "I'm glad you're still going. We'll see you at cotillion rush events, then."

"When does that start?" Lea asked, her voice anxious.

"I don't know for *sure*," Savannah stressed as if she had a clue. She always acted in the know even when she wasn't. "I heard Mary Beth Pearson might be running it."

"Your cousin?" Lauren asked. "Lucky you! She'll give you the easiest tasks."

Cotillion pledging. Rush. Debutante initiation. Whatever you wanted to call it, Mira had forgotten about this secret tradition, too. While the Junior League didn't approve of it, or even acknowledge its existence, over the years it had become customary for former debs to put the current cotillion class through a series of sometimes funny, sometimes mortifying games to prove their worthiness like they were a college sorority pledge class. No one knew who ran the rush till the games ended, but participating was pretty much mandatory. Those who didn't do it were socially blacklisted for the rest of the year, and no one at Emerald Prep wanted that.

"You guys have nothing to worry about." Savannah pushed her bangs out of her eyes. "If it's Mary Beth, and I bet it is, she'll take care of you guys." She glanced at Mira. "She knows who my friends are."

If Mira needed proof that she was no longer in Savannah's inner circle, that was it. Savannah made her feel worse about herself. Weren't friends supposed to do the opposite? The school's reigning queen was never going to forgive her. Mira had chosen Izzie over Savannah, and Izzie had won Brayden, which left Savannah out in the cold. And she did not do the deep freeze well. She liked to cause hell rather than be in it.

"But enough about cotillion," Savannah said, stepping closer to Mira with an expression of deep concern. "How are *you* doing? I would be mortified if I had to go on TV and talk about my dad having a kid he never told us about. Not that my dad would ever do such a thing," she added just as quickly. Lauren tried to hold in a snicker.

"I'm fine." Mira tried not to sound testy. She was glad she had changed out of the outfit she wore on Wendy's show and into her fitted green tunic and capri leggings. She felt like her go-to outfit gave her superstrength, which she needed right then.

"Are you sure?" Savannah frowned, and the wrinkles that formed around her mouth almost screamed in protest. "You look pale, and you have bags under your eyes, but that's nothing that a little under-eye cream can't fix." Savannah rooted around in her enormous designer bag and pulled out an equally expensive eye cream. "This is my mom's. She has horrible bags, too, so this should help." Lea smirked, while Millie looked mildly mortified. She was new to Savannah's group, so she was still learning how cutting Savannah could be.

Mira noticed the saleswoman watching the girls' exchange with interest. The pile of clothes Mira had left were still in the woman's arms. Mira took the clothes from her. "I changed my mind," she said, and dumped the sweaters, jeans, and dress on the counter. "I'm going to take everything." She deserved some new clothes for putting up with Savannah. "I am in a rush, though, so if you could ring me up, that would be great."

"Where are you off to? Another tabloid interview?" Lauren asked with an evil glint in her eye.

"God, no." Mira tried to smile. "*Teen Vogue* called this morning and offered Izzie and me a fashion layout in the magazine." Savannah's eyes widened, so she kept going. "They want to know the real story, not the silly rumors people are spreading."

"*Teen Vogue?*" Savannah repeated slowly, almost tripping over her own words.

Mira nodded. Was it her imagination or did Savannah look jealous? "I am meeting our publicist to discuss whether we're going to take it." She looked at Lea's surprised expression and laughed to herself. "I mean, who knew *Justine* and *Teen Vogue* would be fighting over us? We might do *People*, too." She made a mental note to call Callista later and persuade her to get them in a magazine. Any magazine!

"Wow, you do sound busy," Savannah said, pushing the cheer back into her voice. "So busy that you probably don't even miss having a boyfriend like Taylor. Did you hear Taylor officially asked Millie out?"

"He gave me this." Millie thrust her arm at Mira, showing off a thin silver bracelet with a dangling starfish. Taylor had given her one just like it when they started dating. "Savannah helped him pick it out." Savannah's smug smile returned.

Mira had to hand it to Savannah. She knew how to twist the knife. For a moment, Mira thought the boyfriend talk and the bracelet would make her crumble. Instead, she quickly recovered. "Cute, Millie! I'm surprised Savannah helped him pick that one, though." She frowned. "The one Taylor got me tarnished quickly." Millie paled, making Mira feel slightly bad, but she couldn't back down now.

The saleswoman handed Mira the credit-card slip, and Mira turned away from the girls to sign. "Speaking of jewelry, I've been meaning to buy myself something nice to wear for all these magazine interviews. I just have to find the time. My publicist said *Teen Vogue* needs days for an interview and photo shoot. They even want me to paint a picture for them to put in the story. Can you believe it?"

"No, I can't," Savannah said without thinking. When Mira turned around again, she noticed Savannah's posture was stiff as a board.

Mira collected her bags and walked past her. "See you at school!"

Savannah looked jealous! Mira thought with glee as she hurried down Main Street toward Corky's before Savannah could retaliate. She couldn't stop replaying their conversation in her head. The look on Savannah's face when she mentioned *Teen Vogue*, Millie's reaction to what she said about Taylor's bracelet...those moments were priceless! Her friends had made her feel as worthless as a cockroach the past few weeks, but now she felt like she could take on the world. *Who needs those girls, anyway?*

You do, a small voice inside her head said. *Maybe you don't need Savannah, but you do need some friends,* the voice reminded her. Mira's run slowed to a crawl. Since their big fight, she hadn't had anyone to talk to or hang out with. She shopped alone, avoided parties, and spent most of her nonschool hours in her room. That wouldn't do.

She and Izzie had made strides in the friendship department, but Izzie still wasn't someone who would go for manicures or sit with her and gush over a picture of Taylor Lautner's abs in *Us Weekly*. She missed doing that stuff. *How are you going to survive cotillion without friends or a date?* the voice taunted. *Your debut is going to be ruined.*

By the time she made it to Corky's, the popular fifties-style diner practically all of Emerald Prep hung out at, the high she'd been on from taking Savannah down a peg had

51

disappeared. When she slid into an empty booth and looked over the menu, even the famous sweet-potato fries didn't look appealing. She had no desire to sing along with the popular song blasting from the jukebox. She held the menu in front of her face and tried not to feel sorry for herself. The menu was quickly pulled from her hands.

Kellen slid into the opposite side of the booth with a grin. "Hiding from me?"

Normally, the sight of the way-cute eleventh grader who had persuaded her to take a chance on her artwork would have made her feel light-headed. His sandy blond hair, green eyes, and toned physique (thanks to cross-country and track) gave Mira plenty to stare at during sculpting class. She had been looking forward to seeing him all day, but now...She was afraid if she opened her mouth, a sob might escape.

Kellen frowned. "Oh, man, I know that look. My little sister gets it when my mom threatens to turn off *Dora the Explorer* if she doesn't finish her breakfast. Is it your dad?" he asked. She shook her head. "Your mom?" Another head shake. "Izzie?" Third one. His right eyebrow arched slightly. "Maybe you should just tell me what happened."

Mira spilled the story quickly as if she had been holding it in forever. "I ran into Savannah and my friends at Prepsters. Correction: my ex-friends. And they were all 'Oh cotillion is coming—how are you going to survive?' I played it really well, I think, but Savannah's right. I can't show my face at cotillion without them. I'll never survive rush on my own!" She was starting to get hysterical. "You can't do a scavenger hunt without a team, and I have a terrible singing voice! There is no way I'm singing Beyoncé in front of the cafeteria without backup." Kellen's mouth began to twitch. "It's not funny."

Kellen pretended to be serious. "Nope. Not at all."

His expression made her laugh a little. "I know I sound a little insane—"

"A little?" His green eyes were playful. She still wasn't used to seeing him out of a school uniform. His look was definitely casual. T-shirts whose brand she couldn't make out and cargo pants. Today, he had upgraded his ensemble to include a short-sleeve plaid shirt that was unbuttoned over a navy T. It was working for him.

"I'm not crazy." Mira pouted. "I just miss having people to hang out with."

"Hello?" He waved a hand in front of her face. "Person hanging out with you."

"I know. It's just…" Kellen didn't get it. Boys never did. Girl friendships were different. She and Kellen had a lot to talk about, but their relationship was clouded by the fact that Mira had recently realized she had a major crush on him. "You've been great. I don't know what I would have done in the last few weeks without you."

Kellen looked at the neon wall clock across the restaurant. "What are friends for?"

Friends. Did he mean to emphasize the word, or was she imagining it? Boys were so hard to read. She decided to make light of it. "Friends are good at ordering fries and milk shakes." Mira tapped the menu.

"Glad to see you still have an appetite." Kellen waved over a waitress and ordered some cheese fries and two chocolate milk shakes. Afterward, he looked at her quizzically again. "So, cotillion? Really?"

"Yes, really!" she said, indignantly. "Every girl at EP who is anyone does cotillion. It's like a rite of passage."

"Is that what it says in the brochure?" Kellen asked, and Mira glared at him. "I'm sorry. Scholarship students don't do cotillion. It sounds old-fashioned to me."

Mira tried not to look as insulted as she felt. "Cotillion is an honor. People think it is just about making your debut in this amazing dress and going to all these dances that lead up to the big night, but..."

"There is more than one dance?" Kellen looked horrified.

"It's fun!" Mira insisted. "It may sound strange to you, but we take etiquette and dance classes to get ready for our debut, and I've learned a lot in them."

Kellen laughed. "Cotillion *classes*? Mira, you're joking, right?"

"No!" Mira twirled a saltshaker to avoid seeing Kellen's incredulous reaction. "It's not just dance class. The Junior League runs these workshops that teach you how important it is to give back to your community, how to find an internship and network." Okay, maybe she did sound like a cotillion brochure.

"But it's really about the dress, right?" Kellen asked as a waitress roller-skated over with their drinks and fries.

"Okay, yes." Kellen looked vindicated. "But it is more than that, too," she added quickly. "Cotillion is a sisterhood that I've wanted to be part of since I was seven. My mom was a deb, my grandmother was a deb. I've looked forward to this day forever." She bit her lip. "I never thought I'd have to do it alone."

"Savannah and her friends can't be the only ones doing it." Kellen pulled a gooey fry from the plate.

"They're not, but..." Mira was pretty sure she knew everyone in her cotillion class. It was usually the same girls year after year. There was no way Izzie could get in this late in the game, not that she would agree to doing it, either. "I just don't want them to ruin it for me."

"They can't ruin it if you don't let them," Kellen said between bites.

But Kellen didn't get it. Cotillion was supposed to be special. She wanted to try on dresses with her friends, and talk about escorts, and—*escorts*! Every deb needed an escort, and if Kellen was hers, then there was no way the evening would be a failure. She felt a tiny glimmer of hope. "I do know one way to keep the night from being a total disaster," Mira said, picking at a fry. She tried not to sound eager. "I need to find an escort. You know, like a date. But I can't ask anyone—they have to ask me."

"You are not allowed to ask someone to your own dance?" Kellen looked confused.

"Technically no," Mira said. She watched as he stopped chewing. "It's tradition for escorts to be assigned a girl. But if a guy knows a girl is going to cotillion, he can ask her on his own, too. I just hope someone wants to ask me." She pretended to stare at the jukebox.

Kellen took a long sip of his milk shake before saying anything. He seemed to be deep in thought. Maybe he had gotten her subtle hint and was going to ask her to cotillion right now!

"I wouldn't worry about a date too much," he finally said, chewing on another fry. "I'm sure they'll assign you an escort if no one volunteers."

Mira's hands clenched tightly. Boys. Sometimes they were so clueless.

Six

The heated discussion the next day continued even after Hayden pulled into their driveway and everyone got out of the car. Izzie chose to walk behind him and Mira—out of the line of fire—which was a smart move because Hayden was about to say the one thing he knew would make his sister's head explode.

"I forgot the world revolves around Mirabelle Monroe."

"Excuse me?" Mira's wavy hair bounced angrily as her head whipped around to look at Hayden. Izzie thankfully suppressed a smirk because two seconds later Mira gave Izzie a look that said, *Can you believe he said that?*

Izzie replied with her own look, the one she'd patented over the last few weeks to deal with problems of the Mira variety. Those included, but were not limited to, Mira asking whether her headband matched her outfit (Izzie didn't have a clue), if Izzie knew where Mira had left her favorite pair of flip-flops (nope), and whether Izzie would choose Team Peeta or Team Gale if she was on a deserted island and could only pick one boy to spend the rest of her life with (Peeta, of course!). Mira didn't really want an answer—she had already formed her own opinion—but Izzie noticed that if she just nodded and gave "the look," Mira was satisfied.

"Izzie thinks you're overreacting, too!" Mira took "the look" to mean that Izzie agreed. "Any girl in my situation would want to know the same thing!"

Hayden winked at Izzie. She knew he was trying to get Mira fired up on purpose. "You're right. *Of course*, Kellen asked about you during cross-country practice. What else would he be doing? Trying to improve his time? No, all he wanted to talk about today was you," Hayden said patronizingly. "Is that what you want to hear?"

Mira played with the strap on her messenger bag. "Well, it would be nice, but I guess he did have other things to think about." Her face turned pink, and it looked like her cheeks might explode. "So, did he? Ask about me, I mean."

Hayden gaped at her, and Izzie started to crack up. That made Hayden roar.

Mira stopped short and stared at them both as if they were nuts. "What? Hayden never answered my question!"

Hayden finally managed to stop laughing. "Sorry, but

he didn't ask me about you." Mira's face fell. "Don't sweat it. I would never ask a guy about his sister if I liked her, either."

"So you *do* think he likes me?" Mira asked.

"I . . ." Hayden looked at Izzie wearily. "A little help here?"

Izzie backed away, swinging her army-green messenger bag. "Don't ask me. I've got my own boy issues."

"No, you don't." Mira pouted. "Brayden likes you. Everyone at school is talking about it." Izzie had a feeling that the latter half of that statement bothered Mira more.

"Everyone," Hayden agreed, trying to keep a straight face, even as Mira gave him the stink eye. "Face it, Mira. Izzie is more popular than you are now." He hurried ahead of Mira down the path to avoid being hit.

"Thanks. Rub it in! Mono is more popular than me these days," Mira griped, and stomped inside. The three of them filed into the foyer.

Izzie still couldn't get used to the size of the house even after living there for the past few months. Every square inch of it looked like it belonged in an expensive furniture showroom. The Monroes' taste was definitely more traditional than Grams's shabby-chic place, but the vibe was still homey. Well, it had been. With all the bickering and silent treatments going on, the place felt a little frosty now.

"Don't be depressed." Izzie flung her bag on the entry room bench. "Savannah still talks about you," she said encouragingly.

"Well, if you count all the negative stuff she says." Mira's scowl deepened.

"Don't worry, Mira," Hayden told her. "Give it two weeks. By that point some unfortunate girl in the sophomore class will look twice at Lea Price's boyfriend, and they'll have someone new to hate." Hayden dropped his backpack in his designated cubby. "By then, I'm sure you'll have a new group of girls to boss around."

"Thanks." Mira sniffed. That seemed to please her a bit.

The new-friend topic gave Izzie a thought. "Speaking of new people, have either of you ever met Brayden's sister, Dylan?" Hayden and Mira looked at each other warily.

"Of course we've met her," Mira said. "Have you?" By Mira's expression, Izzie figured it was best to shake her head no. "She's nothing like Brayden," Mira told her. "I'm not one to talk"— Hayden coughed—"but when Dylan lived in EC, she had major mommy/daddy drama going on, and not for lame reasons like my-mom-won't-let-me-put-red-streaks-in-my-hair-for-the-swim-meet."

"Well, it was unreasonable." Izzie thought of the week before. "I told your mom it would wash out."

"Dylan has done everything you can think of to make her family's life more scandalous than an episode of *Real Housewives*." Mira began to tick off the indiscretions on her fingers. "Wearing an off-white dress to cotillion, getting several tattoos, showing up tipsy at one of her mother's dazzling self-thrown birthday parties. Dating a guy from out of town who worked at a tattoo parlor in Harborside." Mira's eyes widened. "I'm sure he was really nice," she added quickly, "but it was still a scandal."

"Forget I brought her up." Izzie wasn't about to get into an argument with Mira about Dylan. Personally, none of the supposedly scandalous things Dylan had done sounded *that* bad. They sounded like things a person would do to forget they lived somewhere like Emerald Cove. And that was a feeling Izzie understood completely. She kept waiting for the day that she woke up and finally felt like she belonged there, but she wasn't sure that day would ever come.

Aunt Maureen's laugh brought her back to the present. It was coming from the kitchen and it was followed quickly by their father's. The last time Izzie heard him laugh like that was when Connor painted his face like Darth Maul with her aunt's lipstick.

"What are they doing home?" Mira's voice was anxious, just like Izzie's stomach felt when she heard Bill's voice. "I thought they were at a fund-raising rally in Raleigh."

Hayden shrugged and headed toward the kitchen. "I guess it ended early."

Izzie used to find Emerald Prep the most stressful part of her day. She looked forward to hurrying back to the Monroes', where she could sit and watch whatever Kaitlin Burke movie was on ABC Family in peace. But now it was the opposite. She dreaded coming home and finding *him* there.

Hayden looked at them strangely. "Aren't you guys coming? I thought you wanted something to eat."

"I'm not hungry," Izzie said quickly.

"I had a big lunch," Mira seconded.

"I thought you guys said you skipped lunch." Hayden sounded suspicious. He pointed to Izzie. "You said you had a meeting with Mrs. Fitz."

Mira forgot for a moment about needing a cover. "You had a private meeting with Mrs. Fitz? Why? What are you talking about? Tell me," she said excitedly.

"Nothing." Izzie looked at her feet. "I just had a few questions about the club."

"Like what?" Mira pressed. "I gave you a Social Butterflies orientation kit, right?" Her face crumpled. "You're not quitting, are you?"

"No," Izzie said. "I like it." As much as it killed her to admit it, the stuffy, prestigious Emerald Prep Social Butterflies club she had joined by default was growing on her. Some of the girls may have been in the group for the status, but there was no denying the group's commitment to charity work. That's why she had stopped in to see Mrs. Fitz. Izzie had half a dozen ideas for events clogging her brain, and she wanted to run them by their club director in private. She wasn't ready to share them in front of the group yet. "I wanted to know what the final number was that we raised for the community center," she lied. "We raised close to nine thousand dollars."

"That's amazing," Mira said. "The center must be thrilled."

Izzie could still feel Hayden's eyes on them. "I thought you were going to the kitchen for a snack."

Hayden loosened his EP tie and shook his head. "You guys can't avoid him forever."

Yes, I can, Izzie wanted to say. But she didn't. Instead she watched as Hayden swung open the door between the dining room and the kitchen. She could just make out Bill's navy pin-striped suit as the door swung closed.

"This isn't fair!" Mira complained when Hayden was out of earshot. "I've been dreaming of that chocolate cream pie in the fridge since third period."

"Since when do you eat pie?" Izzie asked.

Mira shrugged. "Since I have no one to look good for."

"Please." Izzie wasn't playing into her pity act. "Look good for yourself."

"Mira? Izzie?" Aunt Maureen called out. "Are you two home?"

Aunt Maureen knew they were, but this was her polite way of getting them to show their faces rather than run upstairs.

"We might as well face the fire and get a cookie out of it," Izzie said.

Seeing her uncle/dad/liar didn't get any easier. No matter how big he smiled, or how nicely he asked about her day, Izzie still couldn't stop thinking about how he had let her down. He had given her a roof over her head and new clothes to call her own, but he hadn't given her what she'd needed the most: a sense of family. Aunt Maureen had done that, which was why even though she had been in the know, Izzie couldn't be mad at her.

"Hi, girls," Bill said cheerfully. He took off his reading glasses, the ones Izzie always thought made him look intimidating, which was probably why he never wore them on television or for photos. "Did you have a good day?"

Mira was too busy staring at the chocolate cream pie on the kitchen counter to look at her dad. There was only one slice left. Izzie took an M&M cookie. She did not want to face Mira's wrath over that piece of pie.

"Mom, did the mail come yet?" Mira asked.

"Not yet," Callista told her. "We've been waiting for it ourselves. *O* is supposed to send us an advance copy of the article they did on your father."

"Haven't they heard of e-mail? It's quicker," Izzie said, and Bill chuckled. Izzie didn't look at him.

"They said something about not wanting the layout to be misconstrued." Callista leaned her long arms on the counter. She had a yellow legal pad in front of her, and it looked like she had been taking notes. "How was school?"

"Super as always," Hayden smirked. "Well, unless you're Mira or Izzie."

Callista's face clouded over. "Are you still having a hard time? God, I hate high school! What do you two have to do with any of these politics?"

"Mira's former best friend is Holden Ingram's daughter," Bill explained.

Callista groaned. "No wonder school is miserable. If that girl is anywhere near the snake her father is…" Callista glanced down at her dessert plate, embarrassed. "That was wrong. Sorry. I just get so mad sometimes!" She looked at Bill. "The Ingrams are trying to ruin a super candidate like your dad by backing that one-trick pony Steven Fray. It makes me sick to think about the money they're throwing at him."

"Holden Ingram has come out publicly to support your father's new opponent for the ticket," Aunt Maureen explained, her face grim. "He's a rookie district attorney who is riding the family-values wave. As if marrying the secretary you got pregnant is family values!" Aunt Maureen's voice had a hard edge Izzie hadn't heard before. She seemed so stressed these days. "The Ingrams are determined to get Fray nominated instead of your father." She looked at Izzie worriedly. "Fray also supports Holden Ingram's coastal revitalization project and wants to start by tearing down half of Harborside Pier, including the community center."

Izzie felt like she had just been sucker punched. Her former community center was always in jeopardy of not having enough funding, but now someone was trying to take a wrecking ball to it.

"I don't want you to worry, Isabelle," Bill told her. "I'm going to do all I can to make sure no one touches the community center unless they're renovating it." She knew he had withdrawn his support of Mr. Ingram's project.

"Thanks, Unc—" Izzie paused. "I'm sorry. I don't know what to call you anymore, and I can't keep pretending not to call you anything or say 'hey, you.'"

He took a sip of coffee. "What do you want to call me?"

"*Dad* feels weird." Izzie felt her cheeks burn. That sounded mean. "*Uncle* doesn't work, either, though, right? Since that's clearly a lie?" She had noticed sometimes it was harder being angry at Bill than just letting things go.

"If calling me Uncle makes you comfortable, then do that," he said thoughtfully. "Or just call me Bill."

"But not in public," Callista said hastily, and everyone looked at her. "It's so forward—well, for down here. I don't know how that would go over in the polls."

"I'm more worried about what Izzie wants," Bill said, looking directly at her. "If you want to call me Bill, call me Bill."

Izzie thought for a moment. Did she really want to get used to calling him something else when she was just getting used to *Uncle*? "I think I'll stick with *Uncle Bill* for now." He nodded.

The rest of the room was so quiet, Izzie could hear the sound of the dishwasher running in the background. Mira broke the ice with a strange new topic.

"So, Callista, I was wondering…" Mira twirled a lock of her hair around her finger. "Any chance *Teen Vogue* might want to interview me and Izzie?"

"Why would we want to do that?" Izzie looked ready to have a heart attack.

Callista munched on an M&M cookie. "I think that's a super idea! I'm sure they'd love to have you. I'll make some calls. I know the editor at *Justine* personally."

Mira squealed, and now everyone was looking at her. "What? I want to help the campaign." She stared at them innocently.

"Yeah, that's the reason you want to be in a magazine," Hayden said wryly.

Izzie didn't have time to wonder what Mira's real reason was, because two seconds later, the front door slammed so hard, their coffee mugs shook, and Connor bounded in. He dropped a pile of mail on the table. "Cookies!"

Aunt Maureen handed him one and started sorting through the mail. When she came to an oversize, thick cream envelope, she stopped. Before Izzie could figure out what the invite was for (an invitation for a spinning-class-for-asthma-relief fund-raiser had come the day before), Mira snatched the envelope from her mom. The two of them ran their fingers along the calligraphy that spelled out her name. Then Mira carefully broke the seal, pulled out an invitation, and shrieked.

"I've officially been invited to cotillion!" She let herself collapse on the island in relief.

"Was there really any doubt?" Hayden asked.

Mira didn't answer him. Instead, she waved the invite in Izzie's face. "Look!"

Izzie took the invitation and read it herself.

Mirabelle Monroe is cordially invited, after three years of service and hard work, to participate in this year's cotillion class and make her debut at Emerald Cove Castle on the Cliffs on Saturday, December 13, at 7 pm. All cotillion members are expected to participate in this fall's classes, which consist of both etiquette and dance. . . .

Izzie stopped reading. "*This* is what you're excited about? Another dance? Doesn't this town get tired of parties?" It never ceased to amaze her how many bashes EC had and for such silly reasons. Last week, they attended a garden party to celebrate the new park playground.

"Cotillion is a big deal." Mira took the invitation back

before Izzie could get chocolate on it. "Why does no one get that?"

Aunt Maureen hugged Mira. "I do. It feels like only yesterday I was taking you to your first precotillion dance class. I'm so excited for you, sweetie."

"What makes this dance different from the nine trillion other black-tie events EC has? The cheesy white gloves and bridal gowns?" Izzie asked her.

"No. I mean yes," Mira said, getting flustered. "White gloves are cool! I'm sure Kate, Prince William's wife, wears them for official functions."

"But why do *you* need to wear them? You're not a princess," Izzie reminded her.

"Shh!" Hayden put a finger to his lips. "I'm not sure anyone told her that."

"Why did Mira get two letters?" Connor held up a second cream envelope that had been buried in the unopened mail. Izzie could see her name from clear across the kitchen counter and she practically spit out her iced tea.

"No way," Izzie said, backing away as if Connor were waving a ticking time bomb. "Send it back! I am not going to cotillion." She looked at Aunt Maureen. "How could I get invited? I didn't even sign up."

Aunt Maureen looked guilty. "I submitted your name back in August, when you first got here," she explained before

Izzie could freak out. "I didn't think you'd get in this late, but if the Junior League picked you, with no prior training, then they must accept you as a member of this community and our family."

Izzie snorted. "The only thing they accept is that they're stuck with me."

"That's not true," Aunt Maureen said. "Everyone knows you single-handedly planned the first Social Butterflies event of the season. You're a natural Junior Leaguer waiting to happen. They obviously realize that."

"Me? A Junior League member? No way." Izzie shook her head. "I'd rather eat bark than sit at a meeting with those Southern belles. I've heard them at parties," Izzie told the others. "They think the town's Founders Day is more important than the Fourth of July."

Aunt Maureen looked teary. "After all that we've been through, you getting an invitation is such an honor for this family. I'd love nothing more than to see both my girls make their debut together."

Both my girls. Did Aunt Maureen just say that? Izzie knew her aunt really cared about her, but she and Mira also cared about this backward, totally-past-its-prime tradition. Cotillion was *so* not Izzie. It sounded time-consuming—and ugh, the white gloves! Izzie glanced at her fingers, which were sticky from the cookie she had eaten. There was no way she was wearing white gloves! Still, there was her aunt to consider. She looked so hopeful. Mira's expression was the same. She was clutching that invitation as if it were an invite to the Oscars. How was she going to let them down?

"I think cotillion sounds ridiculous." Izzie felt the need to repeat that one more time. "But if you really want me to do it, then I guess I will." Mira and Aunt Maureen sandwiched her within seconds. This family was too touchy-feely. "It'd better not conflict with swim meets or visiting Grams or Social Butterflies," she said, trying to find a way to breathe and talk while being hugged so tightly. "I just signed up for that club, and I don't want Mrs. Fitz to think I'm a slacker already."

"It won't." Mira bounced up and down in her heels. "The Junior League makes sure classes don't conflict with our regular schedules." She shrieked again. "Isn't this great? I don't have to do cotillion alone! I mean, we can do it together," she corrected herself. Another squeal escaped her lips. "I can't wait to go dress shopping!"

Izzie wondered what she had just gotten herself into.

"Do we get to go to this ball, too?" Callista asked.

"Of course," Aunt Maureen said happily. "We'll be buying a whole table for the event. It's Bill's job to present the girls to their escorts." Her face took on an almost dreamy quality, like it did whenever she watched George Clooney movies. "I've always imagined that moment he brought Mira down the stairs, which are lit with candles and—"

Callista cut her off. "Bill is part of this, too? This is super!"

She was practically foaming at the mouth. "I've been looking for something exactly like this to give to news programs and the papers—a true father-daughter moment showing Bill at his finest. We need something feel-good like this right now."

"I have waited forever to escort Mira down those stairs," Bill told her, happy to see the smiles on everybody's faces for a change. Mira and Izzie watched as he slid the pie plate over to his dish and took the last slice right under Mira's nose. "To do this with both my girls would be incredible."

"Perfect!" Callista scribbled notes furiously.

"No." Mira's voice was barely audible, but Izzie heard her.

"What did you say, sweetie?" Aunt Maureen asked as she placed the now empty pie dish in the sink.

Mira stared at her dad's plate, waiting to see him take a bite. "I said no." Her voice was stronger. "I don't want Dad presenting me."

"Mirabelle," Aunt Maureen said in a hushed voice.

"I'm serious." Mira stared angrily at her dad's plate. "I won't pretend we're something we're not!" Her voice turned into a full yell. "You were a coward, Dad, and I won't let you pretend everything is okay just to save your stupid party ticket!"

Izzie was shocked. She wasn't used to hearing Mira flip out like a reality TV star.

"I understand you're upset, but let's not make any rash decisions. Cotillion is still over a month away," Bill said. Izzie could hear the hurt in his voice.

But Mira wouldn't back down. "I've made my decision. I won't go with you, and I know Izzie won't, either." She glanced at Izzie meaningfully. Even though Izzie felt uncomfortable, she gave Mira "the look." Relief flooded Mira's face. "You can't make us change our minds."

"Maybe we should take our snack to the living room," Aunt Maureen said hastily, herding a bewildered Connor away. "I think we've had quite an exciting day. Maybe the girls need some space." She gave Mira a stern look, but Mira ignored it.

"Nice, Mira," Hayden said when everybody left the room. "How could you—"

"Bite me, Hayden," Mira shot back venomously. Hayden pushed his plate back and walked out, disgust written all over his face.

"How could he start with me?" Mira said, getting visibly upset. "Hey, would you mind letting Dad present you at cotillion?" she said, mimicking Callista's voice. "Are they crazy? What would make them think I would even consider that?" Mira's chest went up and down. "I don't care how it looks for his career. I don't care if this sinks him! He doesn't deserve to present me, and I won't change my mind."

Mira was never unhinged. It didn't matter what someone did or what name Savannah called her. Mira always held it together. Izzie didn't know how she did. But for the first time Izzie could remember, Mira was a mess.

"No one understands why I can't get over this," Mira said, her voice strangled. "But I can't."

"I understand," Izzie said quietly.

Mira looked at her. "You're the only one who can." She leaned her head on Izzie's shoulder and then turned in for a hug.

This time, Izzie didn't want to stop her.

Seven

"Mira! Wait up!" Izzie's loud voice ricocheted off the buildings in Emerald Prep's main quad.

Normally, Mira would have flinched at Izzie's tone. It was one she felt should be reserved for football games, not for flagging down your sister, but today there was no one around to hear Izzie but Mira. Half the school was at a football game. It was Friday, and all after-school sports had been canceled so that students could attend the Cardinals' final football playoff game against St. Elizabeth's Holy Rollers. If the Cardinals won, they'd play in the first round of the fall state championships next weekend. Mira kept walking.

"Mira! Hell-*o*!" She could hear Izzie running across the grass. Within seconds, Izzie had caught up with her. "Why are you ignoring me?"

"I didn't hear you," Mira said innocently.

Izzie folded her arms across her chest and glared at her. In her EP uniform, she did a good impression of one of Savannah's mean girls. "Don't give me that. You heard me calling you after the Butterflies meeting, but you ran off anyway."

"No, I didn't." The truth was, she didn't want to hear Izzie mouth off about their meeting. Mira had completely let Savannah take over, and she didn't want a lecture about it.

Izzie sighed. "Whatever. I just wanted to know how you could let Savannah walk all over you like that."

See? There it was, right there. She could already read Izzie like a book.

Izzie's hazel eyes were practically on fire. "You let her take over the whole meeting! We got stuck listening to her talk about her trip to Hilton Head instead of deciding what our next club project was going to be!"

"It was an interesting slide show, don't you think?" Mira squeaked.

Izzie scowled. "Slide show? She flipped through pictures on her iPhone."

Mira shrugged. "Same thing. Besides, Mrs. Fitz was riveted."

"No, she wasn't." Izzie pushed her bob out of her eyes. "She was waiting for you to take the ball back, since she couldn't get a word in, either. Now we have to wait till next week. It will be a month since we've planned anything."

"That's okay," Mira said. "We're lucky if we do three or four events a year."

"What?" Izzie's voice reached maximum volume again.

"We only plan a few events a year," Mira repeated. "That's how the club has always worked. Our parties are so good, we don't have to plan more than that."

"But you meet weekly!" Izzie was flabbergasted. "And we raised so much money at the Falling into You Fest! Think about how much good we could do if we did even more stuff. I'm not talking about more lame dances, either," she said before Mira could even suggest it. "There are so many easy ways to raise money. We could do a car wash at the school for parents. Or we could have a takeout night where we cook so the parents don't have to. Not that the parents around here actually cook, but you get the idea." Her eyes were bright with excitement. "We could have a babysitting night in the sports complex. Parents could drop off their younger kids for a flat fee that is cheaper than a sitter and..."

Mira let Izzie rattle off at least five more smart ideas before stopping her. "These are good. Why didn't you bring them up at the meeting?"

Izzie shrugged. "I don't know. I just ran the fall fest. I can't exactly suggest all the other events, too." She looked at Mira pensively. "But I was hoping if you opened the meeting up to ideas, I could have at least mentioned one."

Mira frowned. "I didn't want Mrs. Fitz to ask if I had any ideas. I've had a lot on my mind lately. Besides, I didn't want to sit there and listen to Savannah shoot down everything I said. It's bad enough that I have to stare at her smug face all day in class and—"

"You're cochair of a charity club," Izzie snapped. "You're going to have to think about something other than your own problems sometimes."

Mira rolled her eyes. "Whatever. Can we just get out of here?" All she wanted to do was go home, put on a DVR'd episode of *The Bachelorette*, and eat a Twinkie.

Izzie grabbed Mira's arm and gave her "the look." That's what Mira called it. The one that said Izzie didn't believe a word coming out of her mouth and she wanted real answers. She could be such a bully that way. Must be a Harborside thing.

"Promise me you won't let Savannah get to you," Izzie said. "There are already enough people in this town who are scared of that girl. We don't need to add one more to the list." The two stood in the nearly deserted courtyard and stared at each other.

"I'm not afraid of her," Mira said, even as her hazel eyes darted back and forth.

"She's not out here," Izzie said, reading her thoughts. "Everyone seems to be at the football game." Izzie looked in the direction of the stadium and sighed. "Watching football is about as fun as rubbing sandpaper on a wall, but I promised Brayden I'd go. Want to come? Violet and Nicole are going, too."

Oh, how their roles had been reversed. Izzie had people to hang out with, and she had none. The stadium was on the other side of campus, but Mira could picture her former friends there having a good time without her. "I'm not in the mood to have fun."

Izzie seemed baffled. "I never heard you say that before. What's with you?"

"I'm not like you, okay?" Mira snapped. "I'm not ready to take on the world by myself!"

"What does that mean?" Izzie looked at her quizzically.

"Just forget it," Mira said. She was embarrassing herself, and she hated that. Izzie said and did what she wanted and didn't care what the fallout was. Not everyone had the guts to act that way.

"Poor Mira." Izzie pretended to pout, which only irritated Mira more. "So you're not number two on the food chain at EP anymore. People still like you—probably better now than they did when you hung out with Savannah. You're just too wrapped up in your own pity party to see it."

"If this is you being nice, I'd hate to be on your bad side." Mira hiked her messenger bag higher on her shoulder and started to walk away again. Izzie could make her so mad sometimes. Usually when she was right.

"Are we interrupting?" Violet's hesitant voice came from out of nowhere, startling them. Izzie's good friends Nicole and Violet had somehow snuck up on them.

Even though every girl at EP had the same uniform, people had a way of making it their own with accessories. Violet had on those large rubber bracelets that said things like *sneaky*. Nicole's nails were painted a sparkly pink, and she was wearing several oversize rings. One was a giant horseshoe. Izzie had traded her pricey ballet flats for beat-up black Converse sneakers (technically, there was nothing in the EP handbook that said she couldn't wear them—Mira and her mom just thought they were ugly). Mira stuck with the basics, accenting her ensemble with her favorite plaid headband.

"No," Mira said, and smoothed her hair, pushing it behind her right ear. She smiled as if she didn't have a care in the world. "How are you guys?"

Violet pushed her long, straight dark brown hair away from her face and looked at her warily. "We're good. Pretty much the same as we were five minutes ago in the Butterflies meeting."

"Sorry," Mira shifted awkwardly. "Force of habit."

"Ready to go to the game?" Nicole asked Izzie, bouncing up and down on her toes like an overeager Labrador retriever.

Izzie hesitated, glancing at Mira. "We're kind of in the middle of something."

Violet's phone started to ring, distracting them. "It's my mom." Mira watched as Violet's face paled. "She probably found her cashmere sweater I stuffed in the back of my closet. I wore it without asking, and a pen exploded over it." She winced as the phone kept ringing. "I better walk ahead and meet you guys at the stadium. I don't want any of you to hear my mom practically reach through the phone and strangle me."

"Good luck!" Nicole said. She was tall, even taller with her blond hair piled high on her head in a bun, and she towered over Mira. "Want to come to the game with us?"

Nicole was the second person to ask her in the last five minutes. She looked down at her black ballet flats, the same ones Savannah always wore. It was nice of them to offer, but she felt awkward all the same. These were Izzie's friends. She couldn't glom on to them now that she had none of her own. "Thanks, but I'm heading over to the art studio. This abstract painting assignment I have due next Tuesday is kicking my butt."

"Is the art studio even open today?" Izzie asked, looking around the deserted campus. "I know there is a game going on, but it's kind of creepy, isn't it? One minute—"

Swoosh!

Mira's arms were pulled behind her back, and a blindfold was placed over her eyes before she could figure out what was happening. Something told her she wasn't in danger, so she didn't fight back. The others apparently didn't have the same gut feeling. Nicole was screaming, and Izzie was yelling things like "*Get off me, punk!*" Mira could hear Izzie's fists flying. She felt someone bang into her and fall to the ground.

"Would one of you tell this one to stop?" a girl complained.

Mira didn't recognize her voice. "You're not being abducted, sugar! We're trying to take you to your first cotillion initiation!"

Cotillion initiation! Yes! She wasn't expecting it to start today, but maybe the ritual was just what she needed to get her mojo back.

Nicole stopped fighting at the word *initiation*, but Izzie was still resisting.

"*Oeuf!*" Someone must have just gotten socked in the stomach. "This one thinks she's a street fighter. Someone help me hold her!"

"She's the new Monroe girl," another girl said. "She probably *is* a street fighter! Wow, honey, you've got some strength! Save it, though. You're going to need it."

"I am not a Monroe!" Mira heard Izzie grunt. "But if you hurt me or my friends, I swear, I'll…"

"Izzie, calm down!" Mira yelled as plastic handcuffs were placed on her wrists. "Didn't you hear them? This is for cotillion! It's our initiation."

"Initiation?" Izzie growled. "*What* initiation?"

Mira bit her lip. Maybe she had forgotten to mention this part.

On purpose.

"What does kidnapping have to do with white gloves and dresses?" Izzie asked again, getting suspicious. Mira was glad she was blindfolded so Izzie couldn't find her and deck her, too. "Mira?" she warned. "Unless they duct-taped your mouth shut, I know you can answer me."

The girls in charge laughed. "This one is going to be fun to watch."

"Uh, I kind of left initiation out," Mira squeaked. "Just go with it. Please?"

She heard Izzie sigh. "Your IOUs are stacking up."

Someone tugged on Mira's arm, and she let herself be led along. She wondered where they were taking them. "Just relax. This is going to be fun."

"Fun," Izzie repeated, sounding like it was anything but.

"You're going to love it," Nicole seconded. "I have been dying to do cotillion initiation ever since I signed up to be a deb. I love a good dare."

"You see?" Mira tried to sound confident since the girls in charge of the initiation could hear her every word. "This is tradition, like the dance itself."

"You and your stupid traditions! I didn't sign up for any initiations," Izzie grumbled. "I didn't sign up for any of this! I'm supposed to be at the game right now watching Brayden, and now God knows where we're going! Thanks."

"Mira Monroe, please explain the initiation to Isabelle Scott," a charge barked.

"Izzie," she heard her new sister correct the girl.

Mira thought carefully about what she wanted to say

next, since she had an audience. "Cotillion is like a sorority, and when you pledge for a sorority, you have to prove your worth during rush week. This is the cotillion version."

"I have to be tested before I can wear a white gown? I'm out." Mira heard Izzie start to struggle again.

"Izzie, you go along with this, or you're out of cotillion," warned the girl. "You should know no one gets hurt, no one has to do anything dangerous, and no one—I repeat, no one—talks about cotillion initiations. Got it?"

"Please?" Mira had been reduced to begging and not the pretty kind. It was the kind she used when she was young and wanted a new Barbie at Target. "You're going to love this! You think well on your feet. Please? Mom so wants you to do cotillion. You'll kill her if you drop out. Please, Izzie? Puh-leeze?"

Izzie groaned. "You owe me big-time, Mira."

Mira knew that was Izzie's way of saying yes. She was glad Izzie wasn't able to see her smile.

It felt like they walked forever. At one point, Nicole asked where they were going, and she was told not to ask questions. When Mira heard cheering, she knew they were near the stadium. That's when they came to a halt.

"Now that everyone is here, let me welcome this year's recruits to their first cotillion hazing!" Mira didn't recognize this voice, either, but she was so excited, she cheered along with the other girls who had apparently been assembled. Her heart was pumping out of her chest. She couldn't believe it was finally her turn to be part of this society.

"I don't have to tell you guys how this works," the girl continued. "If you've lived in Emerald Cove long enough, you know. Cotillion initiation is a tradition as important as cotillion itself. If you pass our tests, you make your debut in some overpriced gown while your dad tears up and escorts you down your first aisle. If you screw up—or talk about our hazing to anyone—don't even *think* of showing your face at the Emerald Cove Castle on the Cliffs December thirteenth. Got it? We will be everywhere these next few weeks, watching you, giving you assignments. Sometimes you won't even know we're there. Think of me as a guardian angel with a mischievous streak. Do as I say, know the cotillion code, and I'll put in a good word with the powers that be. I might even upgrade your status to potential cotillion captain. Cotillion captains are picked by former debs, so you've got a shot at my job if you do yours well enough. Finally, none of you will know who I am till I see fit. In the meantime, listen and you'll learn a lot."

"Excuse me?" Savannah's drawl was undeniable. "I was told Mary Beth Pearson was captain this year, but you don't sound like Mary Beth."

The girl laughed. "Mary Beth Pearson? She wishes. Don't speak unless spoken to, Savannah Ingram. You already have two marks against you."

"Me?" Savannah stammered. "What did I do?"

"You're *you*. Be warned, princess. I'm watching you personally."

Mira tried not to grin. She suspected Izzie might be smiling for the first time since she was handcuffed.

"Recruits, your first assignment starts now. If you haven't already guessed, we're near the Emerald Prep football stadium. The Cardinals are down seven-to-three, and this crowd could use some cheering up. You're going to do that by singing for them."

That was all they had to do? That didn't sound so bad.

"Now for the fun part—you're not a halftime show. You're going to stand up in the bleachers during the game, block their view of Taylor Covington making a pass and Ryan Hodgkins scoring a touchdown, and you're going to sing your little hearts out. You're going to sing a Lady Gaga song, even if they throw things at you."

Mira heard nervous laughter. Singing as a group wasn't so bad, was it? She felt her cheek poked and she jumped.

"Ladies, you'll notice someone is touching your face." Someone screamed. "If you're going to sing Lady Gaga, you should look like Lady Gaga, don't you think?"

Someone squeezed cold gel onto Mira's hair and started pulling it. *Oh God!*

"Your hair and makeup needs to be Lady Gaga–worthy, which is what we're making it. Next, we'll bring you to the stadium, remove your blindfolds, and send you inside. We'll be watching you, and you're being judged, so don't even think of trying to sneak out without doing this task." Mira felt sick, but maybe that was the cloud of hair spray covering her. "When you're done, you can go. You'll get your next assignment soon enough."

After much poking and hair pulling, they were marched over to the stadium. They were instructed to sing their cotillion theme song the entire way as a warm-up. After being warned not to open their eyes till they counted to fifty, their blindfolds were removed.

"Forty-eight," the girls counted in unison. "Forty-nine... fifty!"

Mira opened her eyes and looked around. Everyone was laughing. Or more like screaming. Girls had their hair teased up as high as it could go. Some had crazy ponytails sticking out of weird parts of their head. Others had white makeup. A few had Gaga-like sunglasses. There were fifteen girls total. Everyone Mira had suspected would be there—Lea, Lauren, Savannah, Nicole, and Izzie—plus a few other girls she didn't know very well. When Mira and Izzie spotted each other, they started to crack up.

"Do I look atrocious?" Izzie asked.

"Actually your makeup is kind of nice." *And mild for Gaga.* Izzie's face had been completely covered in glitter, and her short hair had been slicked back.

"How is mine?" Mira asked anxiously.

Izzie grimaced. "I would have made you look much worse."

"So I don't look bad?" Izzie wouldn't answer her. "What is on my face?"

Nicole walked over. Her blond hair had been teased into a bird's nest, and someone had put on her a bright blue hat that had an old telephone glued to the top. Her makeup was almost fluorescent.

"Where is Violet?" Izzie asked, her glitter almost blinding in the afternoon light.

"She isn't doing cotillion," Nicole said. "Her mom thinks it's archaic. I texted her. She said she's going into the stadium to take pictures of us." She glanced at Mira. "Cool hair."

Mira touched her head. "I wish I could see. Izzie won't tell me anything."

"You don't deserve to know," Izzie told her, but Nicole pulled out a mirror and showed Mira her face.

"*Oh. My. God.*" Mira inhaled sharply. She did not even look like herself. She had green hair! *Green hair!* A long purple streak went down one side and her cheeks were painted bright purple. Her eyebrows were a pasty white.

"Do you think this stuff washes out?" Mira asked, trying to mask the panic in her voice. Nicole gave her a look that didn't seem too optimistic.

"Now that is funny," Izzie said, and pointed to Savannah.

Savannah's normally angelic face had been transformed

into a fiery devil. She was wearing a red wig with devil horns, and her whole face was painted red except for heavy black eye makeup. Mira didn't recognize it as a Gaga look, but maybe it wasn't one. Maybe it was just supposed to represent how evil Savannah was. Either way, Savannah was practically in tears, and Lea, who looked like Gaga's alter ego, Jo Calderone, tried to calm her down. Izzie took a picture with her phone before Savannah could stop her.

Savannah stomped over. She looked more terrifying than usual with her red face and devil horns. "Delete that!" she hissed. "Right now!"

Izzie slipped the phone back in her pocket and jutted out her chin. "Make me."

Savannah was smart enough not to try that. "They made me over this way on purpose, you know. Only potential cotillion captains get put through the paces, and I am definitely going to be cotillion captain one day." Her eyes became slits, which was pretty creepy with that makeup. "And then I'm going to make everyone else's life hell."

Izzie rolled her eyes. "I kind of suspect the reason you look like the devil is because our cotillion captain, whoever she is, knows you *are* the devil."

A simultaneous symphony of pings kept Savannah from responding. Everyone reached for their phones. It seemed all the girls had received the same text.

Enough whining about your makeovers. Get in there already!
You have seats on the left side of the bleacher section. Row
B. Remember to smile! We're watching!

With some nervous laughter, their oddly dressed group reluctantly filed into the stadium. Mira wasn't surprised to see the place packed. Eighty percent of the crowd wore red (the Cardinals) or blue (the Holy Rollers), but their team spirit was no match for the Lady Gagas. People stopped cheering and stared at the girls as they walked by. Even some of the players on the field noticed them! They found their seats and stared at the scoreboard. The Cardinals were now up ten-to-seven, and it was third down.

"They're going to kill us if we stand up and sing right now," Lea said. She had a huge lightning bolt cap on her head.

"We don't have a choice," Lauren said, but she didn't budge, either.

"Savannah, your mom is sitting directly across the field," Lea pointed out.

"Don't let her see me," Savannah hissed, ducking behind Lea. She peeked out from behind Lea's shoulder and frowned. "Oh, God! The football team is laughing at us! I am not doing this." She thought for a moment. "I'll be the first Ingram in history to not make cotillion." She covered her face with her hands. Mira didn't tell her that the red paint ran all over

90

them. Others started to murmur their agreement and fears. Their cotillion class was quickly falling apart.

Izzie stood up to face the others. "You can't handle one little dare? You guys are supposed to be the perfect belles."

"We *are* belles," Savannah snapped. "And doing this"— she motioned to her ensemble—"will ruin that."

"No, it won't," Izzie told her. "If anything, this will just make you look cooler. Everyone is going to know we're doing something mysterious if we stand up and sing together. It will all be over in five minutes, and then you can dive under the bleachers and hide until our next initiation. But if you don't do this," she warned, "there won't be another one." Lea paled. "So? Everyone with me? Let's do this!"

Mira couldn't believe Izzie's take-charge attitude. Her Gaga look was sort of kick-butt. Maybe that helped, because the others seemed to listen to her. A few stood up with Izzie. Savannah, Lea, and Lauren were the final three to join them.

Izzie looked satisfied. "Okay, then. On the count of ten, we sing. One, two..."

They attempted to do Gaga proud. Mira sang the best she could, the whole time scanning the crowd for Kellen. Thankfully he wasn't there to witness her humiliation, but Hayden was. He was sitting in the bleachers a few rows up, and he had a look of deep satisfaction on his face as he videoed the whole thing on his phone! Great. He'd show this to all her future boyfriends. Even if he didn't, she was sure someone else would humiliate them by posting this on YouTube.

"*Sit down!*" a guy wearing red face paint barked.

"Shut it!" said another guy.

Someone threw a paper cup at Lea, and then a rain of wrappers started coming down on them. Savannah looked like she might burst into tears, but Mira started to laugh, and so did the girl standing next to her, who had a black lightning bolt painted over her right eye and her strawberry-red hair piled on her head in an oversize bow. She thought her name was Charlotte. They had never really talked before. Now they were both hysterical from the adrenaline of embarrassment, and Charlotte had her arm draped around Mira's.

When the Gagas hit their last off-key note, the group flew out of the stadium as fast as their feet would carry them. Savannah, Lea, and Lauren kept running, but Mira, Izzie, and some of the others stuck around. Most were laughing as they tried to fix their hair and remove their crazy makeup. Everyone was talking a mile a minute about what they had just pulled off. Mira had to admit, it was insane, but probably the most adventurous thing she had done in a long time. Izzie, the one cotillion participant who *hadn't* dreamed of making her debut since she was young, was the one who had gotten them to complete their first assignment. She wanted to thank Izzie, but the minute she saw her sister's deadly expression, she decided that might not be the best idea.

"You're dropping out, aren't you?" Mira said quietly.

Izzie tried to run a hand through the gel in her hair, but it got stuck. "I was ready to quit an hour ago."

Mira's heart sank. It was official. She was doing cotillion alone. She couldn't blame Izzie for wanting out. She didn't know what she was getting into when she agreed in the first place. But when she looked at Izzie, she saw that she was smiling.

"Then I thought about missing everything they're going to do to Savannah. They clearly don't like her." Mira perked up. "And watching that might make this whole stupid initiation thing worthwhile."

Mira tried not to get excited. "Just to be clear, does this mean you're staying?"

Izzie smirked. "I'm not going anywhere."

It might not have been the reasoning Mira was looking for, but she'd take it.

Eight

"Go, Mimi! Go!" Izzie shouted, jumping up and down so hard that the metal bleachers shook beneath her feet. She tried to scream loud enough to be heard over the crowd in the cavernous Harborside Community Center pool, but that was pretty tough to do especially when Kylie's cowbell was louder than all of them.

"You go, squirt!" Kylie screamed, ringing her cowbell furiously.

Izzie had no idea where she had gotten the thing, but Kylie said the bell was good luck. Kylie used to bring it to all of Izzie's swim meets, and she figured the same luck would apply to a junior team meet. She rang the bell faster as Mimi Grayson—the guppie whom Izzie had taught to swim for a year—inched out her competitor and raced to the other end of the pool. Izzie could feel her voice give out as little Mimi hit the wall. The buzzer sounded and it became official. Mimi had won her first-ever swim race.

"Wow, who knew a race among seven-year-olds could be this exciting?" Callista put two fingers in her mouth and gave a loud whistle.

Izzie laughed. "You can't beat this kind of excitement on a Saturday morning."

"It beats watching two screaming toddlers while your brother snores and your sister refuses to answer your calls," Kylie said. Izzie patted her arm. She knew Kylie got stuck on babysitting duty way more than any sister deserved. When Kylie's mom gave her the morning off, she jumped at the chance to join Izzie for the peewee meet. Kylie looked relaxed in jeans and a striped T, her bedhead disguised under a Braves cap.

"My original plans weren't much better." Callista pushed her glasses up on her nose. "If I wasn't here, I'd be at Starbucks by myself reading the *New York Times*."

Izzie knew what it was like to be a full-time babysitter—she had been one for Grams the last six months she lived with her—and what it felt like to be an outsider. She felt bad for Callista. It had to be hard being from New York City and not knowing a soul in Emerald Cove. That was why, when Callista asked if she could see the community center Izzie talked so much about, Izzie didn't feel funny about inviting her along with Kylie.

"Are you going to go down and congratulate the squirt?" Kylie asked Izzie. They watched the curly-haired kid accept high fives from her teammates.

"You should," Callista agreed. "Didn't you bake the team victory cookies?" Izzie had told her all about her star pupil.

"Victory cookies?" Kylie shook her head. "You mush."

Izzie watched the girls and boys standing by the edge of the pool, listening to their next instructions from Coach Bing. He had also been Izzie's coach in Harborside. "I don't want to distract them. I'll see them when the meet is over."

"Did you give lessons to most of the kids down there?" Callista asked.

Izzie nodded. "Most mornings before lifeguarding and sometimes after, too."

"Did you get paid well?" Callista asked, and Kylie laughed.

"Are you kidding?" Kylie hugged Izzie, practically smothering her. "This crazy girl did it for free. It ate up a ton of her free time, let me tell you."

Izzie shrugged. "Lessons are pricey. Even those fees are waived sometimes. My coach waived mine," Izzie said, remembering. "When he saw how well my mom taught me to swim, he said there was no way he'd feel right about keeping me out of the pool." Izzie kept her eyes on Mimi, who was talking a mile a minute to a girl in a bright orange swim cap. Izzie had always had a soft spot for the tiny brunette, even though she was supposed to be impartial. Maybe it was

96

because Mimi's story so closely mirrored her own. Mimi was being raised by her grandparents.

"Free lessons. That's pretty generous of you," Callista said.

"That's Iz." Kylie rang her bell again. "Generous to a fault."

"Not everyone would be the same way," Callista said. "Especially when this place had so many memories of your mom."

"Yeah, that was hard a little bit." Izzie looked down at the pool. "The smells, the sounds…Once in a while, when I'm here, I even forget she's…" There was no need to finish that sentence. While Harborside Community Center held mostly good memories, sometimes it did make her sad.

"And yet, even if this place bums you out sometimes, I bet you'd rather be living here than Emerald Cove any day," Callista said bluntly, then blushed. But that could have been because it was hot in the room. She took off the cardigan she had on over her tank top. "Sorry. I shouldn't get so personal."

"No, it's okay," Izzie told her. "This is the only life I knew and I loved it. Emerald Cove has given me a lot of opportunities, but if my mom were still alive, then yeah, warts and all, I'd rather be here."

"I wish you were still here, too," Kylie said quietly. "But I'm happy you've got a family now." Izzie leaned in to Kylie affectionately while keeping her eyes on the next heat.

Izzie couldn't help noticing how different this pool was compared to the state-of-the-art one at Emerald Prep. The tiles surrounding the pool here had to be from the seventies, giving the place a dated vibe. There were cracks in the ceiling, the roof tiles leaked, and the single-pane windows had seen much better days. They had a permanent film over them that made the sky outside always seem cloudy. There was only one pool, and it had two lap lanes that had to be put up or taken down depending on the class going on at the same time. Izzie's high school pool had six lap lanes, a separate stroke pool, and even a sauna. There was so much Izzie wished she could give back to Harborside and the community center the way it had given so much to her.

"I can understand wanting to be in two places at once," Callista told her. "I was a military brat. We moved every two years from the time I was two till I was sixteen. Just when I started liking a place, we moved again." She wiped her glasses, which kept fogging up. "You want what you can't have, I guess."

Izzie knew she felt that way sometimes.

Kylie pointed to the pool. "You've been spotted, Ms. Celebrity Coach." Mimi must have noticed Izzie because the whole group was jumping up and down and waving instead of paying attention to the meet. Coach Bing blew his whistle to bring them back in line.

"I can tell this place does a world of good." Callista leaned her elbows on her knees and watched the team. "I will keep on

Bill about doing shout-outs for the center where he can, okay?"

Izzie was grateful for all Callista had done. "I appreciate you listening to me go on and on about my old life. Kylie has to hear about it all the time, but you didn't sign on for this when you agreed to spend your morning off with me."

Callista put an arm around her and looked across the pool. "Any time, my friend." Suddenly Izzie felt her stiffen. "What is your dad—sorry, Bill—doing here?"

Izzie's eyes followed Callista's. Bill had walked into the pool area with the director of the community center. Both Bill and the director looked serious.

"Did you tell him about the meet?" Callista asked. Izzie shook her head.

"Whoa, is he fighting with the director?" Kylie asked. "Not cool."

They seemed to be in the middle of a heated conversation. Usually in public, Bill was always "on." He never missed a handshake. Here, several people noticed him, but he was too busy to say hi or even smile. What was he up to, and why hadn't he told her he was going to be there? Izzie's foot started to tap the bleachers madly. Her mind was spinning. Maybe Bill was backing Mr. Ingram's bill again. He wouldn't. Would he?

"What is he doing here?" Callista wondered aloud. "He didn't have a stop here on his schedule unless..." She stopped herself and side-eyed Izzie worriedly. "Don't stress. I'm sure whatever his reason is, it's a good one."

"I'm sure it is," Izzie seconded. But looking at the steely expression on Bill's face, she wasn't sure she believed that.

~

After she congratulated Mimi and the team, said hi to some friends at the center, and assured Callista she was fine getting back to EC on her own by bus, Izzie headed onto the boardwalk with Kylie to breathe in the cool, salty sea air. Kylie had suggested they head to Harborside Pizza to get some lunch, and they walked part of the way in silence, just taking in the beauty of the desolate beach. Izzie was thankful for the quiet. She couldn't stop thinking about Bill and why he had been at the community center that morning. Why had he looked so angry? And why hadn't he told anyone—not even Callista—that he was going? Everything about his visit gave her a bad vibe.

"I'm not sure I can stomach pizza today," Izzie said as they turned off the boardwalk and neared Harborside Pizza. A gust of wind, always stronger by the water, blew her slightly sideways, and she buttoned up her navy peacoat to keep warm. The weather was so different from just a few days ago.

Kylie held her stomach. "I can't say the idea of melted

cheese and the pool chlorine still burning my nostrils is a good mix, either. We can eat somewhere else if you want, but we've got to go to Harborside Pizza first. We're meeting someone."

"Who?" Izzie wasn't so sure she wanted company. If Kylie had invited Molly and Pete, the afternoon was definitely going to be weird. Things hadn't been the same among all of them since Izzie moved.

Kylie's dark eyes looked devious with the addition of the black liner she was into these days, but her face was one huge grin. "Take a look for yourself." She motioned to someone walking down the block.

"Hey, girls." Dylan smiled as she strutted toward them, looking like she belonged on a catwalk. A catwalk for Harley-Davidson clothing, that is. Her upper body was buried in a weathered leather bomber jacket that she had paired with skinny jeans and worn knee-high brown boots. Her honey-colored hair sprayed around the wool collar of her jacket like she was in a windstorm, which they kind of were. Certain blocks bordering the boardwalk were wind tunnels.

"Dylan hung out with my brother last night, and when I told her you and I were hanging out today, she asked to come along," Kylie explained. "Do you mind?"

"Not at all." Izzie had been hoping to run into Dylan ever since they met at Scoops, but she hadn't seen her around EC, and Brayden never talked about her. Izzie had a feeling Dylan Townsend knew all of EC's secrets, and she couldn't help wondering what some of them were.

The smell of pizza dough wafted out of Harborside Pizza, and Dylan wrinkled her nose. "If I eat another slice, I'm going to turn into a pizza. Can we go someplace else?"

"We were thinking the same thing," Kylie said. "What do you have in mind?"

"How about that place we went to with Charlie right before I left for school?"

"Yes!" Kylie said, and looked at Izzie. "I actually hadn't even heard of it till Dylan took me, but you're going to love it."

"Love where?" Izzie slipped her hands into her pockets to keep warm. She looked at Dylan. "Are you telling me you know someplace I don't when I'm the one who has lived in Harborside for the past fifteen years?"

"Lived—past tense," Dylan corrected her. "And that doesn't mean you know all the cool haunts." Dylan linked arms with Izzie and steered her and Kylie down the street. "So where have you been hiding?" Dylan asked.

"Um, school?" Izzie said as if it should be obvious.

Dylan laughed. "Oh, right, the hallowed halls of Emerald Prep," she mocked sarcastically. "I'm glad I don't have to worry about school till January. I can just chill down here with Kylie and the gang." She pushed a slouchy black leather bag with braided rope straps higher on her shoulder. Izzie had always wanted one just like it.

"So that would explain why I haven't seen you around EC," Izzie said.

"If I stand still for more than ten minutes, my mom signs me up for things like the Emerald Cove Greeters' movie mixer." Dylan shook her head. "No, thanks."

"A movie mixer?" Kylie repeated the words as if they were in a foreign language. "What the heck is that?"

"Be happy you've never had to go to one," Izzie told her. "Aunt Maureen dragged me to one my first week there. Before the movie, you hang out in the lobby and have crab dip and lobster rolls."

Dylan grinned. "Welcome to EC."

She led the girls onto the main drag for a few blocks like a true townie. Then she turned onto a narrow side street that Izzie didn't recognize before pulling them into a restaurant called Pit Stop. Izzie had never heard of it, and she was pretty sure why. The place had old tables, plastic backyard chairs, and red-and-white gingham tablecloths, but it was packed with college kids. No one even seemed to care that there was a huge line for a table. Leave it to an outsider-turned-insider like Dylan to find this place.

"Isn't this great?" Kylie yelled in Izzie's ear over the hard rock music blasting. "Dylan knows the owner."

A cute guy in a messy apron walked up to them at the back of the line. Izzie read the writing on his apron: *Our place is a* Pit, *but you won't be able to* Stop *coming once you try it.* "Hey, beautiful," he said to Dylan. "Bring some new friends with you?"

"Kylie knows the deliciousness that is this greasy dive, but Izzie is a Pit Stop virgin," Dylan said. "Tragic. A former local who has never had your chili lime burger."

His brown eyes opened wide. "We've got to fix that. Girls, ditch this line and follow me." He led them through the crowd to a bar area that was, in fact, not a bar. It overlooked the tiny kitchen, which had smoke billowing out from the open flame grill. "Three chili lime burgers with garlic fries coming up."

"You rock, John Boy," Dylan said, getting herself situated on the high swivel stool. She looked at Izzie. "Cool, right? Do I deliver, or do I deliver?"

"It smells amazing," Izzie said, looking around as she parked herself on a high stool next to Kylie, who was practically salivating, and not over the food. The place was filled with cute guys just Kylie's type. "How did you find this place?"

"It's right across the street from where I got one of my tattoos." Dylan flipped over her wrist to reveal tiny Chinese symbols. "Do you have a tat?"

Kylie laughed. "Iz has a fear of needles."

"No, I don't," Izzie said. She'd given Grams's insulin

shots daily when they lived together. She just couldn't imagine getting a tattoo herself. "I haven't found one I like enough to live with permanently."

It was a good thing Izzie had quick reflexes, because a guy behind the counter shot three plates toward them, and Izzie caught hers before it slid off the counter. The burger on the plate was massive, as was the mound of fries.

"I think your next cotillion dare involves permanent ink." Dylan watched Izzie's reaction. "Kidding!"

Izzie exhaled. "How did you know I was doing cotillion, anyway?" Izzie asked. She took a huge bite, and the juice oozed out of the side of the burger onto her hands.

Dylan gave her a look similar to one Mira might. "I know everything that goes on in that town, including initiations."

"You know about the initiation, too?" Izzie dropped a fry.

Dylan grabbed it and dipped it in ketchup. "Of course. I'm surprised you let yourself get roped into that charade."

"I know you want to fit in," Kylie agreed between bites, "but I cannot see you at some old-school ball where the girls have to wear wedding gowns. That does not sound like you at all."

"It's not, but it means a lot to my aunt," Izzie explained, feeling like she had to defend herself. "She was a deb, her mom was a deb, and Mira didn't want to do it alone. It is killing me, though. Cotillion is *so* not my thing." She looked at Dylan curiously. "You must've had to make your debut. How did you survive?"

Dylan laughed. "I fought my mother tooth and nail for years—till I found out about the hazing. That part is *awesome* because everybody—from the self-professed queen bee to the lowest on the totem pole—has to participate if they want to keep their reputation intact. Initiation is a common denominator."

That was Izzie's favorite part about cotillion, too, actually. Izzie was glad someone else saw it her way.

"Besides"—Dylan raised her perfectly arched right eyebrow—"when you get to dress up like Lady Gaga and interrupt the precious Cardinals' football game, how can you not have a little fun?"

Wow, she really did know everything about EC. "How did you know about that?"

"Gaga?" Kylie repeated. She nudged Izzie. "You've been holding out on me."

Dylan grabbed her phone and quickly pulled up a photo from that afternoon. Kylie laughed so hard, Diet Coke came out of her nose. Izzie quickly filled her friend in on the dare.

"Brilliant, no?" Dylan asked Kylie. "And who do you think came up with the Gaga worshipfulness?" She leaned back in her seat and put her hands behind her head. Izzie gaped. "Yep, I'm not just home to torture my mother. I'm part of the initiation group. Who else could come up with something as diabolical as a Gaga sing-along?"

Izzie was in awe. "Thanks for not painting my face red."

Dylan's blue eyes gleamed. "You're welcome. I had to save the devil face paint for my favorite Southern belle. Or should I say, my mother's favorite. That girl deserved a little payback for the way I've heard she's treated you."

Izzie couldn't help being impressed. Dylan was coolness personified. She took risks, she didn't seem to let anyone or anything get to her, and she had everyone's number. The fact that she had grown up in Emerald Cove and hadn't let it swallow her whole made her even more appealing.

"Initiation is the whole reason to do cotillion," Dylan told her. "My mom and her friends can't stop it, because they only vaguely know what's going on. Besides, none of them wants to be the one to admit their daughter is taking part in it. Initiation lets you take a nice jab at EC and its whole backward system." She took another bite. "That's why I'm helping out. Besides, if you do a good-enough job, you might make cotillion captain in a few years, and that is the gravy on the biscuit. So I hear."

"Can I apply for cotillion captain so I can kick Savannah's butt?" Kylie asked.

Dylan grinned mischievously. "Sorry, Ky. Only EC debs may apply for that gig." She patted Kylie's hand. "Don't worry about Savannah. I'll see to it that she's covered."

Dylan gets it, Izzie realized. *She thinks the same way I do.* And when she looked at cotillion the way Dylan did, making her debut didn't sound so bad. In fact, it might actually be fun. The hazing seemed like just the right amount of approved rebellion she needed to survive a town like Emerald Cove.

"So? Think you'll stick with it?" Dylan asked.

The garlic and the salt from the fries left a bittersweet taste in Izzie's mouth. "Yeah." She chewed slowly. "I think I will."

Dylan smiled and took another bite of her burger. "Just what I was hoping you'd say." Her cell phone interrupted them, and Dylan's cheerful demeanor quickly dampened. She answered her phone. "What do you want, Mother?" she said coldly. "I don't have to check in every hour. I'm eighteen." Dylan rolled her eyes at Izzie and Kylie. "I'll be home when I'm home." Pause. "What does it matter who I'm with?" Her dark mood lightened. "My friend Kylie. No, you don't know her. She lives in Harborside. Yes, *that* Harborside. You know, that dangerous town on the water where gangs roam?" Dylan high-fived Kylie. Then she caught Izzie's eye. "I'm with Brayden's new girlfriend, Izzie Scott, too."

Izzie didn't think her face could get any hotter, but it did.

"Yep, the other Monroe girl. *Girlfriend.* That's what I said." She winked at Izzie. "I don't know, Mother. Maybe he doesn't want you to know. I wouldn't." Izzie started to sweat. She thought she could actually hear Brayden's reserved mother yelling. "Bye," Dylan said sweetly, and hung up. "That woman," she said to Izzie and Kylie as she tossed her phone in her oversize bag, "should not have been allowed to have children."

"You and your mom really don't get along, do you?" Izzie asked quietly.

"Not. At. All. Do you get along with your dad?" Dylan was blunt. "I hear he's a pretty decent guy—when he's not denying long-lost children."

Izzie was a little surprised at Dylan's candor, but she didn't let on. "We're not talking right now, but eventually I'll have to forgive him, I guess."

"Are you sure you want to after what you saw this morning?" Kylie was referring to Bill's mysterious appearance at the center. Izzie didn't answer her.

"Well, I don't know what happened earlier, but I, for one, don't forgive and forget easily," Dylan told them. "My mother lied to me one too many times, and I've completely written her off." Dylan was pensive. "Do yourself a favor—stay as far away from my house and my parents as you can. They will sprinkle you with Splenda and eat you for breakfast."

Izzie's stomach churned, like it wanted to get rid of the half a pound of burger she'd just eaten. "I don't think that will be a problem. Brayden and I aren't going out."

"Please!" Kylie rolled her eyes. "Surfer boy is *so* into you!" Izzie blushed.

"Kylie's right. My brother likes you." Dylan pushed the

fries around her plate like she had lost her appetite. "It's totally obvious even if he won't tell me himself."

"Why don't you guys get along?" Izzie wondered. Dylan seemed like a fun sister to have.

"I adore my brother, but we don't see eye to eye on EC," Dylan said cryptically.

"Really? Brayden hates how superficial it is," Izzie said. "He says it all the time."

"He avoided EC like the plague this summer," Kylie added.

Dylan shook her head. "You guys don't get it. My brother says he wants to be different from our parents. Not so hung up on appearances or concerned about privilege. But if that's true, then why does he go along with everything they say?" Her blue-green eyes darkened. "He's still playing football, going to their ridiculous charity events. If he hates their world so much, why doesn't he accept me for being my own person?" She took a sip of Coke. "Brayden's rebellion is a phase. Mine is a way of life."

Izzie suddenly felt cold. Dylan couldn't be right, because if Dylan was right, then that meant that Brayden could never be with someone like her. She thought back to how Brayden behaved when he first ran into her at Emerald Prep. He acted like he didn't even know her. Was she really just a phase of his?

I like you. He had said that to her, more than once. He

110

had kissed her, too. Then Izzie looked at Dylan. She bucked the system just like Dylan did, and if Brayden didn't like her, then...

"I think you're cool, which is why I feel like I have to warn you. EC destroys people like my brother," Dylan said quietly before meeting Izzie's eyes. Izzie felt like all the noise had been sucked out of the restaurant. Dylan took another bite of her burger. "But hey, what do I know? You two are really cute together. I am sure it will all work out."

Dylan's mood had shifted perceptibly. Brayden's sister was smiling right at her, but for a split second, she saw a flash of Emerald Cove on Dylan's face. It was a look that screamed Savannah Ingram.

Nine

"Are you *really* reading that thing again?" Izzie asked, her lip twitching slightly.

"*Yes.*" Mira considered the question insulting, and she hoped her face conveyed that. Hayden was driving her and Izzie to their first official cotillion event of the season, a mother-daughter tea, and instead of using the drive time to complain about how itchy her white gloves were (like Izzie was), Mira was looking over her cotillion handbook again. "There could be something in here that I missed. I don't want to show up unprepared."

"Unprepared?" Hayden laughed. "You've been practicing your whole life."

Mira sniffed. "Not my whole life." *Just the past ten years.* She glared at Izzie and tapped the laminated handbook on her lap. "It wouldn't hurt for you to look at this instead of one of your weird pirate mystery novels."

"Those are worth reading," Izzie said, and Mira was hurt. "But I'm sure the cotillion handbook has important things in it. Why don't you, uh, read me something from it?" It looked like it killed her to say that, but Mira turned to the very first page and read.

The Emerald Cove Cotillion Club, run by the Emerald Cove Junior League, has had the same mission since it started in 1948. We hope to empower young women with confidence for their future careers and lives. Our program covers new etiquette and character-development topics such as dating courtesies, positive self-esteem, job interviews, scholarship applications, and how to handle peer pressure. Attendance is mandatory for classes, as is a dress code. White gloves are required for all dance classes. Please select a closed-toe shoe and pick dresses that cover you up appropriately. No backless, strapless, or slip dresses! A party or church dress is suitable. Knowledge of the following dances will be expected: fox-trot, samba, rumba, waltz . . .

Izzie interrupted, "The rumba? Seriously?" She glanced at Hayden in the rearview mirror. "Surviving cotillion training seems harder than the SATs."

"It's just as important," Mira said tersely, and Izzie gave her a look that could turn someone to stone. "Okay, so the SATs are probably more important, but—"

"Yeah, the SATs only count for a little thing called college," Hayden cut in. "Cotillion is preparing you for life." He and Izzie laughed.

Mira flung the book onto the seat. "I should have done this alone."

Izzie squeezed Mira's white-gloved hand with her own. "I'm just teasing. This stupid luncheon has me all worked up," she admitted, and Mira winced as Izzie unwound her hand and pulled off one of her white gloves with her teeth. "I feel like I'm playing dress-up! You, on the other hand, could make a Hefty bag look elegant."

Mira had to admit her first dress of the season was pretty perfect. The pale blue cocktail dress had rosettes along the collar to give it "something" but was still plain enough to be appropriate for a luncheon with the women of Emerald Cove. "That's very sweet of you to say. And you do not look like you're playing dress-up. You look pretty."

Izzie looked down at her wine-colored dress. It had darts and a wide matching belt that accented the bell-shaped skirt. Very un-Izzie, but she had refused to go shopping, so Aunt

Maureen had picked it out without her. "These gloves are itchy, and the dress makes me feel like I'm forty-five. I can't believe you talked me into this."

"On Friday afternoon, *you* were the one into this," Mira reminded her.

"That was different," Izzie said. "We were all in the same boat. Here, I'm in foreign territory. I can't believe they invite debs from as far back as the 1940s to this." She sank lower in her seat. "And we have to make small talk with all of them."

"You're going to do fine," Mira promised. She looked out the window as Hayden drove through the Sea Crest Resort's iron gates. "Tell them about the work you're doing to revitalize your community center. Junior Leaguers eat that stuff up."

Izzie seemed to think about that. "They do?"

Mira nodded. "Mom says everyone is always trying to one-up one another in the giving department. And you do it because you like to, not to win brownie points."

"Hear that, Iz? You actually *want* to help people!" Hayden pulled under the resort's vine-covered awning just in time, because Mira was ready to strangle him.

Mira could understand why Izzie felt nervous. The Sea Crest would intimidate anyone who wasn't used to five-course meals on a daily basis. The resort was a tourist destination for travelers from New York to Florida, for both its rich history and its lavish accommodations. Not only did it have a five-star hotel rating for its serene beach location and turn-of-the-century vibe, but its original building was also a state landmark. Victor Strausburg, Emerald Cove's founder and emerald-mining tycoon, had made his home in the four-thousand-square-foot plantation home that was part of the hotel that stood today.

"You're going to be fine," Mira told Izzie as they left Hayden behind and walked to the lobby. "I'm nervous, too," she added. "I can't believe Callista is meeting us here instead of coming with us. What if she runs late?"

Mira's mom had planned on attending the event with both girls, but that Sunday morning, she'd found out she had to go to New York with their dad. Callista had booked him a last-minute spot on *Meet the Press* to be followed by a political meeting of the minds with a senator and his wife. Mom had felt bad about missing the tea, and Callista had offered to stay back and fill in for her.

"Callista knows if she's late, your head will spin around like in *The Exorcist*," Izzie said to her sister. "She'll be here." She glanced at her phone again.

"Haven't heard back from Brayden?" Mira asked.

"He usually texts me right back," Izzie said. "I've texted him twice, and I haven't heard from him. I have no idea if he's coming." She made a face. "It would be nice to have a dance partner I like."

"He'll be here," Mira assured her. "His mom's name is on every cotillion form we get. There is no way she would let her son get out of being an escort." She smiled at Izzie. "And there is no one he'd rather be an escort for than you."

Izzie still looked anxious. "I hope you're right."

Mira wasn't sure why Izzie was so worried about Brayden, but she didn't pry. She was too busy staring at the bustling lobby. Women were holding glasses of sweet tea and chatting as a pianist played softly in the background. A giant satin banner welcoming this year's cotillion class hung in the lobby. Last year's debutantes could be recognized by the white gardenias they wore, while this year's pledges were being pinned with hydrangeas. Every year, the Junior League picked a different flower to anchor their theme. This year's ball was Winter White, and Emerald Cove Castle on the Cliffs was going to be transformed into a lilac-and-white wonderland.

It took Mira a minute to realize that Izzie wasn't next to her. She turned around. Izzie had stopped dead in the middle of the lobby.

"Are you okay?" She touched Izzie's arm, and Izzie jumped. "You're so white." She examined Izzie's chin. "Did you forget to use bronzer?"

Izzie pushed Mira's hand away. Her eyes kept darting back and forth among the women and girls scattered around the room. "I'm fine."

"Okay." Mira was afraid to push. All she needed was for Izzie to freak and bow out of cotillion before they even officially started. She looked around for the sign-in table. She

117

spotted half a dozen girls standing in a line and practically yanked Izzie over. "Okay, this is it. You've been reading your handouts, right? You know the cotillion motto and pledge?"

"You think someone is going to quiz me on it?" Izzie asked incredulously.

"You never know." It was always a good idea to know your cotillion protocol. "Last year's class is here. They might ask us some stuff. I bet some of them were the ones who gave us our Gaga makeover."

Izzie moved up. They were next. "I wonder what they have in store for us."

A woman with a pin that said *Cotillion Class of 1978* looked at them. "Name?"

"Mirabelle Monroe and Isabelle Scott," Mira said pleasantly.

The woman checked their names off a list and handed them Tiffany-blue name tags that had their names written in a loopy scroll. "Is your mother joining you for our tea today?" Mira had been dreading this question.

"Excuse me! Pardon me!"

Mira turned around. Callista was squeezing through a cluster of people in the middle of the room. Mira was relieved—until she saw what Callista was wearing. In any other situation, the outfit would be perfect. But at the EC cotillion tea, Callista's cream-and-teal spaghetti-strap sundress with the short-sleeve sweater and espadrilles looked like beachwear.

"I'm here!" Callista said as she made her way to the table. "Callista Foster," she told the woman. Callista laughed while the woman winced. "I'm filling in for their mom, Maureen Monroe, who had a last-minute press commitment in New York. She wanted to be here, but you know how it is."

Miss Cotillion Class of 1978 looked Callista up and down. "In the future, Ms. Foster, please follow the same dress code as our cotillion class." She smiled thinly. "We must set a good example, after all." She wrote Callista's name in swirly script on a badge and handed it to her.

"Yes, thank you!" Callista said, and turned to the girls. She gave them a face. "Dress *code?*"

Mira looked around nervously. "Don't say anything you wouldn't want repeated at these things. Even the perfume has ears."

"Sorry." Callista yanked up the top of her dress and Mira wanted to die. "Sorry. Well, here is something you want the whole room to hear: *Teen Vogue* called me back. They want both of you for a story and photo shoot."

"Yes!" Mira yelled before remembering where she was.

"You'd have to do the photo shoot with your dad, of course," Callista added, and Mira's face fell. "I know, awkward. But this opportunity is huge! Think about it."

"Okay." Mira tried not to sound defeated. She couldn't

119

stand being in the same room as her dad. How was she going to do a photo shoot with him?

"Super! Mind if I slip off to the bathroom to touch up for Miss Cotillion 1978 before we head inside?" Mira and Izzie both nodded.

"Why do you want to do *Teen Vogue* so badly, anyway?" Izzie asked when Callista had walked away.

It's a chance to show I still matter, she wanted to say, but not when Lea and Lauren were just a few feet away. They were preoccupied with a purple notecard. Probably another party invite she wasn't getting.

Savannah, on the other hand, had no problem spotting them. She strode toward them in four-inch heels, looking practically regal in a simple navy shift dress.

"Hi, girls," she said, holding a thin-stemmed glass of sweet tea. "I'm glad you are here. I was worried you wouldn't show your faces after the story in the paper today."

Someone with an obviously long camera lens had taken pictures of the family arguing over dinner on the outdoor patio one night. Mira wasn't even sure she remembered what the fight had been about, but it didn't matter. Their angry faces in the photos did all the talking. The headline said: **Are the Monroes' Family Values All for Show?**

"Why wouldn't we show up?" Izzie asked sweetly. "We have nothing to hide. At least no one seems to think either of us are the devil."

Savannah smiled coldly. "I don't know what you're talking about. I wasn't even at the game. I was visiting my grandparents," she lied. "The three of us went riding." She brushed her hair away from her blue eyes. "How's your grandma doing in her nursing home?"

Mira winced. That was a low blow even for Savannah.

"Hey, Savannah?" Izzie pointed to her right ear. "I think you still have a little red paint right there."

Savannah reddened and turned to Mira. "Nice dress." She cocked her head. "Didn't I see this on clearance last week at Prepsters?"

"No," Mira squeaked. "I've had this for a while." Why did she let Savannah get to her? She should say something tart like Izzie, but before she could think of a comeback, a gorgeous guy who could have doubled for Bradley Cooper walked up to them. He looked overdressed in a tuxedo, but what really stood out were the purple envelopes in his hand.

"Hello." He passed out the cards that had each of their names on it. "I suggest you read these discreetly. Good luck."

Izzie and Mira looked at each other. Savannah walked off. She obviously knew what Mira hadn't realized before. The envelope had information about their next hazing. Mira felt her lungs constrict. The hazers expected them to complete a dare at the welcome tea? Were they insane? She opened the envelope and pulled out the note.

121

Mirabelle Monroe:

"We promise to embrace, honor, and accept our womanhood." Such beautiful words for a cotillion motto, don't you think? That's why we want you to make sure everyone at this luncheon-both debs of old and new-hears the cotillion pledge before it's time to head home. We'll be watching to see how you do. Remember: Discretion is key!

XO,

Your Cotillion Captain

"I don't know where they come up with these ideas," Izzie said after reading the note. "My dare of the day is that I have to force everyone who has hot tea to add ice to it." She chuckled. "That should be interesting. What does yours say?"

Mira felt clammy and weak. The envelope dropped from her hands, and Izzie swooped in to rescue it. "I have to recite the Cotillion Club pledge to everyone I speak to," she said in a monotone voice. "I'm going to sound ridiculous! I've been practicing so hard to get ready for today, and now all my conversation starters are going to be ruined because I have to say the cotillion motto." Izzie started to laugh. "It's not funny!"

"It's a little funny," Izzie said. "At least now we don't have to suffer through an afternoon of prim and proper boringness. We get to do something fun." She bounced on her toes excitedly. "I can feel the adrenaline pumping through my body already."

Well, at least she didn't have to worry about Izzie ditching cotillion today. The hazing ritual lightened her mood.

Callista walked back over. Her makeup and hair seemed much more cotillion-tea-worthy after a quick touchup. She flashed them a big smile. "Someone said we're supposed to move into the ballroom. Ready for your proper entrance into society, ladies?"

"I was," Mira said under her breath. *Now I'm not so sure.*

Too bad she didn't have a choice. Mira headed toward the ballroom and prepared to face the music.

Ten

The Sea Crest ballroom was so decked out, Izzie thought they had walked into someone's wedding reception by mistake. There were cascading flower arrangements full of hydrangeas on every table, antique china, tiered plates with tea sandwiches, lilac satin tablecloths and napkins, and Waldorf salads being brought out by waiters in tuxes. The room filled up quickly, and everyone seemed to know one another. Not only was the ballroom breathtakingly beautiful and expensive-looking, so was every woman and girl in it. Instead of looking ridiculous in their prim Chanel skirt suits and Talbots threads, they all fit in perfectly, just like Mira. It was Izzie who was out of her element, and she was sure it showed. This was why she didn't want to do cotillion. It brought up too many emotions that she still hadn't gotten a handle on yet. *I don't belong here*, a nagging voice in the back of her head reminded her. Izzie tried to push it away, but she could still hear it. She had felt so confident a few minutes before, but now she felt a little ill.

What she needed now was Brayden. He would see her face and make a joke about high society, and instantly she'd be at ease. They hadn't talked about her doing cotillion till Brayden figured out she was one of the Gagas at the game. Even then, all he wanted to discuss was her glittery hair. Now she wished she had brought up the escort topic. If he knew how crucial it was for him to be there, he would have come. She checked her phone one last time, but there was still no text. She was on her own.

Izzie exhaled. How was she going to keep a straight face when she approached EC's elite with a pair of ice tongs?

"I guess it is time to face the music," Izzie said as they picked up their table cards. They both looked like they were going to a funeral. "I'm going to get ice."

"Ice?" Callista's expression was bewildered. "Why do you need ice?"

"Callista?" Mira put a hand on the publicist's shoulder. "Have I ever told you about the cotillion code of honor? Let me recite the pledge for you." She cleared her throat. "We promise to respect, honor, and accept our womanhood by..." Izzie made her exit.

Ever since Dylan told her she was involved with initiation,

Izzie felt like she was being watched. The idea that she could be forced to do something crazy at a moment's notice was both terrifying and exhilarating. Today, she had reason to be worried. Former debs were everywhere, observing members of her cotillion class taking part in their latest hazing.

Nicole hurried by her, trailing a woman wearing a *Miss Cotillion 1984* sash. "Miss Bronson? Did you know the first Emerald Cove cotillion class started in 1948, three years after World War II ended and the town's Junior League decided to…"

Izzie headed for the kitchen. Her note had said a purple ice bucket would be waiting for her there. On her way, she passed Lea, who surprised her mother by spraying her neck with a putrid-scented perfume while they were in the middle of talking.

"Lea! I already am wearing Chanel Number Five," her mom snapped.

"Funny, I don't smell Chanel," Lea said nervously. She caught the woman next to her mom off guard by spraying her, too. The woman sneezed. "Bless you! This new fragrance by, uh, Sassy, emphasizes the eternal beauty that comes with a winter hibernation.…"

Izzie hurried through the kitchen doors before Lea could spritz her, too. A busboy handed her a bucket and led her to an ice machine. *That was easy*, she thought when she exited the kitchen a few minutes later. Lauren was standing nearby, turning a deep shade of purple.

"Excuse me!" EC's mayor said when Lauren blotted her mouth with a napkin.

"You're excused, but the speck of mayo by your mouth isn't." Lauren tried to sound breezy as she followed the mayor's bobbing head with her napkin. "Got it!"

Izzie took advantage of the mayor's distraction and quickly dropped ice cubes in her teacup and those of two other women standing with her. When the women saw what Izzie had done, they were flabbergasted. Even Lauren stopped blotting mouths for a moment.

"That tea looks too hot," Izzie said, trying to sound as conversational as Lauren just did. "I thought you could use some ice." But she wasn't sure she could pull off breezy. The three women scurried away.

"Ice?" Lauren snapped. "How'd you get off so easy?"

"People like me. Haven't you heard?" Izzie dropped a cube in Lauren's china teacup while Lauren blotted Izzie's mouth. Then they glared at each other, and Lauren walked away. Izzie spotted Mira and Nicole and headed in their direction.

Mira was holding her hand to her heart. "We promise to embrace, honor, and accept our womanhood by…" As she spoke, Izzie stuck a piece of ice in her cup.

"Izzie, did you know that cotillion classes in the 1950s

127

were held all year on Saturday mornings and consisted of both etiquette classes and dance lessons?" Nicole asked. She was wearing a deep green cocktail dress that made her look like an elegant Jolly Green Giant. "Escorts were few after the war, as most boys went off to work." She stared at Izzie miserably. "How long do we have to keep this up? I'm running out of facts I remember!"

"Hopefully we'll be told to take our seats soon," Mira said, her eyes darting around the room. Izzie watched as her face froze. "Oh, hello, Mrs. Townsend!"

Mrs. Townsend? Izzie's palms began to sweat. Brayden's mom was coming their way! Even though she was tiny, Mrs. Townsend looked intimidating in a short, chic bob, tailored suit, and pearls. Izzie didn't see a resemblance between her and Brayden, but Dylan looked just like her. That must have driven Dylan nuts.

"Hello, ladies," Mrs. Townsend said crisply. Her mouth barely moved when she talked. It was held in a very small but decidedly permanent half smile, half frown. "Are you enjoying our welcoming luncheon so far?" Mrs. Townsend asked.

"Yes, Mrs. Townsend. What a lovely affair," Nicole said as if on autopilot.

"I particularly love the foreign tea bar," Mira added. "It's so nice to experience teas from around the globe."

Izzie was going to gag. Nicole and Mira sounded ridiculous! This was not the president. Why were they trying to impress her?

"Yes, well, you know how important we think it is for you girls to learn about different cultures," Mrs. Townsend agreed.

Tasting teas from foreign lands taught them about foreign culture? She has to be kidding! A microscopic sound that resembled a snort escaped Izzie's lips. Mrs. Townsend caught it, but Mira was even quicker. She held out her hand.

"Mrs. Townsend, I know we've met before, but I wanted to formally introduce myself. I'm Mirabelle Monroe, Bill and Maureen's daughter."

Mrs. Townsend extended a slender hand that dripped in diamond jewelry. Thankfully, she had been distracted. "It's lovely to see you, dear. How is your mother?"

Mira smiled. "Fine. She sends her regards, of course, and she told me to tell you that whatever you need in way of monetary contributions for upcoming dances, just let her know. She hated to miss today, but it is so important for her to support our father on his upcoming political run. Have you met Isabelle yet?" Mira asked, barely taking a breath.

Mira amazed Izzie sometimes. The sweet Southern belle thing came so naturally to her, even when she was facing someone as intimidating as Abigail Townsend.

Mrs. Townsend turned to Izzie with interest. "No, I haven't had the pleasure." She held out her hand. It was ice-cold. "It's a pleasure to finally meet you, Isabelle. I've heard quite a lot about you." Whether that included good things (anything Brayden might have said) or bad (Savannah's and the Ingrams' whispers), Mrs. Townsend didn't say.

"Thank you. And I you," Izzie said, causing the woman's half smile to turn down slightly. Izzie realized her gaffe, but it was too late.

Brayden's mom watched her closely. "I'm impressed that you've chosen to take on an endeavor as ambitious as cotillion having had no training prior to this year." Mrs. Townsend took a sip from the delicate teacup in her hand. "There is so much to memorize and so many behaviors to learn. I hope you don't find it too overwhelming."

Izzie tried to shake the impression that Mrs. Townsend was being condescending. "I'm a very fast learner," she said, but her words didn't have the same warm impression on Brayden's mom that Mira's did. Mrs. Townsend glanced at her ice bucket.

Was she really expected to perform her task on the cotillion director? It was practically social suicide. But if she didn't do her job, her cotillion captain might notice.

"A few waiters felt the water was too hot for tea," Izzie started to explain, and before she could freak out, she took her tongs and picked up an ice cube. "Ice?"

"No, thank you," Mrs. Townsend said, but Izzie followed her cup with the tongs.

"Mrs. Townsend," Mira said hurriedly, "I know you've heard it a thousand times, but I would be so honored to recite our cotillion pledge for you."

"Really?" Mrs. Townsend sounded surprised, but it was hard to tell because her expression was permanently frozen.

As Mira started to say the words Izzie had only memorized the night before, she moved in closer with her tongs. Mrs. Townsend had nowhere to run.

"Let me cool that down for you," Izzie said. Before Mrs. Townsend could stop her, she dropped the ice into the cup and sent hot tea sloshing over the sides. Mrs. Townsend gasped as the tea hit her cream suit jacket. It was official: She had botched her first meeting with her potential boyfriend's mother. "I'm so sorry. I . . ."

"Here," Lauren said, appearing out of nowhere with napkins. "Let me help." She dunked the napkin in Izzie's ice bucket and grabbed Mrs. Townsend's lapel before she could stop her.

"Ice can remove anything, Mrs. Townsend," Nicole jumped in, her face a deep shade of scarlet. "It can even, uh, clean emeralds."

"Emeralds?" Mrs. Townsend tried to discreetly push Lauren off her.

"Yes, my mom uses ice to clean her emeralds all the time," Nicole said. "Speaking of which, did you know members of the first cotillion class received an emerald pendant when they made their debut?"

Savannah's gasp could be heard throughout the room. "Mrs. Townsend, what happened to your beautiful Dior suit?" Izzie's heart sank further. By now, it was probably inside her stomach.

"Savannah, dear, thank goodness," Brayden's mom backed away from Izzie and the others as if they were dangerous. "I'm so glad you're here. Don't worry about my jacket. I'm sure the cleaners can get the stain out," she said even as her eyes told Izzie otherwise.

"I hope so! It's such a gorgeous suit. I remember when you wore it to see Brayden and me off on our first date." Izzie felt her blood begin to boil. "How did you stain it?" She suspected Savannah already knew the answer.

"Savannah?" Nicole interrupted sweetly. "Isn't there something *you* need to ask Mrs. Townsend?"

Thanks, Izzie mouthed. Her friend winked.

Savannah's face quickly turned the color of Mrs. Townsend's raspberry herbal tea. "Well, yes, I ..." She shook her head and started to softly sing their cotillion club song. "We are the members of the Emerald Cove Cotillion Club." Her voice cracked. "We come from mothers, both near and far. And we're here to say ..."

Izzie started to laugh before she could stop herself. Out of all the assignments, Savannah's had to be the worst. The girl could not carry a tune, and she suspected their cotillion captain already knew that. At least there was something

Savannah Ingram couldn't do. Izzie was so busy laughing, she didn't feel the ice bucket lift from her hands.

"I think if anyone needs ice, they can ask the waiters, don't you?" Mrs. Townsend's eyes were as cold as the ice in the bucket.

Izzie felt too flustered to respond. If she was caught without her ice bucket, who knew how the cotillion captain would make her pay? But she couldn't pry the bucket out of Mrs. Townsend's hands, either. She'd have to find another one. "Yes, Mrs. Townsend."

Mrs. Townsend smiled thinly and tucked the bucket under her arm. "Savannah, that was lovely. Why don't you walk me back to our table so I can get my welcoming speech? The rest of you should take your seats. We'll be starting shortly."

Savannah gave Izzie a self-satisfied smile before walking away with Brayden's mom. Izzie wished she could trip her, but that would only make things worse.

You don't belong here, the voice said again. *But she does.*

Izzie watched as Savannah chatted effortlessly with Mrs. Townsend.

"She's been talking this talk since she was in Pull-Ups," Mira said quietly. "Don't let her get to you. You belong here as much as she does."

Sometimes Izzie felt as if Mira was a mind reader. Today that skill irked her. "I'm going to get more ice," Izzie said gruffly, and hurried to the kitchen before Nicole or Mira could stop her. She waited till the kitchen door closed behind her before letting the tears roll down her cheek.

"How are you holding up, rookie?"

Izzie jumped. Dylan was standing a few feet away, munching on a tea sandwich from a tray about to go out.

"Fine. Well, not really." Izzie quickly wiped her eyes. At least there was someone here who knew what she was going through. "I'm dying out there."

She smiled. "No, you're not. You did a nice job going toe to toe with my mother." Izzie couldn't help but look at what Dylan was wearing. Her ensemble was definitely not up to cotillion code. The strapless dress showed off her tiny legs and her ankle tattoo. Her hair was full of volume. Southern demure it wasn't. "She's not the easiest person to face off with," added Dylan. "Just ask Brayden."

Brayden. She still hadn't heard from him. Izzie pulled out her phone again. No new text messages. "Have you seen him today? Is he feeling okay?" Izzie asked.

Dylan looked at her oddly. "Yeah. At least he was at breakfast. Why?"

Izzie's heart sank. Was he ignoring her, or did he just forget to charge his phone? "Forget it. I have to find another ice bucket. Your mom stole mine." She didn't want this to turn into another conversation about her and Brayden's chances of relationship survival.

You two are really cute together. I am sure it will all work out.

She couldn't stop thinking about Dylan's expression when she had said those words. It was pure Savannah, but that was ridiculous because the two were nothing alike.

"Why do you need an ice bucket?" Dylan asked as she fiddled with her long beaded earrings, which were similar to the pair Izzie was wearing.

Izzie froze. "Did I say ice bucket? I meant I needed a cup of ice. To chew on."

Dylan chuckled. "It's okay." She threw her half-eaten cucumber sandwich in the garbage. "I'm the one who wrote this initiation. I write all of them." Her expression was full of satisfaction. She put a finger to her lips. "That's the part I left out the other day at lunch. I don't just help out with initiation. I'm in charge of it."

Izzie was surprised, but not as surprised as she should be. Who better to make EC's future debs squirm than the girl who bucked the whole system? "Everything makes sense now!" Izzie realized. "No wonder Savannah has the most miserable assignments."

Dylan laughed. "You've caught on quick. As captain, I have the power to do things like tell you to forget a new ice bucket. You've passed your second test." Izzie grinned. "Sit the rest of this task out—just remember: not a word about who I am to anyone. Not even Mira or Nicole." Izzie pretended to seal her lips. "I knew I could trust you." She headed to the kitchen door. "See you out there, pledge."

It took Izzie a few moments to let Dylan's confession sink in before she was ready to head out and hear the rest of Mrs. Townsend's speech.

"We live in a very unusual time," Mrs. Townsend was saying from the podium. An EC Junior League banner made of lilac silk hung on a wall behind her. Izzie tried to discreetly hurry across the room to her seat. "In today's world, a child might know what this month's Happy Meal toy is and yet not know the proper way to hold a fork." Murmurs of agreement could be heard throughout the room. "It's time to swing the pendulum back to a time of civility and grace, the way our mamas and our grandmamas raised us. Manners are not optional. Thank-yous shouldn't be prompted, and cell phones shouldn't be at the dinner table." There was lots of nodding from the mothers, Izzie noticed as she sat down, and Mira gave her a dirty look for being late.

"When you are part of a cotillion like the one the Emerald Cove Junior League has successfully held for over fifty years, then you know you are raising your daughter well," Mrs. Townsend concluded. "I thank you for your continued involvement in shaping the future women leaders of our country, and I look forward to another great season."

Everyone applauded. Savannah and her mother actually stood up and gave Mrs. Townsend a standing ovation. Dylan, on the other hand, was sitting at the same table, and she barely looked up from her phone.

"Thank you." Mrs. Townsend looked pleased. "And now I'd like to start off this afternoon's dance lesson by introducing our cotillion class to some of their potential escorts."

The escorts were here? Izzie looked around, feeling butterflies in her stomach. Maybe this was why Brayden hadn't texted her back. He wanted to surprise her.

"I hope I don't get stuck with some guy who sweats too much," Mira groaned.

"I hate the ones who want to stand too close," Nicole whispered. "Just because you're dancing with me does not mean you get a free feel."

"Now, ladies, for today's session, I have done the assigning," Mrs. Townsend said. "These are not your permanent escorts. As is tradition, an escort must ask you to go to cotillion, but that does not mean you can't drop a proper hint now and then to one you want to go with." People laughed. "Your date for this afternoon will find you and lead you onto the dance floor to practice the fox-trot before lunch is served."

Izzie's heart stopped. If Mrs. Townsend was doing the assigning, that meant...

Instinctively, Izzie's eyes went to Savannah. When she spotted her, her heart felt like it did when she accidentally belly flopped off the high diving board.

Brayden was there after all. But it wasn't Izzie he was

137

walking toward; it was Savannah. Izzie watched painfully as he took her arm and escorted her to the dance floor. Brayden didn't even glance her way. He had eyes only for Savannah and she for him.

"Izzie, are you okay?" Nicole asked quietly, watching the scene unfold.

"I'm sure he didn't have a choice," Mira said. "He'd much rather be with you."

Maybe Brayden didn't have any control over whom his mom assigned him to, but he could have texted her back. He could have warned her. *Is he embarrassed to be seen with me?*

You don't belong here, the voice in her head whispered again, and this time, Izzie listened.

Eleven

For the first time in a long time, Mira and Kellen were at a loss for words.

They stood side by side in the frigid Emerald Cove Masterpiece Gallery and gazed at the wall-size painting they were supposed to critique for art class.

Mira had her notebook out and a pen in hand, but she couldn't think of a single thing to say about this bizarre piece of modern art. It looked like it had been painted by a three-year-old. The artist had literally thrown large blotches of red, violet, and yellow paint at the canvas and then pushed pieces of rusted metal through the back of the painting, ripping parts of the canvas. Bark and tree branches hung from the metal like necklaces. The work was called *Changeling*. She would have titled it *Junk*.

She glanced at Kellen out of the corner of her eye. He could have passed for an art buyer in the navy sports coat he still had on from an earlier school ceremony. She looked dressed down in comparison, in jeans and her favorite pale green shirt, the one with the cute scarf attached. Kellen had barely given her outfit a glance. He kept looking at his notebook every few seconds to jot something down. What was he writing? There wasn't anything to say about this painting except how horrible it was! If she handed something like this in to their art teacher, Mr. Capozo, she would get a big, fat F.

The art gallery curator walked over. She could have been Gwyneth Paltrow's twin. She removed her thick-rimmed black glasses—the kind Mira suspected girls wore to look smart—and smiled. "The Stefano Paramore is something, isn't it?"

"Yes," Kellen said. She thought she saw his mouth twitch. "It is *something*."

"Such fine craftsmanship," Gwynie said, admiring one of the steel beams. "He worked months to get this right."

Kellen shook his head solemnly. "You can tell."

The woman's blond ponytail swished like a horse's tail when it meets a fly. "We've had several calls about it. A potential buyer is coming in this afternoon."

"What is the asking price?" Mira had to know. Were there really people out there interested in a piece like this?

"Twenty-six thousand dollars," the woman said without blinking. The phone rang, and she hurried to answer it, which was good because she missed Mira's gaping mouth. "Tell Mr. Capozo if any more of his students want to see *Changeling*, they should get here soon. I'm sure it will be sold by next week."

"We'll tell them to rush over," Kellen promised. "They won't want to miss this."

"Please tell me you're kidding," Mira whispered, the horror all but unmistakable in her hazel eyes. Kellen winked. "Thank God! How is this considered art?"

They looked at the ginormous eyesore again, and Kellen could barely contain his laughter. Neither could Mira. The curator glanced their way. "Let's get out of here." Kellen led her to the exit. Mira tried hard to keep up with his long strides. She did not want him letting go of her arm.

"What about the rest of the assignment?" Mira asked. "We're supposed to write about five different paintings."

"I know someplace better." Kellen pushed the gallery doors open, and she felt a rush of warm air as they stepped onto Main Street. Even though it was fall, anything would be warmer than that igloo they were just in. "How do you feel about a field trip?" Kellen asked. "Where we're going, we can tackle our art assignment and eat."

"Food and homework tackled? I'm in." Her heart revved

slightly. Kellen was inviting her someplace with food! Corky's had been her idea. This one was his. Did that make this a date? "Where are we headed?"

"You'll see," he said, looking a lot like her brother Connor when he was trying to get away with something he shouldn't. Kellen let go of her arm, and she tried not to appear disappointed. "Do you have a bus pass?"

"A bus pass?" she repeated, this being the first time the words *bus* and *pass* had ever crossed her lips in the same sentence.

Kellen shook his head. "Come on, princess. I'm taking you to my town. It's time someone shows you how the other half lives."

Before Mira knew it, she was on the M14 bus headed for Peterson, crammed between an older woman carrying a grocery bag that smelled of red onion and a guy listening to his iPod so loud that she could have sung along. Kellen was standing in front of her, acting like a cushion every time the bus stopped short. He had his feet planted squarely on the ground, slightly apart, and he seemed to be balancing like he was on a surfboard. Peterson was a fifteen-minute ride from Emerald Cove made thirty minutes with the bus stops, and she spent the entire time wondering what Kellen's town would be like. He had told her Peterson was nothing like Emerald Cove. Did that mean it was a carbon copy of Izzie's

142

Harborside, check-cashing stores on every corner and bars on the windows? If it was, how was she supposed to react? She'd put her foot in her mouth too many times with Izzie, and she did not want to do the same with Kellen. He may have teased her about being a princess, but she was determined to prove him wrong. But when she stepped off the bus at their stop, she wasn't prepared for what she saw.

"*This* is Peterson?" Mira looked from the picturesque street to a cute baby in a pricey stroller. She half expected the baby to explain herself.

"Were you expecting something else?" Kellen asked.

"No." Mira's face heated up as she spotted the Starbucks on the corner right next to a dog-grooming shop. She felt like such an idiot. Again. "It's really cute." *Just nothing like what I thought it would be*, she didn't add.

Peterson's tree-lined square looked exactly like Emerald Cove if you took away the boutiques and the Apple store and replaced them with a music shop and a barbecue restaurant that had a giant cow statue out front. Metal sculptures jutted out of the walkways. A sketch artist worked on a bench nearby. Kids walked by in the same jeans and Ts she wore. The outdoor seating at a café was full. She could already tell the town had a cool, laid-back vibe.

"You thought Peterson was going to be like Harborside, didn't you?" Kellen seemed to have read her thoughts.

"That's okay, I get that a lot at EP. People hear scholarship and they immediately think I live in a trailer park."

"I didn't say that, I just..." Mira took a deep breath, thinking about what she wanted to say. "Okay. I didn't say it, but I did think it. Forgive me?"

"I am not mad." A crooked grin spread over his face. Mira watched two kids walk by with ice-cream cones. "I already know how you think, Mirabelle Monroe."

She wasn't sure if that was a compliment, but she decided to take it. Something was still eating at her, and she couldn't hold it in. "So why do you go to Emerald Prep if you live someplace like this?"

"Ah, she continues her downward spiral, ladies and gentlemen." Kellen applauded to those around them, and she narrowed her eyes. "Why don't *you* go to public school?"

Well... She didn't have an answer for that one.

"Uh-huh. Just what I thought." Kellen studied her like he had that awful painting. "Just because I live someplace cool doesn't mean I don't want to go to a school that has a state champion fencing team."

"You don't fence." The smell of crepes from the nearby bakery was making her hungry.

"True." Kellen turned left onto another equally cute block. "My parents are big on education, and Peterson's fine, but if I could go to Emerald Prep for next to nothing, why not? I took the test, got almost a full ride, and here I am. My only regret is that my benefactor is the Ingrams. I wish they weren't, but what am I going to do? My parents have a lot more on their minds than my scholarship sponsor." His face darkened. "My dad's company keeps talking about moving their headquarters to another state."

"Can they do that?" Mira tried not to sound worried.

"Maybe." Kellen shrugged. "He doesn't talk about it much, but he needs his job. My mom was laid off over the summer, and money's tight. But enough about my family's drama." His green eyes looked greener in the late afternoon light. "Any other questions on your list? My favorite color is cobalt blue, in case you were wondering."

"Okay, clearly I need to stop talking," Mira said.

Kellen stopped in front of a store that had flyers covering the windows. The sign said *Sup*. What the heck was Sup?

"You're making that look again." Kellen imitated Mira's doe-eyed nervous expression perfectly. He even tried to push his sandy blond hair behind his ears, like she often did, but his wasn't long enough.

She crossed her arms. There was only so much teasing she could take. "Are you going to make fun of me all afternoon? Because I could take a bus right back to Emerald Cove right now."

Kellen viewed her skeptically. "I'd like to see you figure out the bus schedule."

"I could." She tried to think of ways she could get

145

home if she had to. "I mean, I'm sure someone could show me how."

Kellen shook his head. "Why don't we just finish our assignment first?" He held the door open for her. A thumping bass beat from some new Pitbull song was being played so loudly, the tables were vibrating. They appeared to be in a coffee shop, but there was a stage at one end where a lonely microphone stood unattended. The dark purple walls and the Goth-looking chick making cappuccinos behind the counter didn't exactly warm up the vibe. Where had Kellen brought her?

The song ended, and Mira could hear Kellen again. "What do you want?"

"Are we taking this to go?" she asked hopefully. She didn't have any antibacterial wipes on her to scrub down those dingy-looking tables.

"No, we're here to do our art assignment," he said as if it should be obvious. "This is an art house. Well, an art house *and* a coffee bar, but it's pretty well known. They've displayed a lot of work from up-and-coming artists in North Carolina."

For the first time, Mira noticed the walls. They were covered with paintings, and those that couldn't fit were propped up on easels. A few of the funky metal sculptures she had seen on the street were in miniature form near the espresso machine.

She walked over to the wall to examine a painting that

caught her eye. It was of an old man in a frayed sun chair watching a small child jump in the waves. "This is a George Piner," she said in awe. They had learned about Piner in class. He was the first painter in their area to get his work displayed at the MoMA in New York.

"I'll leave you and Piner alone while I get us some drinks," Kellen said.

The brushstrokes of the ocean were so vivid, she wanted to touch them. She pulled her notebook out of her bag and started to write. It was much easier now that she had something inspiring to look at.

When Kellen returned a few minutes later, she had already taken pictures of the painting and written a page of notes. "Wow, you really are hooked on this one."

"I keep wondering what the old man is thinking." She stared at the picture. "Is he sad that he isn't young anymore, or is he thinking about how happy his own life was at the beach?" She glanced at Kellen sheepishly. "Maybe I'm just reading too much into it."

"I think that's what you're supposed to do with a painting." Kellen took a seat at a table nearby and pulled out his notebook. "At least I do. There are so many different ways to look at someone's work."

Mira wanted to see more paintings. She stopped at a tiny canvas painted in bright colors. It was a comic strip about a robot whose parents adopt a coffeemaker and say it's the robot's brother. Mira cracked up. "Have you seen this one?" she asked. "It's hilarious!" Her eyes caught sight of the small name tag to the right of the painting: *Artist: Kellen Harper.* Mira spun around. "You did this one?"

"Guilty. I worked on it here." He looked at it for half a second. "It's not my favorite comic, but Lily, the owner, insisted on putting it up."

Mira was impressed. Kellen's work was in a real gallery. A coffee house gallery, but still. The only place her work was displayed was on their fridge. "I didn't know you liked comics."

"Love them." Kellen offered her his notebook, and she flipped through it. Not surprisingly, small comics filled almost every page. "I like reading and writing them. Manga, too. Not that I'm that good at any of it."

"You *are* good." His sketchbook was incredible.

"I don't usually show people my stuff," Kellen admitted.

"Well, I'm glad you shared it with me," she said, her voice soft, her hands sort of sweaty. *Oh God, please don't let me leave sweat stains on his artwork.* It had to mean something that he was opening up to her. "I don't have a clue what I'm doing in painting," she told him. "I like it, but I can't see my work ever being displayed in public."

"Why not? They run contests at Sup all the time. They just started a new one." Kellen handed her a hot-pink flyer from the coffee counter.

148

WHAT'S SUP, ART AFICIONADOS?

THINK YOU HAVE WHAT IT TAKES TO SHARE ART SPACE WITH THE LIKES OF PINER, FEIST, AND ALBRACK? THIS MONTH'S CHALLENGE IS GETTING REAL WITH YOUR ART. SHOW US THE ANGST IN YOUR OWN LIFE THROUGH YOUR PAINTBRUSH. SHOW US YOUR BEST SELF-PORTRAIT. ONE WINNER WILL HAVE THEIR WORK DISPLAYED ON OUR WALLS FOR A MONTH. AFTER THAT, WHO KNOWS WHERE YOUR ART WILL WIND UP?

"You have to enter," Mira told Kellen over the roar of a new song. Oh wait, that was just the coffee-bean grinder. "You would win." She slid the contest flyer toward him.

Kellen pushed it back. "Why don't we both enter?"

She shook her head and tried to send the flyer his way again, but Kellen kept his fingers on it. "I've never really drawn people before." *All I draw is flowers and trees.* How lame was that? Sure, Monet did the same, but she couldn't compare herself to *Monet.* She wasn't sure she could draw something as personal as the lines on a person's face or someone's nose. She glanced at the Piner wistfully. It was so beautiful.

"Why don't you draw yourself at that cotillion luncheon?" Kellen suggested. "You said it was the craziest one you've been to. I'm sure you can come up with some good expressions for people's faces."

"Maybe." She had been looking for a cotillion opening all

149

afternoon so she could bring up her lack of an escort, but now that the moment was here, it didn't seem to fit into the conversation.

"What are you afraid of?" Kellen taunted. He was always up for a dare.

"I'm not afraid." Kellen held her gaze, and she cracked. "Okay, maybe I am a little. I don't draw my personal life."

"That's art," Kellen said. "Why do you think Piner's painting affected you so much? He drew real life. He didn't stick a metal pipe through a canvas and call it a day."

Mira glanced at the Piner again. "What if my painting comes out awful?" She had never sounded so unsure of herself before. She didn't like it.

"Come on. Give it a shot. We can enter together."

That was certainly an incentive. Mira bit her lip.

"If you're that worried about someone seeing it, don't be," Kellen said. "There must be dozens of Monroes in North Carolina."

That was true.

Kellen pushed the paper her way again. Sometimes he could be so stubborn. Kind of like Izzie. "What do you have to lose?"

"Okay." She folded the flyer and put it in her notebook. "But I'm not making promises."

They talked so long after that conversation that the chai tea latte he'd bought her was now lukewarm. "Thanks," she said out of nowhere, making Kellen look up from the notebook he had been drawing in. "It's nice to have someone to hang out with again." Sometimes he made her so nervous, especially when he was staring at her like that.

"Yeah." He looked at her carefully between sips of cocoa. He had a small white line on his upper lip from the whipped cream, but she didn't tell him. He looked cute like that. "I like hanging out with you, too."

And that's when Mira felt it. Hope. The hope that maybe, just maybe, Kellen liked her back.

Twelve

The buzzer sounded, and Izzie hit the pool, her head bobbing above and below the water ten times before she took a breath. She sped through the water with a determined focus. There was no time to worry about where her competitors from St. Alexander's Girls School were. She'd made that mistake before and paid for it dearly. When she finally hit the wall, she felt a moment of panic like she got when she wasn't sure what was going on around her. But when she broke through the water, she heard cheers coming from the red side of the bleachers. She must have won! She took off her goggles and twirled them in the air, jumping up and down in the pool.

"Time for the breaststroke one-hundred-meter race, one minute and nine seconds, a win for Isabelle Scott," said the announcer as Izzie pulled herself out of the pool.

"Nice one, Izzie!" Coach Greff threw a towel around her.

"You are a machine, woman!" marveled Violet, who was standing with Nicole.

Nicole grabbed Izzie's arm and led her to their section in the bleachers. "Look at your triceps! No wonder you powered through two laps! Are you sneaking in workouts?"

"Yes," Izzie lied, still out of breath. "After you guys leave, I do fifty laps."

"Show-off." Violet adjusted her camo swim cap. "You are quickly becoming the star of this team. Coach Greff is your biggest fan."

The indoor pool had a high glass ceiling, but the room was still a hothouse. As Izzie glanced at Savannah across the bleachers through the muggy haze, she could almost feel the other girl's hatred. "Let's hope you-know-who doesn't see it that way. I don't need any more problems."

"She's too preoccupied with cotillion to worry about you," Nicole assured her.

"And she's ignoring the Butterflies because of it," Izzie grumbled. "She missed our meeting the other day because she was shoe shopping for our next dance lesson!"

"Are you surprised? Butterflies isn't her main focus anymore," Violet said. "She has a white dress to buy and a group of fellow debs-in-training to make miserable."

Izzie shook her head. "Mrs. Fitz seemed upset when she and Mira didn't show. Mira at least had an excuse. She had to go to some gallery for an art assignment, but still. Mrs. Fitz told me she feels like no one is taking their club duties seriously, and she's right. There are so many things we could be doing, and instead we can barely get everyone to a meeting."

"Wait till Founders Day planning starts," Nicole warned her. "It's even harder to get everyone's attention then."

Izzie got so frustrated by the Butterflies' lack of drive sometimes that she wanted to scream. They needed a real leader. Mrs. Fitz needed to put herself in charge, but she wouldn't. She was a by-the-rules girl, as she called herself, and the rules said that Savannah and Mira were in charge.

"Why don't you organize the next event?" Violet asked.

Izzie bit her lip. "I know I did the last one, and if no one else wants to get their act together, then maybe I should take over."

"Woohoo! She realizes her power!" Violet fist-bumped her.

"But I can't," Izzie reminded them. "Only a cochair can nominate a new project."

"Those rules are ridiculous," said Violet. "They give Savannah ultimate power, which we all know she does not need."

"She already has too much power," Nicole agreed. "She's even getting her way in cotillion." Nicole turned to Violet. "Savannah danced with Brayden at our cotillion lunch, and she didn't have to cuff him to get him to do it. He asked her!"

Izzie continued to towel off. "Thanks for reminding me."

"I can't believe Brayden would do that to you." Violet pulled the band of her goggles, and they snapped hard.

"Want to know what is worse? He hasn't even apologized," Izzie said, and Violet's eyes widened. "I've barely spoken to him since the lunch, and when I saw him today in class, he acted like everything was fine. I wanted to sock him in the stomach."

"What a jerk." Violet pulled her goggles over her swim cap and removed her red shorts, which said *Emerald Prep* on the butt. Her 100-meter freestyle was coming up.

"You guys aren't being fair." Nicole liked to play devil's advocate, but Izzie wasn't in the mood. "Maybe his mom put him up to it. You have no idea how much control that woman has. She's probably got Brayden under some sort of voodoo spell."

"He looked fine to me," Izzie said. "He danced with her three times, then disappeared. It's like he thinks if he doesn't talk about it, it never happened."

"Now I wish I was doing cotillion." Violet's eyes narrowed. "I wouldn't want to do stupid stunts like your Gaga sing-along, but I would have loved to be at your welcome tea so I could kick Brayden's butt." She sounded like Kylie. When Izzie had told her what happened at the luncheon, Kylie screamed all sorts of things that Izzie couldn't repeat.

"Brayden must be waiting to talk to you alone," Nicole guessed. "He probably had to put on a show for his mom since his sister is doing the opposite. You guys know about his sister, Dylan, right?" Violet shook her head, and Izzie figured it was best to do the same.

"I guess you wouldn't." Nicole pulled her long legs up on

the bench and rested her head on her knees. "She was gone before either of you came to town." She looked at Izzie. "She's one of the debs running our initiation. The tall, skinny one with long blond hair."

"Aren't they all tall, skinny, and blond?" Izzie joked. Dylan had trusted her enough to share her secret, and she didn't want to blow it.

Nicole had already swum the backstroke and the 500-meter freestyle, so she had plenty of time to share gossip. "When Dylan was here at EP, I heard, the things she did were so crazy, her parents had to ship her to a boarding school in New England."

"What did she do that was so wrong?" Izzie couldn't help but ask. "Get drunk at a party or date some guy they didn't like?" That's what Mira had said happened, but neither scenario sounded banishment-worthy. It irked her how quick everyone was to jump to conclusions about Dylan when they barely knew her.

"Think worse," Nicole said. "Dylan drove her mom's Porsche Roadster without a license and crashed it into the horse stables near Harper Browning's farm."

"She's the one who destroyed the stables?" Violet's eyes bulged. "I heard about that when I moved here."

Nicole leaned in closer. "Yep. She wasn't drinking, but the accident happened in the middle of the night, and the EC police chief was the first on the scene. She was in the car with some guy who definitely wasn't Junior League–approved. Everyone knew the story by morning—the police chief's wife is a big Junior Leaguer—and Dylan's mom was mortified. She was shipped out to St. Bernadine's the following week. Abigail Townsend has no tolerance for mistakes, especially from her daughter."

Driving without a license and stealing her mother's car was definitely a mistake, but the accident might not have been her fault, Izzie thought. *The guy in the car could have been anyone. Just because he wasn't from here didn't make the story more of a scandal.* Maybe it was time for her to change the subject. "I don't think Mrs. Townsend has a high tolerance for a lot of people," Izzie said. "Especially me."

"What makes you say that?" Violet stood up and started to stretch for her race.

"She didn't seem too fond of me at cotillion, especially after I got hot tea on her jacket." Violet winced. "Then I got a note from her yesterday saying I needed extra help in the ballroom-dance department. She also said I have less than one week to find a legitimate charity to work with to fulfill my community commitment, or I'll flunk out of cotillion."

"You can't fail out of cotillion." Nicole frowned. "I think."

Izzie pulled the ice-blue monogrammed stationery out of her bag and handed it to the girls. "I'm not so sure of that. Take a look at the note yourself."

"Hi, girls." Savannah had come from out of nowhere. "Nice

157

race, Izzie. Too bad your time wasn't just a teensy bit faster. We would have had the lead." She noticed the blue card in Nicole's hands, and her face lit up. "Did you get a note from Abigail Townsend? I'd recognize her Tiffany note cards anywhere."

"God, do you have the Townsends on radar or something?" Nicole slipped the note back into Izzie's bag before Savannah could reach for it.

Savannah adjusted her pink swim cap. "She gave me a thank-you note just the other day, actually. She wanted to thank me for agreeing to dance with Brayden at the welcome tea." Izzie's back stiffened. "I called her right up and said, 'Mrs. Townsend, why wouldn't I dance with your son? Our families have dinner together every week.'" She eyed Izzie with determination. "'No matter what happened between us, a bond like that doesn't disappear overnight.'" Savannah smiled sweetly. "But don't worry, Izzie. I'm sure you'll be invited over to meet them all eventually. You'd fit right in—with Dylan." She walked away before Izzie could trip her.

Izzie's foot began to tap uncontrollably. Why had Brayden never mentioned that the Ingrams and Townsends got together every week?

"Do not let her get to you," Nicole glared at Savannah walking away. "She's just jealous."

"Of what? All the family dinners she is having with Brayden and Izzie isn't?" Violet said incredulously. Both girls looked at her. "I'm sorry. I know Brayden's a good guy, but first he didn't

158

text you back about being at the welcome tea, then he somehow forgets to mention these weekly dinners? What gives?"

Violet was right. Izzie didn't think she could feel much worse till she felt a tap on her shoulder.

"Hi, Isabelle." Bill looked awkward in a tie and sports coat in the steamy aquatic center. "Great race back there. You, too, girls."

For a split second, she was touched. Bill had come from the office just to see her. She hadn't had family cheer her on at a meet in a long time. Grams had attended many, but in the last year, she had no clue what was going on.

"It's so nice to see you, Senator Monroe." Nicole's voice was chipper, like it was on autopilot. Izzie noticed this happened a lot with her friends from Emerald Cove. No matter how annoyed they were at someone's parents, the minute that adult came into view, their manners took over. Izzie couldn't fake the enthusiasm.

"I should get ready for my next race," Violet told them. "It was nice seeing you, Senator Monroe. Come on, Nic. Why don't you help me warm up?"

Izzie's foot tapped faster now. She didn't want her friends to kiss Bill's butt, but she didn't want them to leave her alone, either.

"Mind if I sit down?" Bill stared at the empty seat next to her.

"I should warm up for my next race, too," Izzie told him.

She glanced at the board. She didn't really have to. There were still seven races ahead of hers.

"I won't stay long." He sat down, and for ten minutes, they watched the race in silence. Violet's heat was going. When she won, Izzie was so happy, she almost hugged Bill.

"It's okay to smile around me, you know," Bill said. Izzie didn't answer him. "You have every right to be mad at me, but I am still going to try to win you over. I used to argue my case with your mom all the time."

The hairs on Izzie's arms may have been wet, but they stood up.

"Chloe was stubborn when we fought, too," he added. "Not that we fought often."

"You didn't fight often, because you only knew her a few months." Izzie's anger was getting the best of her.

"True." He watched the next heat. "But we spent practically every nonworking moment together. You learn a lot about a person quickly when you practically live with them." He studied Izzie for a moment. "You have her mouth—both the shape and the attitude that comes with it. She was big with causes like you are, too. It didn't matter what the cause was." He smiled at the memory. "She'd fight for a street that needed a crossing signal, picket till a school agreed to build a new playground, or fight to keep the vegetable garden in our neighborhood from being turned into a parking lot. Your mom was a one-woman call to arms."

Izzie wished she had the nerve to tell him to stop talking, but part of her wanted to hear what he had to say. She didn't know her mom shared the same need to give back that she did. There was no one left to tell her what her mom was like. Sometimes she even craved hearing her mom's name spoken out loud so it wouldn't disappear.

"Even back then, Chloe was a big swimmer," Bill said. "She'd drag me to the beach at East Rockaway, and she'd want to stay on the sand from sunup to sundown." Izzie turned toward him to hear more, and he did the same, his hazel eyes full of energy. "She was a rabble-rouser, always swimming out beyond the ropes. Anything to tick off a lifeguard. Chloe said she had spent her life in the ocean and no one knew it as well as she did. She used to have an expression about it actually. Something about glory, I think."

"No guts, no glory," Izzie said quietly. Their voices were drowned out by more cheering. EC's team was in the lead. Even though everyone else was standing, Izzie and her dad sat locked in their conversation. "Mom used to say the same thing to me when she was teaching me how to swim," Izzie told him. "I remember her liking a challenge. Any challenge."

"I do, too," he said, leaning forward. "We'd make bets over who could make the bed the neatest. Not that I stayed over," he added quickly.

"Of course not," Izzie said wryly. "The stork brought me."

"Exactly." He nodded solemnly. "Chloe was one-of-a-kind.

I loved how she could talk for hours about what she wanted to do with her life and where she wanted to go. She had a map with pins that showed all the cities she wanted to visit."

The last part struck a nerve.

"But that didn't happen, did it? She never got to go anywhere but New York." Izzie felt the fire in her heat up again. "She came home pregnant with me and never left Harborside again."

Bill looked her squarely in the eye. "I may not have known about you, but I knew your mom, and no matter how far she wanted to travel, she never regretted where she called home. She loved North Carolina. She wanted to see the world, but Chloe always said she could never see herself living anywhere but here."

Izzie could feel the ugly seeping into their conversation. "Why did you leave her?"

Bill's face twisted slightly. "She . . . we . . . it just didn't work out." Izzie stared at him so long for clues as to why, she almost didn't hear her name. Her race was next.

"I have to warm up." She placed her goggles over her swim cap.

"Before you go, I have something else I need to tell you."

She was already depressed. Did he really have to make her feel worse?

"There's going to be another story in the papers tomorrow." For the first time, Izzie noticed how tired Bill looked. "Grayson Reynolds, the reporter at the *North Carolina*

Gazette on my beat, claims to have taped a conversation with you and Mira."

"He's lying," Izzie said. "Mira and I aren't stupid. We wouldn't talk about you in public."

He smiled grimly. "I appreciate that. Callista has threatened the paper with slander, but the story is still running. Grayson is a well-respected columnist. We go way back." Bill no longer looked happy. "He has hated me and my policies for years. Just promise me you won't read his story or get upset."

"What does it say?" she asked. Nicole was waving frantically. She had to get over there, or she'd be late for the race.

Bill looked uncomfortable. "It says that you and Mira wish you could be adopted. That you'd rather crisscross the globe with Madonna than be stuck in Emerald Cove with me."

Izzie inhaled sharply. She *had* said that. She and Mira had joked around about it one night while they were watching a story on celebrity travel on E! But they had been half kidding, and they definitely didn't think anyone had heard them. "I'm sorry."

"It's okay," he told her. "I don't want you to worry."

"Izzie Scott! You're up!" Coach Greff yelled.

"Have a great race." He gave her a small smile.

But Izzie didn't have a good race. She lost the 200-meter freestyle relay for her team. She told herself it was because the girls at St. Alexander's Girls School held the county medal in the event. The truth was, all she could think about was her mom. Maybe that's why she finished the meet and knew where she needed to go. She got as far as the Emerald Prep drop-off area before running into the other person she couldn't get off her mind.

"Hey!" Brayden ran to catch up with her. His brown hair was matted to his head from his football helmet, and he was in gym clothes. "I just got out of practice. I wanted to see the rest of your meet, but someone said it was over. Did you win?"

"Yes and no," she said, avoiding his gaze. Technically, he hadn't done anything wrong at cotillion. They weren't officially dating, so he could dance with whomever he wanted. But that didn't mean he didn't behave like a royal jerk. "I need to go. I'll talk to you later."

Brayden's face fell. "You're mad at me, aren't you?"

Um, yes? She didn't want to get into this. She wanted to catch a bus to see Grams and make it home before dinner. "I'll catch you later." She started walking away.

"This is about Savannah, isn't it?" Brayden wasn't giving up. She kept her eyes on the main gate and the bus stop just beyond it. She was so close to getting out of there. "You're upset about Savannah and me dancing together at the welcome tea."

The way he said it—like he had no responsibility, that it just happened—made Izzie furious. She whirled around. "You're more observant than I thought. How could you not warn me that you were coming to the tea and planning to totally ignore me?"

"I didn't mean for it to happen like that. It was wrong." Brayden was visibly upset. "But you have to understand—"

If she didn't get this out now, she might not have the nerve later. "I had to watch you two on the dance floor. And even after that torture, you didn't come over to talk to me. You stayed with her!"

"I'm sorry," Brayden butted in. "I was only there ten minutes. I was going to call you after and explain, but—"

"But you were having their family over for dinner," Izzie guessed.

Brayden winced. "I should have told you everything. I don't know why I listen to Dylan." Izzie's ears perked up. "She said you'd be upset about the dinners, so I was better off keeping them quiet. I know how worried you get about Savannah getting between us, but I shouldn't have kept this quiet. I'm sorry, Iz."

Dylan couldn't stand Savannah. If she told Brayden to keep the dinners from her, then Izzie had to assume Dylan was trying to protect her. The story made more sense now, and unfortunately it also made it harder for her to be mad at Brayden. But there was still the fact that he'd ignored her texts. He wasn't off the hook yet.

"I thought you were hiding something from me," Izzie said, starting to calm down. "I don't trust people that easily and I trust you, Brayden. Finding out you lied to me…"

He walked toward her. "I'm sorry. Really, I am. It won't

happen again." The only consolation was that he looked miserable.

"That still doesn't explain why you danced with Savannah at the luncheon." She did not want to be *that girl*—the one who hounded a boy to death about his every move—but Brayden had to know how hurt she was. "It still doesn't explain why you ignored three texts from me asking if you were coming."

Brayden looked puzzled. "I didn't get any texts." She gave him a sharp look. "I swear. I couldn't find my phone anywhere. My parents just got me a new one yesterday." He pulled a new phone out of his pocket and showed it to her.

She felt slightly sheepish now.

"I know this doesn't change what I did. I still should have told you I was going to have to dance with Savannah at the luncheon," Brayden said. "My parents bullied me into it with the whole 'our family has to set an example' speech and the 'we owe it to the Ingrams' talk." He rolled his eyes. "I'm sick of it."

She wanted to believe him, but she kept thinking about how Dylan said Brayden was his parents' lackey. Dylan said Brayden never said no to them. Was he really going to stand up to them now?

Brayden squeezed her hand. "I should have told you what was going on. It won't happen again. I swear. Give me another shot."

She didn't want to open herself up to being hurt again, but he looked so sincere that she softened a bit. "You'd better be," she warned him. She held on to his hand until the J26 bus pulled up in front of them. "I have to catch this."

"I'll go with you," Brayden told her. He pulled his wallet out for fare.

Izzie laughed. "You don't even know where I'm going!"

"So?" Brayden took her bag. "All I need to know is I'm going with you." He stepped up in front of the opening bus doors.

"Charmer." Izzie pushed him onto the bus ahead of her.

~

A half hour later, they got off at the stop near Coastal Assisted Living Center. By that point, she had filled Brayden in on where they were headed.

"Isabelle! So nice to see you again," said the receptionist as she buzzed her and Brayden in. "I didn't know you were visiting today."

"Hi, Susan. I'm not on the schedule, but I thought if I got here before dinner…"

For some strange reason, the woman hesitated. "She's had a rough few days." Izzie's shoulders tensed. The center had called Aunt Maureen the other night about Grams's condition. Apparently, she had been having all sorts of health problems unrelated to the dementia. It seemed like after one part of Grams's body failed, they had all started to follow suit. Aunt Maureen had said it was nothing Izzie should worry about. The woman noticed Izzie's reaction and gave her a small smile. "But I'm sure she'd love to see you and your friend. Maybe it would help." Susan pressed a *Hello* sticker onto Brayden's T-shirt. "They're setting up for bingo in the rec room. Your grandmother and her friends are being wheeled down now."

Izzie and Brayden walked down a bright blue hallway to the recreation room. Hannah, aka the "fun coordinator," was flinging bingo cards on all the tables. She looked harried.

"Isabelle! How are you, honey?" Hannah asked, eyeing Brayden. "Who did you bring with you today?"

"My friend Brayden," she said. Hannah dropped a stack of cards, and they scattered all over the floor. "Need help?"

"Yes." Hannah passed them both bingo stampers. "Can you put these in front of every chair? This place could use some extra hands. When we have an art project for Thanksgiving, a macaroni necklace craft, or a game of bingo, I'm the only one holding down the fort." She looked embarrassed. "But you didn't come here to hear me complain. How's your grandmother today? Better?"

"I haven't seen her yet." Hannah nodded. Remembering the note from Abigail Townsend, an idea occurred to Izzie. "When are events, usually?" Izzie asked. "Weeknights or weekends?"

"I can schedule them anytime," Hannah said. "Why do you ask, sugar?"

"I'm here once a week to see Grams, and I feel bad it's not

168

more. Plus, I need to do some volunteer work for my cotillion training. Maybe I could help out here," Izzie said.

"You're doing cotillion?" Hannah studied Izzie like a level of Angry Birds she couldn't beat. "I didn't figure you for the type."

"Yeah, me, neither," Brayden agreed, and Izzie gave him a sharp look.

"So what do you say?" Izzie asked. "I'm yours if you want me." There was no way Abigail Townsend could fault her for picking a nursing home.

"Of course I want you!" Hannah said. "You're hired."

"Great!" Izzie grinned. "I'll start now."

"Can I help today, too?" Brayden asked. He cleared his throat. "People say I have an excellent bingo caller voice."

"You're hired. You're both just in time, too, because here they come." The residents began arriving slowly. Izzie spotted Grams near the back of the pack, being wheeled in by her regular nurse, Eileen. Izzie motioned for Brayden to follow her.

She was rattled when she saw her grandmother up close. Her appearance had changed rapidly from even Izzie's last visit. "I'll take her from here, Eileen," Izzie said quietly, and grabbed the handlebars. Grams looked a little paler and thinner than she had the week before, but her blue eyes still lit up her face. Someone had obviously combed her thinning white hair and fastened a tiny pink flower in it.

"Hey, Grams," Izzie said softly, steering her to a table

without chairs, reserved for the wheelchairs. "How are you?" Her grandmother never answered. She just stared ahead, concentrating hard on something Izzie could never see. Her lips barely moved; her eyes seemed to hardly blink. She rarely made eye contact anymore.

"This is my friend Brayden," Izzie told her.

Brayden crouched down and squeezed her hand. "It's nice to meet you, Grams. I've heard so much about you." Grams didn't look at him, but Izzie did. Whenever they talked about Grams, he acted like having dementia was the most normal thing in the world. It was at that moment that she knew she'd been right to forgive him.

"Great to finally meet you, Grams." He touched Izzie's hand. "I'll give you two a minute."

Grams had always been a great sounding board. She didn't give opinions anymore, but it still helped to talk to her. "That was Brayden," Izzie whispered, leaning by Grams's right ear. "He's the one I've been telling you about. I really like him, but his mom is in charge of cotillion, and I know she doesn't like me." She glanced at Brayden across the room. He was testing out different caller voices. She fixed the crocheted sweater around her grandmother's shoulders. "Can you believe I am doing cotillion? Mom would freak. I miss her so much, especially today. Hearing Bill talk about his life with my mom—with Chloe—made me sad."

At the mention of Chloe's name, Grams stared up at

Izzie, the warmth in her eyes returning for a moment. "Zoe, there you are! I was wondering where you went."

Zoe? This was a new one. Grams must have said her mom's name wrong. It used to be hard when Grams thought Izzie was somebody else, but over time, she had gotten used to it. Her grandmother got agitated whenever Izzie tried explaining who she was so Izzie got good at pretending she was her mom. "Hi, there."

Grams touched Izzie's hand. "You were gone too long this time, and you didn't tell us where you were. I told you, silence never solves anything. You have to work through your disagreements. When I'm gone, all you two will have is each other."

This conversation was new. Who was Grams talking about? Izzie felt like she was getting a peek inside her grandmother's diary. What else didn't she know about her mom? Was her mom seeing someone when she died? Was Grams talking about her dad? Had her mom actually mentioned him to her? "You're right," Izzie said. "We need each other." Her heart was beating out of her chest. "Who do I need again?"

Grams's eyes were squinty and her thin lips went straight, like they did when she didn't like something Izzie said. "Don't get snappy. You know who I'm talking about."

Izzie was dying to say "who," but before she could, she saw Grams's expression change. Her grandmother stared at her for half a second in confusion, then looked away, frightened, and stared straight ahead. The old Grams was gone again.

Thirteen

"And that is how you introduce yourself in Japan to a new acquaintance." Ms. Norberry finished her presentation and gave a final bow to the cotillion class as a reminder of what they had just learned. The class bowed in return.

Mira did a complete ninety-degree bow from the waist, as Ms. Norberry said was the custom when greeting an elder, which Ms. Norberry was. Their longtime cotillion instructor dyed her hair blond, was in great shape, and had amazing suits with coordinating broaches, but there was no hiding the fact that she was in her late sixties and had been running cotillion classes for Emerald Cove for the last twenty-two years.

"Lovely, Mira." Ms. Norberry noticed her perfect bow. She was wearing a traditional Japanese robe over her suit. Their teacher loved props. "Why don't we take a fifteen-minute break to get a refreshment, and then we'll talk about why you should always carry tissues in a Japanese public restroom."

Mira could tell Izzie's mood just by her expression. "How to use a Japanese restroom? I had to be up at eight on a Saturday to learn that?" As they walked out of the classroom, she pulled at the dress she had on as if it was constricting her airway.

"International etiquette is very important," Mira said, walking slightly ahead of her into the Emerald Cove Country Club's great hall to avoid making eye contact.

"Yeah, it's right up there with host responsibilities for a dinner party and the proper way to navigate a five-course meal." Izzie was gesturing with her arms. All Mira noticed was that Izzie's polish was chipped.

"Before that class you didn't even know what a shrimp fork was," Mira reminded her. She couldn't help but glance at some of the former debs huddled in a corner.

The former debs were on hand to "offer guidance," as Ms. Norberry called it. What they were really there for that Saturday morning, Mira guessed, was to assign them their next initiation dare. Knowing that, Mira's former friends had gathered around Savannah on one of the antique couches close by. Savannah held their attention as she chatted away about any number of amazing things she had accomplished that week, and the girls seemed to hang on to her every word.

"I've survived almost sixteen years without knowing how to use a shrimp fork," Izzie said, her eyes resting on the emerald choker on display in a glass case in the center of the room. The lock had been upgraded since Izzie and her friends "borrowed" the necklace a few months back. "I think I can continue to muddle through life without knowing how to use one or how to greet someone in Japan."

"If we ever go to Japan on vacation, you'll be thankful you learned." Mira removed her long white gloves so that she could take a linzer tart from the sterling-silver tray a waiter was passing around.

"I won't hold my breath." Izzie took two cookies with her white-gloved fingers.

"Isabelle!" Ms. Norberry swooped in, her wispy yet sharp voice making even the waiter freeze. "Gloves should be removed before dining. Remember your training," she tsked, sounding like a cranky babysitter. "It's not proper for a lady to take two cookies before the rest of the guests have had a chance to take one."

Izzie dropped a cookie back on the tray with a thud, and Ms. Norberry looked like she might pass out. She quickly produced a napkin from her pocketless shift dress and scooped up the offending cookie. "Once we've taken food, we don't put it back," she said before walking away. "Remember to read your cotillion handbook." Thankfully, Mrs. Townsend wasn't around to chime in. She had a meeting at Emerald Cove Castle on the Cliffs about the Winter White Ball. That woman was like the godfather of cotillion, and having her around put even Mira on edge. She could only imagine how Izzie felt.

"Remember to read your cotillion handbook," Izzie said, mimicking Ms. Norberry. Mira gave her a look.

"Toss the handbook out the window, ladies," Dylan said as she came up behind them. "I barely opened that thing, and they still let me put on a puffy white dress."

They had been caught gossiping red-handed. Mira turned around to face Dylan and couldn't help but gape. What was that girl wearing this time? She had on a strapless black dress that barely reached her mid-thigh, and four-inch-high stiletto heels. Dylan smiled at them as she held out a tray of white teacups. "Tea?"

"No, thank you," Mira said even as Izzie took one. "I don't want to get anything on my dress. Ms. Norberry would probably make me go home and change."

Dylan continued to hold out the tray. "You don't look like the klutzy type. Take one," she insisted. Mira was afraid to argue. "Wait till you taste this tea. It's so outrageous, you'll want to drink every last drop." She winked. "See you later."

Mira and Izzie looked at each other and then at their teacups. This obviously had something to do with initiation, but what, Mira didn't know. Izzie practically chugged her tea, and a small drip landed on her chest. Mira quickly blotted Izzie's dress.

"Geez, how thirsty are you?" Mira admonished.

"I think something's on the bottom of the cup," Izzie said, coming up for air. Mira watched as Izzie stripped off a note folded to the size of a thumbnail that had been taped to the underside of the cup. She carefully opened it as Mira drank her tea faster to see if she had a note, too.

```
Number One:
We want to see how well you know your Emerald
Cove history. On the bottom of each of your cups
is a number. Work together as a class and find
all fourteen items based on your clues. After
you find each object, take a picture with your
phone and text it to DEBS4EVR. Rule number one:
Everyone must be in the picture. Rule two:
Finish all fourteen items together or do the
whole thing over another day. Remember, as
always, we're watching!
XO,
Your Cotillion Captain
```

"Mine has a note on it," Mira told Izzie. "I think I got the directions. What does your note say?"

"Number two," Izzie read. "The clue is 'what is green and only gets greener?' What does that mean, and when are we supposed to slip away from Ms. Norberry long enough to find out?"

Just then, Ms. Norberry rushed into the great hall. "Girls,

I've just received an urgent phone call from my aunt Bertha. I don't even know how she had the number here! I need to run over and check on her, but I'll be back by noon at the latest." She made a face. "I apologize for keeping you late today."

A statement that normally would have been followed by groans was met with concern about Aunt Bertha and talk of studying up on their Japanese toilet training. Ms. Norberry was pleasantly surprised. After watching her car pull away, the fifteen cotillion pledges conferred in the center of the room while the former debs stood watch.

"My note just has a frowny face on it!" Savannah said when the coast was clear. "Everyone has a clue but me."

"I guess someone besides me doesn't like you." Izzie smiled serenely.

"So? No one likes you, and you're still here," Lea snapped. Full-fledged bickering broke out, just as a loud clap of thunder rattled the club.

"Great!" Lauren looked at the stained-glass windows. "A thunderstorm. If we have to go outside, we're going to get soaked."

"Why do I think that's the idea?" Charlotte said. She had on an incredible dress Mira recalled seeing in this month's *Vogue*.

"I'm not ruining my new Tory Burch shoes," Savannah told the others.

Mira looked down at her own cute shoes. They'd never survive all this rain. Fighting and complaining heated up.

"Enough!" Izzie barked, startling all of them and making Mira jump. "Do you guys want to whine about your shoes or get this assignment done? We only have about an hour, so let's let Mira read the directions so we can get started."

"Who put you in charge?" Savannah asked.

Izzie glared at her. "I did. Want to fight me for it?" Savannah backed away.

"Wow, someone should tell Izzie Scott to run for class president," Mira heard Charlotte whisper to a girl next to her. "She knows how to even put Savannah in her place."

Charlotte was right, Mira realized, watching Izzie command the room. Izzie was a natural leader. She was always harping on her to get the Butterflies' next event going, but Mira never had the time. If Mrs. Fitz said their next event didn't have to be till January, then who was she to push? But Izzie would push all of them. It made her wonder.

"Mira?" Izzie looked at her strangely. "The directions?"

"Sorry!" She read the directions as another roar of thunder rocked the club.

"How are we supposed to collect fourteen things if only thirteen of us have clues?" Savannah asked them. "Mira has the directions, and my card doesn't say anything. We're going to be short one item."

Izzie shrugged. "Let's hope something about your clue comes up as we go along." Savannah sat down in a huff. "I'll read my clue so we can start."

"She probably forged her clue," Lea whispered loud enough to be heard.

"Lea, that's not nice," Savannah scolded even though she was clearly enjoying herself now that she wasn't on the chopping block anymore. "He denies forging the signature, remember? Too bad he didn't keep a copy to prove it." The girls snickered.

Just that morning, Grayson Reynolds had run a story about Bill Monroe supposedly forging another district representative's signature on an important water preservation bill. Izzie's dad was a mess. "Donald told me to add his name to the bill!" she heard him tell Callista as Izzie sat quietly and ate her Lucky Charms. "He signed a copy as soon as I got to the office. That's not forgery!"

"Is there something you want to share with the rest of us, Lea?" Izzie stared the girl down.

"No," Lea squeaked. She sounded less sure of herself than she did a minute ago.

"Okay, then," Izzie said. "'What's green and only gets greener?'" Everyone looked at one another. Savannah started to perspire.

"Maybe they mean the golf course," said Charlotte. "Isn't that called a green? It's made of grass, so wouldn't it get greener throughout the spring and into summer?"

"Works for me," said Lea, and she took off running, probably just to get away from Izzie, who was still glaring at her.

The sounds of heels across the cobblestone floor echoed

through the room. The group ran past the ballroom and down the stairs to the golf shop, rushing past the men whose sessions had been cut short, and out the door as raindrops pelted their faces.

"Now what?" Lauren asked, staring at the puddles on the golf course. "Are we supposed to take a picture on the green? I thought this was a history lesson."

"Look over there!" Mira spotted a flag on the putting green. The flag bore the Emerald Cove Junior League's insignia. Something was tacked to the bottom of it. She ran over and pulled down a Ziploc that held a piece of paper.

"It's another note!" She ran back to the others under the small golf pro shop awning. "'Golf is not for paupers,'" she read. "'Maybe that's why it's always been played in Emerald Cove, ever since Victor Strausburg settled here. Using his emerald seed money, he built one of the country's first courses. Today, it's part of the Emerald Cove Country Club and is a prize-winning course.'"

Lauren practically tackled a golfer carrying his heavy golf bag in from the rain. "Sir, would you mind taking our picture?"

"Are you serious?" he asked, the raindrops dripping down his forehead. Lauren motioned to the others, who ran out and stood in the rain as it flattened their hair.

"Read the next clue before I melt," Lauren barked when

they were done pretending to smile for their picture. "Who has the second clue?"

"Me!" Charlotte opened her note. "'You know me as the queen of royalty, the starter of it all, but as I sit pale and silent, I wonder what some are saying about me. After all, there were rumors I was a witch.'"

It took all of Mira's willpower not to yell out *Savannah*.

"Pale and silent, pale and silent," Mira repeated to herself. It had to be a person, right? But who was always silent? The cute valet? Couldn't be him. He was tan. She had it! "They must mean the statue of Audrey Strausburg out front."

Nicole covered her head with her sweater to stay dry. "But she wasn't a witch."

"That doesn't mean someone didn't call her one," Izzie said. "Let's check it out."

The group followed Izzie and Mira to the front of the country club. Emerald Cove's founding wife stared down at them with a slight smile, her face lighting up between flashes of lightning. In her stone hands was a Ziploc bag with a note.

Izzie grabbed it and began to read, the rain smearing the ink. "'Poor Audrey Strausburg. Beautiful and rich but despised by the other founding families. They were convinced she dabbled in the dark arts. How else would her husband have found mine after mine of emeralds?'" Izzie rolled her eyes. "Even back then EC had gossips."

Mira ignored her. "Let's get a picture before one of us gets struck by lightning."

"Lea, go get the valet and make him take our picture," Lauren instructed as the group gathered around the statue. Lauren looked around. "Wait. Where is Savannah?" Mira didn't see her, either.

"Someone go find her," Izzie instructed, but no one moved. Mira didn't blame them. Who wanted to be the one to tell Savannah Ingram to get her butt back outside? "Lea? Go." Lea's shoulders sagged, but she did as she was told.

The storm sounded like it was directly overhead now. Mira looked up at Audrey's statue again, standing tall despite the awful weather. Her friends sounded a hell of a lot worse than Mira's. Maybe Izzie was right: What was Mira so afraid of?

"I can't find her," Lea reported a few minutes later. Her hair was starting to frizz.

"Did anyone call her?" Mira asked. People did not summon Savannah by phone, but there was a first time for everything. She stared at Lea and Lauren. "Someone call her *now*. I am not doing this challenge twice because she had to reapply lip gloss." Mira surprised herself with her tone. She noticed Izzie grin.

"Fine!" Lauren huffed. She dialed, cringing at the sound of Savannah's voice when she picked up. "Where are you?" Lauren's eyes narrowed slightly. "Forget your clue! We're at the statue right now with another clue, and you're going to cost us the hunt if you don't get out here and get in this picture."

Savannah didn't take long to show up, but she did look angry. She stared at Lauren like she wanted to make her one of her dog's chew toys. But Mira didn't care whether Savannah smiled for the camera. The important thing was that they had found the second clue and had a photo to prove it. Clues three through thirteen weren't as hard to solve as Mira had thought they would be. They spent the next forty minutes dashing around the Emerald Cove Country Club, running from the women's locker room to the coat-check area to the men's showers. They passed the pool twice, had to borrow three golf carts to ride out to the ninth hole, and finally found themselves back in the great hall. There was only one clue left to find, and it was Savannah's. Mira sensed a mutiny about to happen as the girls ran around trying to think of places Savannah's real note might be. A few were so cold and delirious after an hour in the rain that they actually accused her of hiding her note to keep them from finishing their assignment.

"Maybe you should grovel to the debs," Lea pushed Savannah toward the older girls. "It's time you tried doing it like the rest of us. I. Want. To. Be. Done. With. This. Dare." The hunt had clearly done a number on her. Lea's pretty silver dress had a small tear near her left shoulder from when she had climbed over a bathroom stall in the men's room to retrieve a clue from the air-conditioning vent.

"Fine." Savannah tried to run a hand through the rat's nest her hair had become as she walked gingerly over to Dylan. "Permission to speak?"

Dylan looked at the others before smiling smugly. "Go ahead, Ms. Ingram."

"I've looked everywhere in this building for my clue, and I can't find it anywhere," she said shakily. "I'm not sure what else to do. Can you please point me in the right direction?"

Dylan responded with a sweet smile. "Sorry. Rules are rules. May I remind you your cotillion class has to do this whole hunt over if you don't find fourteen items?"

The others stared menacingly at Savannah.

"Ms. Norberry is going to be back in five minutes," Charlotte reminded them, staring at the clock like it might bite her. "We have to be back in the sitting room looking like we never left, and that's leaving no time to fix ourselves up! What's she going to say about my dress?" She had a black stain on her beautiful dress from a pen that had exploded on her. At least if her dress had to take a trip to the dry cleaners, it was for a good cause. They had been looking for a pen that had the original club seal.

"Everyone, check your notes again," Izzie suggested. "Make sure there's nothing on the front or back that would lead us to Savannah's clue. Any marking could mean something, so look carefully."

Mira looked at Savannah's card again. She had seen that frowny face somewhere else today, but where?

"Three minutes," Charlotte said as if they needed reminding.

Hearing Charlotte's voice made her think of the dress again and the dress made her think of... "Wait!" Mira shrieked. "Didn't one of the former debs have a frowny face on her shirt?" She scanned the group. A brunette with a tiny frowny-face pin on her shirt caught her eye. It was worth a shot. "Do you have Savannah's clue?"

The girl grinned and gave Dylan a look. "I thought you'd never ask." The others stared in shock as the girl pulled a note out of her pocket. "But you're not the one who has to ask me for it. Savannah needs to ask. Nicely."

"I don't remember hearing about cotillion initiations being this juvenile," Savannah mumbled as she crossed the room. "Maybe it's just this pledge class."

The girl dangled the note above Savannah's head like a carrot. Savannah reached for it, and the girl held it higher. "You have to say please," she trilled.

"Please." The girl handed it over, and Savannah read it. Her color slowly paled.

"What does it say?" Izzie asked, and Savannah shook her head. Izzie took the note and read it aloud. "'Savannah Ingram, you've always thought you were royalty.'" Izzie laughed.

"Sorry. Couldn't help myself. 'Now it's time to look like a princess. Think accessories. Don't forget your picture, either.'"

"This is insane," Savannah said, her brown eyes bulging out of her head. "How am I supposed to dress like a princess? And do it in two minutes? What am I supposed to do? Heist the Emerald Cove emeralds?" She stared at the glass case across the room. "Never."

"You had no problem making other people take the emeralds a few months ago," Izzie said, enjoying herself.

One of the girls snapped, "If you cost us this initiation when we have one clue left…" Savannah's people were turning on her.

"I'm sorry, okay? I don't know what they want me to wear!" Savannah looked anxious. The only one who seemed remotely happy, Mira noticed, was Dylan.

"It can't be the emeralds," Mira said. "They're not a princess thing. Tiaras are."

"Less than one minute," Charlotte said, her voice shrill.

"Ms. Norberry's tiara," Lea piped up. "The one she wears to cotillion. She keeps it in that glass case she always brings to class! She says it's to remind us what being a lady is all about, but it's kind of creepy how she…"

Savannah looked at her watch. "Lea! Focus! Where is it?"

Lea blushed. "I think I saw it in the classroom."

The girls rushed into the room to retrieve it. Savannah carefully opened the glass box and lifted the tiara off the pillow. A tiny note floated down from the accessory. Savannah read it quickly, and her shoulders sank again. "You've got to be kidding me!" she wailed. "I'm supposed to wear Ms. Norberry's tiara to class." Mira winced. That was just asking for trouble. "'Tiaras were never worn to cotillion till Grace Kelly made them fashionable with her wedding to Ranier III, Prince of Monaco, in 1956,'" Savannah read. "'That's when a cotillion pledge by the name of Holly Norberry got permission from the Junior League to be the first. Since then, many a cotillion pledge has worn a tiara.'"

"*Time!*" Dylan said, eating up the look of despair on Savannah's face. "You've failed," Dylan said calmly, "unless"— she glanced at Savannah—"you put the tiara on right now, no buts, and wear it to class."

"I can't!" Savannah freaked. "She'll see it, and I'll be kicked out of cotillion!"

"Vanna, you've got to do this," Lea told her. "We *cannot* go through this twice. What if they make us have a scavenger hunt at school next time?"

"Or schedule it for when we're going to be in Paris?" seconded Lauren. "That's only two weeks away. We'd have to cancel our trip."

Paris. Mira's friends were going to Paris for their cotillion gowns. Without her. And where was she going to find her dress? The mall? Her mother was so busy with press engagements, she'd barely even mentioned cotillion dress shopping.

Mira had been thinking about what her dress would look like since the fifth grade, and now she'd probably have to buy something off the rack from David's Bridal.

"What's your answer, Savannah Ingram?" one of the former debs asked.

"It doesn't seem like I have a choice." Savannah sounded defeated. She gingerly picked up the tiara. If it broke, they were toast. "Let's take the picture already."

The girls huddled around Savannah for the final shot. They breathed a sigh of relief once the valet snapped it. But for Savannah, the real test was just beginning. While the other girls went to the bathroom to clean up before Ms. Norberry got back, she stood to the side. Mira couldn't believe she felt bad for her.

"You must be loving this," Savannah whispered, turning the tiara over in her hands as Mira approached her.

"I'm not," Mira said. "I came over here to make sure you were okay."

"Yeah, right." Mira knew she was catching Savannah at a rare raw moment. "Suddenly you've got it all together while everything in my life is upside down. No boyfriend, no best friend, the cotillion captain hates me. This must be heaven for you to watch."

It almost sounded like Savannah wished she could switch places with her. *Her.* The best friend she had dumped. "Savannah, I…"

"Girls!"

Ms. Norberry's voice floated through the room, and Mira stepped in front of Savannah just in time, blocking Ms. Norberry's view.

"I'm so sorry," Ms. Norberry said, out of breath. She had an umbrella in her hand, but she was still drenched. "You have no idea what kind of morning I've had! I got to my aunt Bertha's, and she said she never called! Can you believe? After I drove all the way there?" She shook her head. "I am setting up a doctor's appointment for her next week." She stopped. "What are you all doing out here? Shouldn't you be in the classroom practicing your Japanese bowing technique?"

"We were doing that out here," Mira lied. "Would you mind if we took two more minutes to practice?"

"Of course not." Ms. Norberry removed her jacket and looked at her watch. "I'll see you in the sitting room promptly at twelve ten." Mira blocked Savannah from view till Ms. Norberry was gone. That's when she heard her sniffling.

"I don't want to get kicked out of cotillion," Savannah pleaded in Mira's ear. "You and I have waited for this day forever. If Ms. Norberry sees me with this tiara... *Please* do something."

Savannah was asking *her* for help? Why did she feel sorry for her after all she'd put her through—and would *still* put her through? But it didn't matter. Mira couldn't watch her be tortured. "Wait here," she said, sticking Savannah behind an armchair. She walked over to Dylan and the others. "We've found the items and taken all the pictures. Do we really want to risk Ms. Norberry seeing Savannah in her tiara and banning us from cotillion?" The former debs looked at one another. "That would mean no more initiation and no cotillion class for anyone. Who does that help?"

The girl looked at Dylan, who nodded. "Okay." Mira could hear Savannah exhale. "But don't ask us for anything again, Mirabelle Monroe. Next time you're on your own."

"Thank you," Mira said. She turned to Savannah, but her former friend was already on her way back to the classroom to try to sneak the tiara back into its case without Ms. Norberry noticing. She hadn't thanked her, but Mira hoped she was grateful.

At exactly twelve ten, the girls were seated in the sitting room and the tiara was back in its glass case. Ms. Norberry was five minutes into her lecture about carrying tissues in Japan before she noticed the girls' appearances had gotten very disheveled since their earlier etiquette session. But being the proper lady that she was—and having been the cause of their class delay in the first place—for once, she didn't say a word.

Fourteen

When Izzie left Grams's nursing home Sunday afternoon, she had green feathers stuck to her T-shirt, dried glue under her nails, and Magic Marker all over her hands.

She'd spent the last two hours helping the residents make paper turkey crafts using their handprints, feathers, glue, and crayons. When they were done, she displayed them in the center's windows for the residents' families to see when they came to take them home Thanksgiving weekend. Grams's turkey was the only one not on display. She held it tightly as she walked down the path to the bus stop. She stopped short when she saw Brayden sitting on one of the garden benches. "Let me guess: You're here because you missed being a bingo caller?"

"How'd you know?" Brayden stood up and pretended to

grab a mic. "B19! B19! That's a bingo right there," he called in a deep voice, pointing to a nearby bush. "Next card will be four corners. That is four corners, everyone."

Izzie tried not to laugh. "They might have to hire you full time." Sometimes Brayden could be so cute. Okay, make that all the time. But she tried not to think about that when he was wearing semi-intimidating attire like his Ralph Lauren dress shirt and navy pants with a quilted jacket. She, on the other hand, was tarred in glue and feathers and wearing ripped jeans and a fleece.

"I don't think this place could afford me," Brayden joked, "although I probably would do it for free just to spend more time with one resident's granddaughter."

Izzie blushed. Sometimes she still wasn't sure what to say when he made comments like that. She knew he liked her, but they still weren't technically a couple, and she knew that was partly her fault. Just when Brayden got close enough, she pushed him away. He had hurt her twice before, and part of her was afraid he would do it again. Plus, Dylan's words of caution were still very much in her head. Would Brayden toss her aside when he decided he was done rebelling against his parents?

"Is that a turkey?" he asked, pointing to her hand.

Izzie held up the craft proudly. The glue from the feathers was still wet. "This is the craft I did with the residents today. Cute, right? I got the idea from Connor's kindergarten

192

class. I displayed the residents' in the front windows." She pointed them out. "This one's Grams's."

"Why isn't Grams's up there, too?"

"She's not coming home for Thanksgiving," Izzie said, her arm suddenly feeling heavy. She dropped her hand to her side, the turkey stuck to her fingers by glue. "This will be the first time we aren't together on Thanksgiving since I was born." Izzie hesitated. "She's having a lot of health issues, and her nurse doesn't feel she should leave the center."

Aunt Maureen had spoken to Grams's nurse about bringing her to the Monroes' on Thanksgiving, and the nurse had advised against it. She could handle Izzie's visits, but Grams had started to get paranoid and confused lately, especially about her surroundings. She was also taking two new medications, and her diabetes was making things more difficult. To keep Grams comfortable, the nurse felt it was best if Grams stayed in the same place and stuck to her routine. Izzie wasn't happy about it, but at least she'd known before visiting that afternoon. She had practically done the whole craft for her grandmother herself; tracing her hand, gluing the feathers, dotting the turkey's eyes, and drawing a waddle. She figured if she and Grams couldn't be together that Thanksgiving, at least she could take a piece of Grams with her.

"I'm sorry." Brayden took Izzie's messenger bag from her and placed it on his shoulder. "I guess it's a good thing I picked today, then."

Izzie reached over him and carefully placed the turkey in her bag, praying it didn't get stuck to her English lit paper. "For what?"

Brayden had a mischievous look on his face. "For your surprise." She stared at him curiously as he took her hand. It felt nice to hold hands in public, even if they were standing in front of a nursing home. "No questions. You'll know soon enough."

That seemed fair. She watched their hands sway as they walked to the bus stop.

~

It was probably better that Brayden didn't tell her. If he had, she would have lied and said she had to finish her report on *Pygmalion* (Eliza Doolittle's rags-to-riches makeover hit close to home). Being in the Townsends' massive foyer, which led to rooms in every direction, was making her sweat. Just the walk up the driveway was a workout. The Monroes' house was big, but the Townsends' house was massive. Like the kind she read about in Mira's *Us Weekly* when celebs like Angelina and Brad rented out a house for $45,000 because they were shooting somewhere far from a Four Seasons.

"Are you going to come in or hang out with the coatrack?" Brayden leaned against a wall and watched her.

Izzie felt like an invisible force field was keeping her from going any farther than the foyer. She looked up at the biggest chandelier she had ever seen, which Brayden had just told her was made from crystals from Tiffany's.

You don't belong here.

The voice was back. She was beginning to wonder if Savannah had planted a chip in her brain that said that phrase whenever she felt out of place, which was often.

"No one's home, if that's what you're worried about," Brayden said, leaning against a doorway that had thick decorative white molding around it. "My parents are at a charity event and won't be back till after eight."

"Why would I be worried?" Izzie lied, even as her stomach relaxed. No Mrs. Townsend pursing her thin, pale lips. Yes! She stepped forward.

Suddenly, there was high-pitched yapping and the sound of tiny paws scurrying across the floor. A tiny tan fluff appeared at her feet, growling and barking.

"I take back the no one being home part," Brayden said, scooping up the tiny Chihuahua. "Blackbeard is here to protect us, right, buddy?"

"I still can't believe you named a Chihuahua something ferocious like Blackbeard." Izzie put her palm out for the dog to sniff. He jumped at first, then started to lick her hand. At least she'd won him over.

"What can I say?" Brayden held the long-haired dog out in front of him. "I wanted a big bulldog named Blackbeard, my mom wanted something small and dignified that wouldn't poop all over the house. She won, as usual." Blackbeard licked Brayden's nose, and he laughed. "Not that I would trade this guy in. No, I wouldn't," he said, slipping into baby talk. Izzie smirked as Brayden's cheeks turned pink. "Enough embarrassing myself for one day." He put Blackbeard down, and he scurried off. "Why don't I give you the grand tour?"

Izzie stepped forward. Remarkably, the force field didn't throw her back.

"It should only take an hour," he added. She stopped short and Brayden laughed. "I'm kidding. I can show you the tennis courts and the stables another day."

The last part didn't sound like a joke.

The tour did not take an hour, but it felt like it did at times. One expansive room blurred into the next, as did Brayden's chatting. She was too busy taking everything in to hear half of what he said. Mira had told her that the Townsends were practically a founding family of Emerald Cove and the history displayed proudly throughout the house made that point loud and clear. Original, fraying, yellowed maps of the town were framed in the study. A hunk of unpolished emerald was in a display case. The sitting room had several pictures of Brayden's great-great-grandparents standing in front of this same house over a hundred and fifty years ago. The home had been expanded and updated and barely looked like the old one, but some of the original floorboards had been salvaged to use in the kitchen, which was practically the size of Corky's. By the time they made it to the dining room, Izzie wasn't sure she could look at another piece of Waterford or sterling.

"Iz? You okay there?"

She hadn't realized how hard she was gripping one of Brayden's great-grandmother's antique dining room chairs. She let go, her palms pink. "Yep. All good!"

"Well, then come right in, madam. You'll find I'm a much better teacher than Ms. Norberry." He pulled out the chair in front of her and motioned for her to sit. "Give me fifteen minutes and you'll know the placement of every piece of silver on this table."

"Wait, what?" She sat down and felt him push her closer to the table. She realized the table was set for dinner. Candlesticks burned brightly next to a roast turkey, mashed potatoes, honey-glazed carrots, and cornbread. Brayden noticed the confused look on her face. "I really wanted to make things up to you after I behaved like such a jerk at the welcome tea," he said. "Mira mentioned you were having a tough time with table settings in etiquette class, so I thought I'd give you a one-on-one lesson."

Her cheeks felt hot. "She shouldn't have said that. I'm doing fine." She wasn't. Ms. Norberry even looked frustrated when Izzie put her red wineglass where her white wineglass should be (why did they have to know about wineglasses when Ms. Norberry kept stressing they shouldn't drink?). But those problems were for Izzie to know. Not the boy she liked who grew up in a world far different from the one she was raised in. Dinners with Grams were served on disposable plates or cheap Corelle, not hundred-year-old china.

Brayden sat next to her instead of at the other head of the table, which was fourteen seats away. Izzie didn't know dining tables this long existed. "Get ready to know the difference between your shrimp fork and your dessert fork." He smiled and pointed to his head. "I've got all the tricks you need to know up here."

Izzie tried to push her chair back, but those stupid old chairs were heavy! "This is really nice," she said, struggling to get up. "But I told you. I don't need any help. I'm going to go. I have a paper due in the morning."

"Hey." Brayden grabbed her hand. "Did I do something wrong?" He looked upset, which made her feel worse. "I'm really doing all this for me," he said. "I need to brush up. Last night at dinner I poured soup into my teacup."

She smiled. "Teacups and saucers aren't placed on the table till dessert. Even I know that." *Thanks, Ms. Norberry.*

"See? You know more than I do," Brayden said. "You can teach me."

Izzie looked down at the gold rim on the bone-white china plate in front of her. Why did she have such a hard time accepting help? Kylie teased her about that all the time.

She was used to doing things for herself. What Brayden was doing touched her, but something was still bothering her. "We can do this under one condition." She stared into his blue-green eyes. "I want you to promise me you won't feel sorry for me. *Ever.*"

"I don't," Brayden said simply, and she knew he meant it. "So let me do this without getting a huge lecture from Ms. Independent, Isabelle Scott. Okay?"

She started to smile. "Okay."

Satisfied, Brayden removed the pale green dinner napkin that was shaped like a swan from his plate. "First trick is something Ms. Norberry probably hasn't taught you." He unwrapped the napkin and placed it in his lap.

Izzie gave him a tart look. "I know that. I wasn't raised in a barn."

"Okay, but do you know *when* to put your napkin on your lap?" he asked, and she bit her lip. "Aha! Something the mighty Iz doesn't know. Here's the rule: Never put your napkin on your lap till your host does so first. Once they do, you do, and the meal begins. That napkin sticks like glue till the host removes his or hers at the end of the meal. Then you do this." He placed it on the left side of his plate, but didn't fold it. "Not this." He wadded the napkin into a small ball and threw it across the room.

She laughed. "I bet it would be fun to see the look of surprise on the host's face."

Brayden raised his eyebrow. "I've done that once or twice with my mother. It doesn't go over well." He took another napkin and placed it on his lap. She copied him. "Next: how to figure out which glass is yours and which is your dinner companion's."

"Please explain that one to me because I keep messing up." Izzie placed her elbows on the table, knowing it was a big no-no.

Brayden held out both his hands and made circles with his thumbs and index fingers. The rest of his fingers stayed straight. He held his hands up. "Do you see the *D* and the *B*? That stands for 'drink' and 'bread.'"

Izzie did the same and stared at her hands in awe. "How did you know that?"

"Our housekeeper taught me when I was five," Brayden admitted sheepishly. "I still use this trick all the time."

Izzie shook her head. "Why can't Ms. Norberry break it down this way?"

Brayden winked. "I told you. She's not as good a teacher. You can use this one every time. Just do it under the table. Otherwise, the other guests might look at you strangely."

She grinned. "What else you got?"

They went through the whole course that way, going through every piece of silver, every heirloom dish, every glass. Then they broke with protocol and cleared the table themselves.

"One last question: Did you cook this turkey?" Izzie scraped the rest of the food from her plate into the garbage disposal in the copper sink.

Brayden looked guilty. "It's takeout."

"Good." She placed the china carefully in the dishwasher, wondering if it should go in there. "It's nice to know you don't know how to do everything."

"I can do *almost* everything," he bragged, and then took her soapy hands from the sink and matched them up with his. "Including how to dance."

Izzie laughed as they started to sway back and forth, soapsuds from her hands dripping onto the wooden floor. "Don't tell me we're having a dance lesson, too." Even as she said it, she knew she didn't mind. The early dinner, the dinner-etiquette tutorial—it was all incredibly sweet.

"Hey, I'm an escort, and if you're going to dance with me, I can't have you stepping on my toes." He looked at her seriously, and she stopped swaying.

"I thought you were Savannah's escort."

"At the tea because my mom made me, but when it comes to cotillion, the escorts are the ones who pick their date." He looked at her expectantly.

Was this his way of asking her? Izzie's heart started to beat wildly, but she didn't want to give herself away. After what he had put her through at the welcome tea, she wanted to make Brayden work for it. Even if she was totally going to say yes in the end. "I don't know." She scratched her chin. "What if another guy wants to ask me, and I say yes to you?" She thought for a moment. "The one I danced with the other day was hot."

"That guy with the greasy hair and the fluorescent-green plaid shirt?" Brayden looked insulted.

"I'll have you know he was really romantic. He said my eyes reminded him of the color of the Thing in *Fantastic Four*," she said solemnly. Brayden started to tickle her.

"So will you go with me?" he asked, hugging her from behind when he was done with the tickling. His chin nuzzled her neck. "There's no one else I'd rather go with."

She could feel the goose bumps on her arms. *Yes*, she wanted to scream, but she hesitated. "But your mom—"

"Don't worry about my mom," he said. "I can handle her."

"Okay," she agreed, and turned around. It was almost as if she knew what was coming next. Maybe that's why she closed her eyes and focused on the sound of her own breathing as his lips connected with hers. Even though his soapy hands were getting her shirt wet, she leaned into the kiss. Blackbeard barked, but they both ignored him.

Afterward, Brayden led her into the living room. He pushed aside the cherry coffee table, then walked over to a built-in bookcase with an iPod dock. He scrolled through the songs till he found what he was looking for. Sinatra soon filled the room.

"First dance lesson of the evening is the fox-trot—pretty much because that's the easiest to master," Brayden said, motioning the steps.

He walked over and placed her right hand in his left and his right hand on her left shoulder. Her left hand went on his right arm. She was already confused. "This is easy?"

"It is. You'll see," he said. "It's pretty slow. Just follow my lead and look down. Do like I do but in reverse—if I go forward, you go back. Got it?"

"No."

"Just try it."

Brayden stepped forward with one foot, then the next, while she stepped back with her left, then her right. Next, he stepped sideways, and she did the same—tripping slightly over her own foot.

"You didn't say it sped up!"

"It barely sped up. Keep going!"

It was more of the same. Back, forward, side, box step. Some steps were slow, some fast. It got more confusing when they did the promenade, and then the promenade with a spin. But three Sinatra songs later, she felt like she was getting the hang of it.

"I could be on *Dancing with the Stars*!" she joked, staring at their feet moving in time to the beat.

"See? Ready to learn the waltz?" Izzie dropped her arms. Brayden picked them back up. "You only have less than a month till cotillion," he said, pushing a hair away from her eyes. "We're on a *Dancing with the Stars*–type schedule here."

"Hey, that was my line."

"I'm stealing it." He put on an instrumental tune, then took her hands again. He cleared his throat, and his voice rose several octaves. "Pay attention, Ms. Scott." He sounded like Ms. Norberry. "Ready? One, two, three, one, two, three."

She repeated the pattern of the steps in her head. *One, two, three, one, two three*... She felt like a klutz when she stepped on Brayden's foot, but at least he didn't step on hers. He had dress shoes on, which were much heavier than her flip-flops.

After trying the dance several times, she felt like she was getting the hang of it. That's when Brayden stopped. "Enough work for one day," he told her. "Let's see how you really move." He put Rihanna on the iPod and turned the volume up so high, she could barely hear him. He pulled her toward him and spun her around. Then they separated and danced on their own. Somehow it turned into a mini dance-off.

"When we're at cotillion, I'm going to wow the crowd with this one," Brayden yelled over the music, then proceeded to move like he was an automatic sprinkler.

Izzie cracked up. "Oh, yeah? Well, I'm going to do this. I call it the flyswatter." She started bouncing back and forth, her hands swatting the dead air. "And Ms. Norberry can't rock moves like my bus driver, either!" She put her hands on a pretend steering wheel and drove around the room. Brayden laughed so hard, he sounded like a hyena. She started cracking up, too. She hadn't let go like this in a long time.

"I've got one better," Brayden told her. "This is the Wii remote."

Izzie watched as Brayden danced around like he was holding the Wii remote for a game of bowling or tennis. She giggled so hard, she sounded like Mira. But she didn't care. They were having so much fun that neither of them noticed anyone had come home till the iPod abruptly shut off.

Brayden instantly froze. "What are you guys doing home?"

Mrs. Townsend and Mr. Townsend, Izzie presumed from how much he looked like Brayden, stood in the living room watching them, and they looked less than thrilled. Dylan hovered somewhere in the background.

Mrs. Townsend pursed her lips into what was her version of a smile. A creepy one at that. "We left early. Hello, Isabelle. It's lovely to see you again."

"Hi." Izzie retrieved her flip-flops from the corner of the room. She had kicked them off earlier and now was acutely aware that she was barefoot. It didn't look like anyone went barefoot in that house. She imagined all the Townsends walking around in fuzzy monogrammed slippers.

"Brayden, you didn't tell me you were having company."

She stared at Izzie as she slipped on her shoes. "You told me you had a study group."

"I did." Brayden's voice was more strained and serious than it had been all afternoon. "It was with Isabelle. When it ended early, we came here."

Since when did he call her Isabelle? And they weren't at a study group. Why was he lying? Izzie could feel Dylan staring at her.

"Lovely." Mrs. Townsend's pursed lips looked even thinner. "I didn't know you were in the same accelerated classes." That was a dig if she ever heard one. "If you had told me Isabelle was coming, I could have prepared a snack."

"We had takeout," Izzie said, and instantly regretted it. Mrs. Townsend stared at her, and Izzie couldn't help thinking about what she had on. While the rest of them were dressed for a party, she was in jeans and had glue and feathers stuck to her shirt.

"I'm tired, and I still have calls to make." Mr. Townsend left the room without even acknowledging Izzie in the first place.

"Okay, dear!" Mrs. Townsend turned back to Brayden. "I hope you didn't eat too much. We're going to the Ingrams' for dinner in an hour. I told them you were coming, so I'm afraid you'll have to cut your ... study group with Isabelle short."

"I said study group was earlier." Izzie noticed Brayden's

shoulders tense. "Iz and I are hanging out. Do I really have to—"

"I see that, but unfortunately we have to go. I told them you'd be there, and it wouldn't be polite for you not to show up." Mrs. Townsend looked at Izzie apologetically, but she wasn't buying it.

Izzie waited for Brayden to stick up for himself—and for her—but instead he just stood there and said nothing. He had turned into a robot that followed his mother's every command. She couldn't believe it. Was he really going to leave her to hang out at Savannah's?

Mrs. Townsend clearly knew she had won. "I'll give you time to say good-bye to your friend and freshen up before we leave." She walked over to Brayden and adjusted his collar. "Nice seeing you again, Isabelle. I'll see you at our next function."

"Yeah, bye," Izzie said, even though Mrs. Townsend barely gave her a second glance. She wasn't sure whom she was more mad at. She looked at Brayden. "Thanks."

"Did it look like I had a choice?" Brayden's face was flushed with anger.

"You always have a choice! You just chose not to make one." Izzie seethed quietly, afraid Mrs. Townsend would overhear. "I can't believe you agreed to go there."

"You don't understand how my family works," Brayden

said, his hands motioning wildly. It almost looked like he was doing the sprinkler again, but she wasn't laughing now. "There is no saying no to my mother."

"So if that's true, then how did you get your mom to agree to let you escort me to cotillion?" Izzie asked, and Brayden didn't answer. Izzie felt her chest tighten. "You haven't told her you want to go with me yet," Izzie realized, and he looked away. Her voice was soft. "You know she's going to say no! Look what just happened. She's going to make you go with Savannah, and you're not going to do anything to stop her."

"Geez, Brayden, get a backbone, already."

Izzie had almost forgotten Dylan was there. She was leaning against one of the archways between the living room and the study, watching them fight.

"Are you going to let Mom make your every move till you're thirty?" Dylan asked. "I thought you had finally become your own person, but look at you." She gestured to him disgustedly. "Same old Brayden."

"And same old Dylan," he fired back, sounding angrier than Izzie had ever seen him. "Ironic that they came home early from a charity event when they never miss a minute of one. What did you do? Tell them you were sick?"

"Don't blame this on me. I thought she'd be gone by now," Dylan said. "Didn't I teach you anything about sneaking around?"

"Sneaking around?" Izzie repeated. Was Brayden trying to keep her hidden away so his mother didn't know about them? She was feeling worse by the second.

"All you do is cause trouble, Dylan!" Brayden yelled.

"Hey, you're the one who didn't stand up for your girlfriend," Dylan said calmly. "What's wrong? Afraid mommy won't approve of her because she's too much like me?"

"Shut up!" Brayden snapped. "Why are you here? No one wants you back in EC, certainly not Mom and Dad. Why can't you just go to school and leave us all alone?"

Izzie couldn't believe how mean he was being. She looked at Dylan and tried to see her the way Brayden did. Her red dress, shorter than it probably should be for an event with the Townsends. Piercings, tattoos, and the rebellious look on her face. It was clear Dylan didn't fit in with the Emerald Cove scene. Izzie didn't look the part, either. She was exactly like Dylan, she realized. Was Brayden going to treat her like this someday, too?

"You didn't answer her question, Brayden," Izzie said quietly, and they both stopped arguing and looked at her. "Is Dylan right? Are you embarrassed of me because I'm so much like Dylan? Is that why you won't tell your mom about cotillion?"

Brayden glared at his sister instead of Izzie. "You're nothing like her."

"Yes, I am, and if you don't see that, then maybe you don't know me as well as I thought you did." The hurt in her voice was undeniable.

Brayden exhaled slowly. He wouldn't look at her. "Maybe I don't."

Dylan smiled at her sadly. This was her cue. Izzie was gone before Brayden even turned around.

Fifteen

"Um, Mira? I think your teeth are as white as they're going to get."

At the sound of Izzie's voice, Mira broke out of her trance. She had no idea how long she had been brushing while she stared at her reflection in the mirror. She had been staring at her face a lot lately to prepare for the Sup art contest, and what better place to do it than while brushing her teeth? She studied every laugh line, her less-than-full lashes, the shape of her eyes, the freckle on her left cheek—and yet she was still no closer to sketching. Maybe she should start bringing a pad and pencil to the bathroom. "Sorry," she told Izzie, and discreetly spit out whatever was left of her toothpaste.

Izzie ran a comb through her wavy hair, which had become unruly overnight. "What were you thinking about?"

"Nothing," Mira lied. "I'm just tired."

"Tired, huh?" Izzie teased. "Admit it." Mira looked at her strangely. "You just like looking at yourself in the mirror." She tapped the gilded gold mirror that extended over both sinks. "Maybe I'll get you a new one for Christmas. You need the magic kind they have in Disney movies." Her hazel eyes shone brightly in the bathroom light. "One that tells you how beautiful you are on command."

Mira threw her wet washcloth at Izzie, who tried to jump out of the way. "Gross!" Izzie complained, wiping her white collared shirt that was part of her school uniform. It now had a huge wet mark on it.

Mira laughed. "Please. Gross is chewing on the ends of all your pencils."

"It's called stress relief."

"It's *called* a disgusting habit, just like biting your nails."

"Know-it-all."

"Grump."

Izzie picked up Mira's expensive can of hair mousse like it was a locked and loaded pistol and aimed to spray it at her. Mira, in turn, ripped her towel off her head and held it like a shield. Neither girl heard the knock on the bathroom door.

"Looks like I caught you both just in time!" Mira's mom said chipperly, and both girls lowered their weapons. "Oh good. You're both showered and semidressed already." She pointed to Izzie's uniform. "You're not going to be needing that today."

"I'm not?" Izzie asked.

Mira started to suspect something was up the minute she saw her mom's outfit. She usually wore a dress to her Emerald Cove Greeters meetings on Wednesdays, but that morning she had on a pink button-down shirt and slim-fitting tan pants with heels.

"No school," Mira's mom clarified. "Both of you get dressed in something casual yet classic." She frowned. "Just no jean cutoffs. We leave in a half hour, so you better start packing."

"Where are we going?" Izzie and Mira said at the same time.

Mira's mom smiled. "We're going to New York for Thanksgiving weekend." Mira's heartbeat jumped about fifty beats a minute. Her mom cocked her head slightly and smiled. "It's about time we found you both cotillion dresses, don't you think?"

~

By late afternoon, they were on New York City's famed Fifth Avenue, staring up at St. Patrick's Cathedral. Every time a police siren blared or a cab honked, Mira felt Izzie shudder. She wasn't sure if it had to do with Izzie taking her first plane ride or if it was about being someplace jam-packed and loud, but Izzie seemed out of her element.

Mira, on the other hand, felt right at home. There was so much to see, she didn't know where to look first. She was glad she had put her sketchpad and colored pencils in her pink quilted messenger bag. She was dying to pull them out, sit down on the cathedral's steps, and people-watch and draw. She could draw the woman in the dark shades who had been on the phone for twenty minutes and ignoring her four-year-old son who kept picking up used gum and eating it. Or she could sketch the magnificent cathedral against the backdrop of the homeless guy pushing a broken shopping cart by a group of tourists.

Mira's mom had been to New York numerous times, which may have been why she barely looked twice at St. Patrick's. Instead, she had her eye on her BlackBerry. "So we'll split up for the next few hours while the boys hit FAO Schwarz and the Central Park Zoo and the girls and I go to their dress appointments."

Izzie's eyes darted back and forth with each passing person, almost as if she anticipated being stampeded to death. "You need appointments to shop here?"

"We do?" Connor panicked. "Did you call the LEGO store and make one?"

"Where we're going, we don't need appointments, buddy," Hayden explained. "While Izzie and Mira try on dozens of white dresses that probably look exactly the same, you and I will check out the LEGO store and the polar bears at the Central Park Zoo." Izzie scowled. Mira had a feeling Izzie would rather have their itinerary.

"The places we're shopping are so exclusive that they only see customers who have appointments months in advance," Mira's mom explained to Izzie. She put on her oversize tan shades that made her fit right in with the rest of the women walking by. "We're lucky Callista and your father were able to make some calls and have us squeezed in on such short notice." She absentmindedly brushed lint off their dad's jacket. "That was really nice of him, considering all he has going on right now, too."

"It was a good weekend to get away," their dad said simply.

Before they had left, Callista told them there was a new scandal brewing. Hayden had heard their parents talking on the plane, and Grayson Reynolds's latest piece was the most damaging yet.

Mira's mom fished for the thank-you again. "Busy or not, this whole trip was your father's idea. Wasn't that nice?"

Mira and Izzie side-eyed each other. *Your father.* Mira's mom had started using the phrase to include Izzie now as if saying it enough would make it true. But if Mira didn't think of their dad as a father, how could Izzie? Mira hadn't had a single conversation with him since their blowup in the kitchen over a piece of pie a few weeks ago. She'd always wanted to see New York, and she couldn't help being excited to be there, but thanking her dad for the bribery was hard to swallow.

That's why she was surprised to hear Izzie say it. "Thanks for the trip. I've always wondered what New York was like."

She eyed the group walking by with American Girl bags. "Grams always wanted to see it."

Their dad smiled. "I'm sorry Grams couldn't come. What do you think of it so far?"

"Well, it's pretty big." Izzie accidentally got knocked in the shoulder by a businessman walking by. "She would probably have found it overwhelming. I do."

"You do? I like it," Mira said. Her friends at Emerald Prep all dressed the same out of uniform. Here, no two people looked alike. "I love the feeling that something is always going on. You could leave the hotel at three AM and I bet there would still be people walking down Fifth Avenue."

Izzie zipped her puffy coat higher. "I guess."

"We'll never know, because none of you will be trying that experiment," Mira's mom said lightly.

"You know, your mom found New York overwhelming at first, too," their dad told Izzie. At the mention of Izzie's mom, everyone got quiet. Izzie had told Mira about their dad coming to her swim meet and talking about Chloe. The conversation had seemed to upset her. Mira couldn't imagine Izzie wanting to open up on that topic again so soon.

"My mom didn't love it here, either?" Izzie asked, wrapping her arms around her like armor. He shook his head. "Then why did she stay?"

"She didn't plan on staying forever," their dad said. "But this city surprises you the way it is always changing."

216

"I don't think I could live someplace like this even for a few months," Izzie said, looking around. "There's no grass, no trees."

"There's a tree right there," Mira pointed out. "And Central Park is full of trees."

"That's a park," Izzie reminded her. "Back home grass is everywhere." She looked up at the tall buildings again. "It's just so different here from North Carolina."

He nodded. "It is. Your mom's heart was always down South, but she had a lot of great experiences in this city that I know she wouldn't have traded for the world. I bet if you give this city a chance, you'll like it, just like she grew to."

Izzie didn't ask him anything else, but Mira thought she seemed calmer after that. The next time a taxi whizzed by, Izzie didn't flinch.

Mira's mom glanced at her watch, then shifted the massive issue of *Brides* magazine from one arm to the other. It had at least two dozen folded pages with what Mira guessed were gown ideas. "We better go. You don't want to be late to Heather Yang." Heather Yang was a young bridal gown designer who dressed the hottest celebrity brides. Since wedding gowns were guaranteed to be white, or some shade close to it, debs usually went for them first.

Mira's mom kissed the boys good-bye while the girls walked to the street corner to avoid being swept up in the same good-bye ritual. They turned onto Fifty-First Street

217

and waited patiently for Mira's mom to lead them to Heather Yang's flagship store.

"Why were you being so nice to him back there?" Mira had to know.

Izzie shot Mira an expression reserved just for her. "The man did fly us hundreds of miles to buy a dress." She shifted slightly. "And I like hearing about my mom."

"You said you were mad at him for bringing her up before your race last week," Mira noted.

"I was, but the more I think about it, I don't know...." Izzie stared at a small stretch of blue sky that peeked out above the buildings. "I like learning things I didn't know about her, and he's the only one who can tell me those stories." She stared at Mira sadly. "There's no one else left to do it."

Mira had never thought about it that way before. With Grams so far gone, their dad was Izzie's last link to her mom.

"Besides, it's hard being mad at him all the time when he does nice things for us," Izzie added, and Mira immediately started to protest. "I'm not abandoning you, if that's what you're worried about. I'm still mad at him. It's just...at least he knows he screwed up, and he's trying to fix things. Unlike other people."

Mira knew Izzie had had a fight with Brayden, but she was still too upset to tell her the details. All she knew was that Izzie had come home Sunday night in tears.

"I think it's great you can talk to him, but I can't seem to do that myself." She saw her mom walking toward them.

Mira pushed her dad out of her mind and focused on Heather Yang. She couldn't believe they were actually going to her flagship store! She expected the building to have a flashy sign and a whimsical bridal display in the window, but instead her mother rang the intercom next to a gray nondescript door with a tiny gold plaque that said *H.Y.* Maureen gave their name, the door opened, and a receptionist led them down a white hallway that could have been in any office building in the world. They even got on a dingy elevator for the ride up. She was a tad disappointed.

But when the elevator opened on the third floor, it was a different world. There were huge, poufy wedding dresses with tulle skirts and long trains, modern dresses with hints of pink and lilac in their sashes, and dresses that were so simple they could have doubled as silk nightgowns. There was only one other girl and her mother in the showroom, and she was much older than Mira and Izzie, which meant she was there for an actual wedding dress. Mira resisted the urge to squeal.

"Welcome to Heather Yang, Mrs. Monroe, Mirabelle, and Isabelle," said a woman in a pale lavender dress. "My name is Lana, and I'll be assisting you this afternoon. Can I get anyone a cappuccino before we begin?" They declined.

Mira's smile was ready to take over her entire face. "Okay, then. I've pulled some gowns to start us off based on the information you gave me. I'll show you to the fitting room area."

Mira noticed her folder said the name *Monroe* on it. They had their own file! That's when the reality finally hit her: No matter what else was going on, cotillion was still happening, she was making her debut, and she was going to wear a Cinderella-style gown to do it!

"Girls, don't feel pressured to pick something if you don't absolutely adore it," Mira's mom whispered as they walked down the hall. "I've set up appointments at Vera Wang and Amsale in case you don't see anything here." Her phone rang, and she quietly answered it. "Hi, Callista. Hold on." She put her hand over the phone. "Girls, I'll meet you in the dressing room in two minutes. Try on something dazzling to show me!"

Izzie touched a raw-silk gown with a hoop skirt. "This feels weird. Why do we have to shop at a wedding store when it's not our wedding?"

"Because the only other place you're going to find this many white gowns is at a communion-dress shop." Mira thumbed the organza on a simple fitted dress. "Do you really want to have the same dress as an eight-year-old?"

Izzie read the price tag on the gown and gasped. "This dress is nine thousand dollars! Even if I was getting married, I wouldn't wear a dress that cost this much."

Mira ripped the tag out of Izzie's hand and stuffed it in

the dress sleeve. "Mom knows how much these dresses are. She's been saving for cotillion since I was two!"

Izzie's frown was getting larger. She started tapping her black Converse on the marble tile. "It's just a dance, Mira. Not your wedding day."

She turned Izzie toward the dressing area. "For once, can you just have fun?"

"Hmph," Izzie mumbled, but ten minutes later, Mira could tell even she was getting into it, especially since Mira's mom had told Heather Yang's people what kind of dresses to pull for her. While Mira's gowns were perfect for a *Gone with the Wind* sequel, Izzie's dresses resembled wispy nightgowns.

Mira was only three dresses into the try-on session when she heard Izzie announce, "I found one."

"What?" Mira cried, squeezing out of her own fitting area in a strapless gown that cascaded in silk ruffles to the floor. "You've only tried on four dresses!" But as soon as she saw Izzie's face, she knew there was no arguing.

Izzie was standing on a pedestal in front of a three-way mirror, and her smile was practically glowing. The dress reminded Mira of something a Greek goddess would wear. The white one-shouldered gown was anchored by a petal corsage at the top. The dress suited Izzie's tanned, toned upper arms, and the shirred, fitted bust area gave way to an empire waist. Like it or not, Izzie had found "the one."

"I only tried on *three* dresses," Izzie corrected her. She

stared at herself in the three-way mirror with satisfaction, then turned to Mira's mom with what Mira could only describe as a shy, hopeful expression. "What do you think?"

"I think you look stunning." Mira's mom sounded a little choked up. She walked around Izzie to see the dress from all sides. "I wouldn't try on another gown, either. Wait till your escort sees this. Has anyone special asked you yet?"

Izzie's face fell. "I don't have anyone official yet." She glanced at Mira.

"Well, any guy would be lucky to go with a girl as stunning as you, especially when you're wearing this dress," her mom said. "Don't you agree, Mira?"

"Yes," Mira said with a sigh, slumping against her fitting room wall and feeling the uncomfortable boning in her dress. She had definitely not found "the one" yet, and what happened if she did but didn't have an escort? Kellen hadn't stepped up and asked her. He hadn't even shown his face at an afternoon dance lesson even after all the hints she had dropped.

"So can I get this one?" Izzie asked, looking hopeful. Mira's mom reached for the price tag hidden near the waist of Izzie's dress, and Izzie quickly shut her eyes. "I don't want to know what it costs! Just tell me if it's too much, and I'll keep looking."

Mira's mom laughed. "It's more than fine. It's a bargain." She winked at Mira.

Izzie opened her eyes. "Really? Okay, then I'm going to change, but first I have to send a picture of me in this dress to Kylie. She can't believe we flew all the way to New York to buy a dress." She held out her phone, smiled, and snapped a picture of herself. Satisfied, she hiked up the extra-long dress, revealing her Converse sneakers, and headed back into the fitting room.

Mira was trying on yet another dress she didn't like when Izzie emerged from the dressing room again. "So does this mean I can go?" Izzie actually sounded excited to stop shopping! She looked guilty. "I mean, I can stay and help if you want me to."

Izzie would rather sit through a *Real Housewives* marathon than watch Mira try on more dresses. Her mom would be more help, anyway. Not that she would tell Izzie that. "No, you go sightsee," Mira said encouragingly.

"Actually I was going to try out the hotel's indoor pool."

Mira's mom handed her a hotel card and some cash. "Take a cab. We'll see you at dinner, if not before." When Izzie left, Mira's mom turned to her. "Now it's your turn to find your dream dress. I bet it's the next one you try on."

It wasn't. Neither were the next four. Heather Yang was a total bust. So was Vera Wang. Mira's hopes hinged on Amsale, and those quickly died when her mom got an urgent call from Callista saying Connor had fallen in Central Park. It was just a scrape, but Connor was carrying on, and Mira's mom had to leave.

"I can't wait to see which one you pick," she told Mira

before hurrying out. "I gave my credit card to the woman behind the counter. Use your judgment—you've looked beautiful in everything you've tried on!" She squeezed her tight. "Just pick one."

Mira sat down on an ottoman in the center of the room and stared at the five reflections of herself in the surrounding mirrors. This gown's skirt took up the whole ottoman, but it still didn't feel right.

"Did your prince turn into a pumpkin?" Hayden's reflection appeared in one of the mirrors.

"What are you doing here?" They were talking, but things had definitely been tense between them since their fight a few weeks ago. She still felt bad for yelling at him.

"Dad sent me to get mom. Connor got…"

"Hurt. Yeah, I know. Callista called. She's on her way back. Is he okay?"

Hayden nodded. "Nothing a new LEGO set can't fix. He just wanted Mom."

"Me, too." Mira frowned at her reflection.

Hayden parked himself in an armchair. "What's wrong? Can't pick a winner?"

"It's not as easy as it looks." She stood up, carrying the gown's skirt carefully so it didn't drag on the ground.

"Is the gown the problem, or is this about Dad?" Hayden asked.

Mira squinted. "I don't want to talk about Dad." They

both knew how well their last "dad" conversation had gone. She didn't want to repeat it in New York.

"Fine." Hayden didn't pry, thankfully. "You look great in this one, if you're looking for opinions."

Mira placed one hand on her hip and smiled. "You think?"

"Yeah." His mouth started to twitch. "Kellen will like it."

Her smile evaporated. "Too bad he's not going to see it. He hasn't asked me."

Hayden rolled his eyes. "Cotillion tradition is ridiculous! Everyone knows you ask who you want. If he hasn't asked you, you ask him."

"He doesn't want to go." She stepped into the dressing room to change. Hayden was wrong. This dress was not the one. She hated the ruching at the waist. On to the next. "He thinks cotillion is dumb."

"It is, but if you want to go, and he likes you, then he should go." Hayden acted like it was so simple, Mira thought.

Mira stared at the new dress she tried on. She didn't like this one, either. The sleeves were too poufy. She knew they had to wear a wrap if the gown was bare up top, but she still wanted something strapless. Why did she even pull this one? She took it off and grabbed another gown from the rack without even looking at it.

"I don't know if he likes me," Mira yelled over the dressing room door as she shimmied the dress over her hips. "We've only hung out as friends."

Friends. She was starting to hate that word.

"The *friend* word blows," Hayden said. "But maybe this is a good thing. You said yourself everything happened so fast with Taylor. Maybe if you and Kellen take things slow, you can see if you really like each other first."

Hayden was probably right. She did dive fast into things. Still, the thought of keeping things slow with Kellen bothered her. She didn't look at this latest dress in the mirror. Instead, she marched out to Hayden to rant. "I keep dropping all these hints about how I like him and zilch!" she complained. "With Taylor, all I had to do was flirt and he asked me out, but Kellen…"

"Whoa." Hayden stared at her. "If you want Kellen to like you, get this dress."

What does Hayden know about dresses? she thought. She glanced in the mirror, and her jaw went slack. The strapless floor-length gown had elegant embroidery from top to bottom with a grosgrain ribbon at the waist and a full crinkle skirt underneath. It was sort of old-fashioned and modern at the same time, just like her.

This was "the one."

"Ladies and gentlemen, I think we have a winner," Hayden said, seeing her face.

"Yes, we do!" She swung around, watching the skirt lift in the air like a bell.

"That dress looks beautiful on you, Pea." She heard her dad's voice and froze. He had just walked in the room. "Is that the one you're getting?"

"What are you doing here?" she asked.

Hayden just shook his head. "I'll let them know they can open the champagne," he said, disappearing before things turned ugly. "Mirabelle Monroe is leaving the building with a dress."

Mira shot him a withering look.

"I didn't mean to interrupt," her dad said. "Your mom wanted me to come and get you and Hayden. Connor is happily watching a movie and eating ice cream before dinner, so all is calm at the hotel." He admired her gown again. "Seeing you in this dress reminds me of when you used to play bride. Remember?"

She smiled. "I got the dress for Halloween and wore it everywhere."

"Even to the supermarket, as I recall," he said. "I think I remember you wearing it to one of my first state dinners. Your mom was mortified, but I thought it was cute."

"I don't remember that," Mira said, thinking back. She did wear that little white gown a lot. She might have even begged to wear it to preschool.

"Anything for my Pea," he said, referring again to the nickname he had given her.

Suddenly she felt bad. Izzie might be right. Maybe they were being too hard on themselves and their dad. It was time to get everything off her chest. She held up the bottom of her dress and stepped off the dressing room platform. "Dad, can we talk?"

"I would like that." His voice got stuck in his throat.

She hesitated. Was she ready to have this conversation in the middle of a bridal salon? Well, it had to happen some-where. She took a deep breath. "I know I've been awful to you lately, and I'm sorry. I've been so mad about how everything with Izzie came down. You've never hidden anything from me before, and I didn't know how to react. I think…" Her dad's cell phone ring interrupted her train of thought.

Instead of ignoring the call, he looked at the ID and his relaxed demeanor disappeared. "Mira, I'm sorry, but I have to take this. This is Bill Monroe. Yes, hello, how are you?" His voice regained its natural jovialness. "Did you need a quote for the story and the…" His face darkened. "Yes, I'm in New York. What's that got to do with…No. *No*, I did not use taxpayer dollars to get here." His voice shook with anger, startling an Amsale bridal consultant. "My savings and invest-ments pay for my trips with my family, not my office. No. This is a private family trip and I…"

Her dad obviously didn't care about their relationship if he was willing to take a work call in the middle of her pouring out her guts to him. Whatever the news was, she didn't care. Mira changed out of *the* dress as quickly as she could, slipped past her dad, who was now on a full-blown tear, and hurried to the front of the shop to give the salesperson her gown to be wrapped and shipped to North Carolina. She left the shop before Hayden or her dad even knew she had left the dressing area.

Mira didn't know where she was going, or even how to get back to the hotel. She just wanted to disappear. It was easier to do in a crowd than she'd imagined. Soon, she found herself at Rockefeller Center in front of the famed Christmas tree. It wasn't lit yet, but she stood at the railing overlooking the ice rink and watched the skaters. Families hurried by, looking happy, talking about Thanksgiving, doing normal family things, but she felt like Scrooge. She walked a little farther and stopped in front of a restaurant window. For some reason, she couldn't stop staring at a family having hot chocolate together. They were laughing about something Mira couldn't hear, but there was no mistaking their expressions. They liked one another. Her family had liked one another once. Her own sad reflection in the window against their happy ones was an image she couldn't shake.

She pulled her sketchpad out of her backpack and began to draw.

Sixteen

Izzie placed her hands over her ears. If she had to listen to another minute of this incessant chatter, she was going to scream. Their latest Social Butterflies meeting had dissolved into total chaos, and they had only been together fifteen minutes.

"Ladies." Mrs. Fitz clapped her hands hoping to get their attention. Her forehead was sweaty, and Izzie could see she was growing tired of arguing with them. "Can we *please* get back to the conversation at hand? Save cotillion talk for after meetings."

The girls continued to ignore her. In the middle of Mrs. Fitz's typical meeting opening remarks—the ones that included dollars made and spent, and talk of upcoming Butterflies events—Savannah had announced she had found the cotillion dress to end all cotillion dresses. Now everyone was staring at Savannah's iPhone as she scrolled through pictures of the gown she bought in Paris.

"I can't believe you found a lilac gown," Charlotte marveled, staring at the tiny screen. "You match the cotillion theme."

"I know we're technically supposed to wear white, but my dress has just a *hint* of lilac," Savannah corrected Charlotte. "I called Mrs. Townsend from Paris to make sure it was okay. She loved the idea of me honoring our cotillion theme of lilac and hydrangeas. How could I not get this dress?"

"It had nothing to do with getting your cotillion picture on the cover of the *Emerald Cove Herald*, right?" Violet asked innocently, and Savannah pursed her pink lips. Every year, the week after cotillion, the town paper put the most beloved deb on their cover. Everyone knew Savannah was campaigning for the spot already.

"My real dress is going to be much more intricate in terms of beading and detail," Savannah told the others. "But you can see how the back of the gown is taking shape."

One of the Butterflies gasped. "It has Swarvoski crystal buttons!"

Izzie wanted to strangle Mira for looking. She would not give Savannah the satisfaction.

"Aren't they lovely?" Savannah admired the photo on her phone. "The neckline is the best part. They're going to put a fresh hydrangea blossom in the middle, and chiffon lilac straps will emerge from it and tie behind my neck."

"She looked incredible," Lea told the group. "Prettier than any Disney princess."

Savannah's one out-of-town dream was to be Cinderella in a Walt Disney World parade. She was obsessed with Disney, hence her *Aladdin*-themed sweet sixteen. "Lea, you're making me blush! That is so sweet of you to say."

"Well, it's true," said Lauren, afraid of being overshadowed. "You have to send Disney a picture of you in that gown. I bet they create a new Disney princess after you."

A snort escaped Izzie's lips. "Sorry," she said. "I got a piece of hair stuck in my throat." She glanced at Mrs. Fitz. "Do you think we could get back to the meeting now?"

"Isabelle is right," Mrs. Fitz said, looking slightly relieved that someone other than her had been the one to interrupt Savannah. "We need to get a status update from our cochairs on what our next event will be. Savannah, do you want to lead us?"

Savannah put down her phone. "But our next event isn't till almost spring."

"How can that be? It's only December," Izzie reminded her and the others. "We can pull off another event before then." She clutched her green spiral notebook. She had at least half a dozen ideas in there that she was ready to share.

"If you knew EC, you wouldn't be saying that right now," Savannah told her sharply. "Everyone knows December is busy with cotillion, and once January hits, all anyone can think about is Founders Day in March. There is just no time."

Mrs. Fitz looked at Izzie sadly. "Traditionally, these two events take over the whole town. Nothing gets done till they're over."

"We're all stretched so thin that there is no time to come up with ideas, right, Mira?" Savannah asked. "You haven't thought of anything without me, have you?"

Mira glanced at Izzie helplessly. "Not really, but Izzie…"

Izzie had just talked to Mira about all the easy fundraisers they could be doing.

"You're the cochair, Mira," Savannah reminded her. "We didn't ask what Izzie's ideas were. What are yours?" Izzie wanted to hit her. What ideas did Savannah have?

Mira looked nervous. "I've had some art projects due, and we were in New York last weekend looking for cotillion dresses, too, and—"

"Oooh, did you find one?" Charlotte passed around the box of Munchkins. Everyone swore they wouldn't eat them because of dress fittings, but they always did anyway.

"Yes," Mira said, and got out her own phone to share a picture. "At Amsale."

Izzie interrupted her. "I know the rest of you think that

dance is the only thing happening in the world, but it's not. People still need help, and there are so many things we could do as a group that wouldn't take up a lot of extra time."

Lea whispered to Lauren, "God, why is she being such a downer?"

"Okay, Izzie. What are your brilliant plans?" Savannah folded her slim arms across her chest.

If Savannah thought Izzie had nothing to offer, she was wrong. Izzie opened her notebook. "What about Habitat for Humanity? There are plenty of areas outside Emerald Cove that work with them. We could volunteer on a Saturday to help build a house."

"That's a pretty good idea," Mira admitted.

"It's a great idea," Violet seconded.

Lea didn't agree. "My daddy won't even let me near a toolbox at home, and you think we're going to be able to help someone build an actual house? We're not contractors. I don't think we're allowed to do such a thing."

"We're not building a house by ourselves." Izzie tried to be patient. "We're all given a task, and there are people who oversee and tell us what to do."

"Any other easy ideas?" Savannah tapped her long nails on her desk.

"Well, we could also sell Otis Spunkmeyer cookies." Izzie produced a few sheets on the company that she had printed out. "Their fund-raising program really works in our favor. We could sell tubs of cookies for any cause we choose."

"That sounds like a lovely idea," Mrs. Fitz said optimistically, looking at the girls. "And not very time-consuming. I bet you could sell a few boxes in an afternoon."

"I stopped selling cookies in Girl Scouts," said Lea as she chomped her gum.

"The Girl Scouts aren't the only ones who sell cookies," Mira tried.

Lauren rolled her eyes. "What are you going to suggest next? A car wash?"

"Well, now that you mention it," Izzie started to say.

Lea's gum bubble popped. "*No way.* What are we? Maintenance workers?"

"The Butterflies do *tasteful* events," Lauren chimed in. "We don't do manual labor. We organize charity polo matches and do variety shows."

"Yeah, your variety-show act last year was real tasteful," said Violet, her oval eyes as dark as her pin-straight hair. "Didn't you wear a sparkly silver two-piece corset?"

"Corsets are very retro," Lauren said with a sniff.

"Girls, no fighting." Mrs. Fitz said.

Planning meetings with Emerald Prep's prestigious girls' club, the Social Butterflies, was always a nightmare. The room was usually split down the middle—half the girls liked splashy events that they could lord over friends who couldn't afford the price of admission; the other half of the room remembered the club motto—charity first, self second. Mira had always sided with the first half of the room with her club cochair, Savannah, but recently she had started to see things through Izzie's eyes, and the world had begun to look different. Izzie just wished Mira was ready to admit that out loud.

"Isabelle, let's hear your car wash idea," Mrs. Fitz encouraged.

"It's not brain surgery," Izzie said. "There are a zillion limos, town cars, and Range Rovers at drop-off. We could charge five dollars for cars and nine for SUVs and limos. It doesn't cost us anything to do a car wash—all we need are hoses, some soap, and buckets, and we could raise hundreds of dollars."

"But we'd get wet," Lea said as if it wasn't obvious. "And dirty."

Everyone started to talk at once, and the volume kept increasing.

"Cochairs, what do you think?" Mrs. Fitz asked wearily.

"It was good of you to try to come up with some ideas, Izzie, but none of these seem worth our time," Savannah said. "I think, and I'm sure Mira would agree, that we just do what we always do—pick up this discussion after cotillion and Founders Day."

"But," Mira tried to speak up, "Izzie has so many great…"

"Agreed?" Savannah held up her hand to vote. Most of

the room followed suit. "Wonderful. See you next week, girls!" She hurried out with her minions behind her.

The others were back to discussing everything from who still didn't have a gown for cotillion to the ever-persistent rumors that lingered from last cotillion, in which Leann Ryder wore a custom Stella McCartney dress that supposedly cost $35,000.

Izzie slammed her notebook shut in frustration. It didn't make much of a sound since it was just paper, but Mrs. Fitz seemed to get the meaning. So did Mira, who lingered in the background.

"I'm sorry, Isabelle." Mrs. Fitz took a seat next to her. She removed her costume jewelry earrings as if they were weighing her head down. "I'm sure you don't think too highly of me for how I ran that meeting."

Izzie didn't say anything. Even she knew you didn't bash a teacher to the teacher.

"Getting the girls excited about events is an uphill battle I have every year, and it only seems to get worse the closer I get to my retirement." She paused. "Or maybe *I* get more frustrated the closer I get to retirement. I know this isn't the way our club should run, but it's hard to argue with our cochair when her parents are the biggest boosters Emerald Prep has, aside from your dad, of course."

The irony wasn't lost on Izzie, but this fact only made her angrier. The idea that Savannah could ruin her personal life and school activities was infuriating. "Isn't there anything we can do?"

"I wish there was." Mrs. Fitz smiled at Izzie. "If it is any consolation, I thought your ideas were excellent. Emerald Cove is lucky to have you."

Izzie laughed. "That's the first time anyone has said that."

"Well, it's true." Apparently she wasn't joking. "Since you came to town, our club has flourished. Your fall festival is the best event we've ever had. Even the headmaster said so."

Izzie's eyes widened. "For real?"

Mrs. Fitz started packing up her things. "Yes. I can see now why you are doing cotillion."

That seemed like a strange leap. "Why is that?"

"You're a natural at community service, and it shows in every idea you have," Mrs. Fitz told her. "Hasn't anyone ever told you that before?"

Her aunt had said something similar to Izzie when she had received her cotillion invitation, but Izzie had just assumed Aunt Maureen said that to get her to do cotillion. Maybe she was blending into Emerald Cove better than she'd thought. Brayden or no Brayden, Mrs. Townsend's approval or not, she might just have a real place here.

Mrs. Fitz seemed sadder than someone should who was paying compliments. "I only wish you had been here last spring. If you had run for the Butterflies chair, I have a feeling we would be doing a lot more than we are now," Mrs. Fitz said, unaware that Mira was still in the room. "Well, you're only a sophomore. There is always next year."

But we aren't even halfway through this one, Izzie thought. There is so much they could tackle if Mrs. Fitz would stand up to Savannah and the others. But she knew their teacher wouldn't. Mrs. Fitz didn't want to push community service on them. She wanted them to want to do it themselves.

Izzie grabbed her notebook and met Mira at the door. "Ready to go?" Kylie had persuaded her sister to let her borrow her car, and she was driving into town to take them to Corky's. Izzie wasn't in the mood to go anymore, but Kylie was already on her way.

"I'll meet you there," Mira said, acting odd. "I forgot I have to go over our fund-raising numbers to give them to the editor at the *Weekly Emerald Prep.*"

Izzie didn't argue. She was at the driveway in the main part of campus within minutes. The afternoon had turned gray, and a light mist had started to fall. She perked up when she saw Kylie waiting, her sister's prized Charger chugging loudly and sending plumes of black smoke into the air. She ran to the other side of the car and opened the door. That's when she heard someone call her name. Hayden was running across the quad.

"I give it ten minutes before the sky opens up," he said, running over. "We ended practice early, but I can't reach Mom and I saw you walking." He glanced at the car.

"Hayden, you remember my best friend, Kylie, right?" Izzie asked. "I think I introduced you two at the fall dance."

"Was that before or after Mr. Senator admitted he was your dad?" Kylie asked.

"Um…before?" Hayden looked at the car. "Is this a 1971 Dodge Charger?"

"Yeah." Kylie's head popped out the window. "You know cars?"

"I wouldn't say it was a Charger if I didn't know." Hayden picked at the peeling paint. "Is this the original color?"

"'Top-banana,'" he and Kylie said at the same time. Izzie's stomach was growling. She just wanted to get in the car, already.

"I take it you know a thing or two about cars, too," Hayden said to Kylie.

"Maybe." Kylie studied him, and the car backfired a hello. "I know this one."

"Me, too," Hayden ran his hand along the hood. "Our dad has a mint 1971 Hemi Charger."

Kylie glared at Izzie, who said, "I didn't know what the car was. I don't speak car."

Kylie turned to Hayden. "I have got to see that car."

"Anytime," he said. "Dad only takes it out if it is just the right temperature and weather, so it spends most of its time in the garage. Sad, really."

"If it's as mint as you say it is, I don't blame him." Kylie looked at Izzie. "Is he coming with us to Corky's?"

"He can if he wants." Kylie normally didn't like new people, so Izzie was surprised to hear her ask. "Mira is meeting us there."

Hayden studied Kylie. "I'm in. I would suggest testing this baby's four-twenty-five horsepower on the way, but we'd get a ticket on the way into town."

Kylie liked that idea. "Let's take it on the highway first! It's only a little backtracking." She looked at Izzie excitedly. "You're not that hungry, are you?"

Izzie held her stomach. "Well..."

"Great!" Kylie started the engine. "Iz, can he ride shotgun?"

"Fine." Kylie held up the front passenger seat so Izzie could slide in the back while Hayden went around to the other side. Izzie fell into the leather seats that had seen better days and closed her eyes. Maybe if she slept while they rambled on about cars, when she woke up, they'd finally be at Corky's.

Seventeen

Mira stepped away from her easel and tried to judge her latest work the way China Chow from the *Work of Art* reality show would.

If she had time to start over—which she didn't—there were a few things she would have done differently. The restaurant window could have used more shading. The family at the table was too scrunched together. She had used too heavy of a brushstroke on their faces. And then there was the image of herself staring through the window at the family—did she draw enough emotion on her own face? Mira could have criticized her decisions all day, but she knew she had to put down her paintbrush. She had been working on her self-portrait ever since seeking refuge in the studio after the Butterflies meeting heard round the world. The week hadn't gotten any easier, and Mira was exhausted.

She sat down in a chair in front of the easel. The room was eerily quiet, but Mira liked it that way. She was not one of those painters who could rock out while they worked. She liked silence so she could hear her own thoughts, and her thoughts today were on Kellen and what he'd think of her work. His opinion was the only one that mattered to her, and he was going to be there any second. They had agreed to meet at the art studio at school for their own private unveiling.

"Sleeping on the job?" Kellen walked in with his canvas tube slung over his shoulder. While Mira preferred to paint on canvases already mounted, Kellen liked to work with a piece of canvas that he could stretch and frame later—if the painting was worthy.

"I am throwing in the paintbrush." Mira stood up to greet him. Just the sight of him gave her goose bumps. "If I don't stop painting now, I'll never stop. I'll keep adding details till I ruin the whole thing."

Kellen poked his head around her easel. "Can I see it?"

Mira blocked the canvas. "No! We have to do it at the same time and make a drumroll." She rolled the sound off her tongue. "Don't you think that would be fun?"

Kellen shook his head and smiled. "You're a bit much with the fanfare, but okay." He popped the top off his tube and used clips to pin his canvas to the easel. Mira tried not to peek as he turned his easel to face hers. They both stood in front of their work. "Ready?" He made a drumroll noise with his tongue, and Mira did the same. Then they both stepped over to the other's easel.

Mira was at a loss for words. Kellen's self-portrait was so realistic that it looked like a photograph. The artsy modern twist told her otherwise. Kellen saw himself as Two-Face, that character in *Batman*. The left side of his picture was decidedly Kellen at Emerald Prep: his hair neatly combed, his navy blazer pressed, his red tie knotted to perfection, his smile faint. He was the friendliest guy she knew, even if he wasn't the most outgoing. That burst of energy was saved for the Kellen she was beginning to know, the one who appeared on the right side of the portrait. This Kellen wore a paint-splattered T with the Big Brothers Big Sisters logo on it (he mentored a boy Connor's age) and lacrosse shorts, and had slightly messy hair. There was paint under his nails and a running insignia painted on his wrist. His smile was much bigger and, if possible, his right eye brighter.

Mira stared harder. "Is the right side of your face wider?"

Kellen stood so close, he grazed her shoulder. "I can't believe you caught that." He reached over her to point something out with his hand. "It's slight, so I don't look cartoonish, but I wanted to show the side of me I prefer—not scholarship boy, the real me."

His work was amazing. "If you don't win, I might have to

boycott Sup, and that would be a shame because their Oreo cheesecake was out of this world."

"Get used to the cheesecake famine, then, because you are the one who is going to win." Kellen put both hands on her shoulders and turned her around. "And you said you couldn't paint close-ups. Liar."

"I'm not lying." Mira was keenly aware that Kellen still had his hands on her shoulders. "This is the first time I've ever done one."

"You should do it more often then. You nailed it."

The painting was full of raw emotion. She had used the image of the family in the restaurant that she had spied on in New York and turned it into a scene with her own family. She painted herself staring through a restaurant window as her family happily sat inside and drank hot cocoa without her. She was trying to say that she wished she could be part of that family again and she feared she never would be. She painted each of her family members in agonizing detail. Her dad was at the center, laughing at something Hayden and Connor said. Izzie had a serene smile on her face, like she had finally found where she belonged. Mira's mom's frown lines she had earned since the campaign began were erased. If someone wasn't looking closely, they might miss the ghostly girl sitting next to her family. It was a mirror image of Mira outside the window, but this one was relaxed and happy. She had drawn her to represent the girl she used to be before her world was flipped upside down.

"What do you think this painting is about?" Mira asked.

"It's you now and then," Kellen said. "It's brilliant."

"What if people think the girl at the table is a ghost? I don't want them to think I'm dead. I'm just trying to say the old me is gone, and the new me is confused about what happened to my family. That's why I'm on one side of the glass, and they're on the other." Maybe she was getting too deep. "I'm not making sense."

"You're making total sense." Kellen looked at her carefully. "But I hate to think you believe your life is over."

"I don't always think that." She looked down. Their bodies were practically touching. "Sometimes I'm happy." *Like now*, she thought.

When Mira looked up, their eyes locked. Neither of them looked away. She was acutely aware of the wall clock ticking above their heads, and she kept thinking the longer they stood there, the less chance they'd pull away. Then he leaned down and kissed her. Their arms slowly wound around each other, her hands making their way to his hair, which she'd wanted to run her fingers through forever. The moment was better than she'd imagined, but the kisses were almost desperate, like they'd both waited too long to do this, and she found Hayden in her head. Was she rushing things with Kellen? If she got together with him now, would she fall into the same relationship she had with Taylor? And didn't Kellen say he didn't want to be a rebound?

"Wait," she mumbled through their kisses, feeling the panic choke-hold her. She pulled away and tried to catch her breath. Their noses were still touching, which made it doubly hard to concentrate on what she wanted to say.

"Maybe this is happening too fast," she said, hating the words even as she said them.

He looked at her. "I thought you wanted this."

"I do!" she said. She knew she was being confusing, but she had to figure out who that girl looking through the window was first. She looked into his green eyes searchingly. "Can you give me time?"

Kellen played with one of her curls. "You are very confusing, Mirabelle Monroe. But okay." She exhaled. He was still staring at her intently. "Under one condition: You let me be your escort for cotillion."

"Seriously?" Mira squeaked, and before she knew it, she was throwing her arms around his neck and kissing him again.

She had a date for cotillion! First a dress, and now an escort! Things were looking up.

When they finally tore themselves apart, Kellen held on to her waist. "So this is your definition of taking some time?"

She laughed. "That was a thank-you kiss. It's different."

Kellen leaned forward, his face lowering to hers. "Then I want a thank-you kiss for your thank-you kiss." She obliged. They still hadn't untangled themselves when Hayden walked in a few seconds later.

"My eyes!" Hayden startled them, and they quickly let go and stepped away from each other. "Dude, that's my baby sister you're pawing there."

"Hayden," Mira whispered, her cheeks flushing hotly.

"What?" Hayden dropped his gym bag and walked over. He had changed into his running clothes. The season was over, but some of the guys still ran the indoor track to keep in shape. "I'm playing the role of protective older brother. Sue me." He shook Kellen's hand. "We're cool, as long as you finally asked her to cotillion."

"Hayden!" This was getting embarrassing.

"You wanted him to ask you, didn't you?" Hayden teased. "Isn't that why we all had to fly to New York only to have you sequester yourself from the family for the whole weekend so you could paint? She found a dress, by the way," he told Kellen.

"Thanks, Hayden," she said through gritted teeth. "We're going to cotillion together, so you can drop it."

"Well, technically, I asked to be your escort," Kellen said with a sly smile. "You didn't actually accept." He glanced innocently at Hayden. "I need a formal acceptance to escort her, right?"

"Definitely." Hayden kept a straight face. The two of them stared at her, waiting to see her blush.

She wanted to kill them both. "Kellen," she said in her most proper voice, "I accept your invitation."

"Oh, all right," Kellen said, his mouth twitching. "Since you agreed so graciously."

Hayden applauded. "Now that that's settled, I'm supposed to get you home for dinner—if you're actually eating with us tonight."

"I'm thinking about it," she said. "I've just got to clean my brushes first."

Hayden didn't hear her. Instead, he was walking toward Mira's easel. "Did you paint this?" he asked before she had a chance to jump in front of the painting. "This is good." His eyes widened. "Is that us? And is that you? Did you die or something?"

"See?" she complained to Kellen. "It looks like I'm a ghost."

"It doesn't." Kellen turned to Hayden to explain. "That is the ghost of Mira past and the girl outside is Mira present."

Hayden didn't look convinced. "Has Mom or Dad seen this yet?"

"No." Mira removed the canvas from the easel. She placed it in her large art bag. "And they're not going to. I was going to enter it in a contest, but I know I can't. This painting would cause a lot of problems. Dad has enough as it is."

Kellen understood. He watched the news. "You would have won, you know."

"Maybe," Mira said wistfully. "It would have been nice to go up against you."

"I'll beat you next time." He winked. "At least now I have

a shot this month. They don't publicize the prize money, but the winner gets five hundred bucks."

"Seriously?" Hayden asked.

Kellen nodded. "I don't joke about money."

Mira didn't say anything. She knew Kellen's family wasn't poor, but he had mentioned money being tight now and again. The last thing she wanted him to worry about was buying her a Christmas gift, if that's what he was thinking.

"We should finish cleaning up," she said to change the subject. She picked up a crumpled piece of newspaper and noticed the name *Monroe*. She smoothed it out. Her dad's face stared back at her from the cover of the *North Carolina Gazette*. It was a paparazzi-style photo of him holding his hand up to the camera. He never did that.

ANOTHER MONROE LOVE CHILD FOUND! PLUS: RECEIPTS FROM THE NEW YORK TRIP HE TOOK ON NORTH CAROLINA'S DIME!

"The *Gazette* is trash." Kellen said over her shoulder, and she jumped. She didn't want him to know how bad things were. She hadn't realized it herself. This must have been what her dad was yelling about on the phone in Amsale.

Hayden scanned the article. "No wonder Dad seemed so stressed in New York."

"Do you think any of this is true?" Mira worried.

"No, but people love Grayson Reynolds, and if he says it is true, people believe it," Hayden said grimly. "Why do you think the photographers were still waiting when we got out of the car at school this morning?"

"That guy is nothing more than a gossip columnist," said Kellen.

"Gossip sells," Mira said, feeling worse by the second. "Especially about our family." She cleaned her brushes and placed them back in their holder while Kellen did the same.

"Someone must be feeding Grayson this stuff." Hayden took the paper and shot a three-pointer into a trash can across the room. "He has to be getting it from somewhere. Dad's opponent, the one the Ingrams were backing, dropped out, so it can't be him."

Then who is it? she wondered. She turned to Kellen. "I should go. Are you staying for a while?"

He nodded. "My mom has to come into town for her hair appointment, so I said I'd hang around and get a ride home with her later."

"When is she supposed to be done?" Mira asked.

Kellen looked at his watch. "Not for another two hours."

"I can't let you beat me to the punch on another master-piece," Mira said. "Have your mom pick you up at our house. I'm sure my mom already made dinner."

Kellen hesitated. "Are you sure? I don't want to put you out."

"You're not." Mira grabbed his arm. "Let's go."

Hayden patted Kellen on the shoulder. "Good luck with her, man. She can be bossy."

Kellen grinned. "So I've noticed."

~

When Hayden pulled into the driveway, Mira was surprised to find Callista waiting.

"Hi, guys." She was fidgeting with her glasses, which was something she seemed to do only when she was nervous.

"Kellen, my dad's PR guru, Callista," Mira said. "Callista, this is my…"

"She doesn't have a title for him yet," Hayden told Callista. Mira glared at him.

Callista didn't crack a smile. "Did you guys eat yet?" She pulled two twenties out of her pocket and handed them to Hayden. "Why don't you go get something? Connor is probably hungry. I'll go get him for you. Have you seen Izzie? She should go, too." She adjusted her brown frames absentmindedly.

"Callista, what's going on?" Mira asked.

"Nothing. Why?" Callista checked her phone for messages. She glanced nervously at Kellen.

"It's okay," Mira said. "He knows."

Callista sighed. "It's another *Gazette* piece by Grayson Reynolds—your father has lost his mind over this one! There are lawyers in his office right now, and he told me to keep you guys away. He's threatening to sue Reynolds and the *Gazette* about the story they wrote about him misappropriating state funds. He thinks suing makes him seem less guilty." She ran her hands through her hair. "I don't know what to do. We need a turn in this campaign, or your father is not going to have a chance." She grimaced. "Even I can't fix every political scandal, and this one is a doozy."

If Callista was saying that, then Mira had to assume her dad was in really bad shape. "I'm sure something will work out."

"I hope so." Callista's eyes locked on Mira's art bag. "Did you paint something today? You keep promising to show me your work." Her voice lightened considerably. "Let me see!"

"This one isn't done yet," Mira said hastily, but it was too late. Callista grabbed the bag and slid the painting out of it. As soon as she saw Callista's face, Mira felt sick. "Wait a minute. Is that your dad? And you?" Her eyes widened.

Mira grabbed the painting. "Yes, but you don't have to say anything. No one is going to see this. I'm putting it deep in my closet so it can collect dust."

Callista's face relaxed. "Good. We have enough on our plates already." She glanced back at the house. "I should get back. Since you know what's going on, you guys don't have to go out to eat if you don't want to. Just to warn you, though, with everything going on, your mom didn't cook."

Hayden looked at Mira and Kellen. "I'm kind of beat. Mira, want to make us those English muffin pizza things Mom always makes? Please?" he pleaded.

"Okay." It might be nice for Kellen to see how well she could move around in a kitchen. "Are we going to get in Dad's way in there?"

"As long as you make me one, too, you can barricade yourselves in the kitchen," Callista agreed, and they all headed up the walkway.

"Can I use your computer before we get sequestered?" Kellen asked. "I forgot to e-mail my social studies paper, and it's due tomorrow." He pulled out his flash drive.

"Sure." Mira opened the front door and lowered her voice to a whisper so she wouldn't disturb her dad. She pointed to the staircase. "My room is up the stairs, down the hall, last door on the right."

"Thanks," he said, and headed up while Mira walked to the kitchen to get started.

Callista tapped the bag still on her arm. "Don't forget to put that away," she said. "You don't want to leave it lying around."

"You're right." Mira ran back to the stairs. "Hey!" she said, ready to ask Kellen to hide the painting for her. Then she hesitated. Did she really want a boy she liked snooping around her closet? But this was Kellen she was talking about. He wouldn't care if her shoe rack was a mess. "Can you stick

254

this in my closet for me?" She handed over the bag. "And don't look at the mess!"

"I'll do the whole thing with my eyes closed," he promised. Mira watched him head upstairs. He had a really cute butt.

"By the way, this was just dropped off for you." Callista pulled a bright yellow envelope from her pocket. "It looks cotillionish. At least someone is getting some good news today." Mira's name was written in script across the front. She knew without even opening it what this note was about. It had to be her final initiation hazing. Her palms began to sweat as she opened the letter and began to read.

Mirabelle Monroe:
You are cordially invited to your final cotillion initiation! It will be a group event because they are so much fun to watch. Meet us on Main Street at 3 pm this Saturday, and wear your favorite Emerald Prep gym T, the shortest shorts you can find, your EP knee-highs, running shoes, and a boa. The rest, leave up to us. See you soon!
XO,
Your Cotillion Captain

Eighteen

Izzie stood on Brayden's doorstep clutching an Entenmann's cake. She stared at the Townsends' doorbell. It seemed to taunt her. *You scared?* it said. *You should be.*

She was scared. Her first visit to Brayden's house had been a disaster. She hadn't seen Brayden since their fight, and he and his family had taken an extended holiday vacation in the Cayman Islands. She kept waiting for him to call her, but he didn't. She was so hurt, she didn't pick up the phone, either. Who knew what he was thinking?

But that Friday afternoon, a text from Brayden came while she was at the nursing home starting the residents' holiday decorations (she needed weeks to do them since she had to cover Christmas, Hanukkah, and Kwanzaa to satisfy everyone).

BRAYDEN'S CELL: I'm back from the Caymans. Sorry about last wk. We should talk. Meet me @ my house tonite @ 6 for a dinner w/my rents & we'll show them why I adore U.

Izzie wasn't the kind of girl who accepted a text apology, and she let him know that.

IZZIE'S CELL: A text sorry? Get over yourself. You can set one less place setting because I won't be there.
BRAYDEN'S CELL: I know apology stinks. At cousin's baby's christening & can't talk, but want 2 see U. Please come tonight and I'll do the best groveling U have ever seen.

That was a little better. She texted back that she would consider it, but who was she kidding? She was going! It was easy making Santa hats out of cotton balls after that. She played the evening out in her head, imagining Brayden's big-time apology. Maybe their fight had even spurred him to reconnect with Dylan. She was only beginning to learn how sibling relationships worked, since she'd never had one before now, so who was she to judge? She'd texted Dylan over the break, too, but didn't hear back from her. Maybe they didn't have cell service in the Caymans. She knew she'd see her that coming Saturday afternoon. She had gotten a note about her final initiation assignment earlier that day.

Before heading to Brayden's, she called Mira to let her

know she wouldn't be home till after dinner. Then she asked the nursing home receptionist where she could find the closest bakery. There was no way she was showing up at the Townsends' empty-handed. Too bad the only thing she could find was a quickie mart, hence the Entenmann's cake. She took the bus and then the town trolley—a historic track that made only a few stops—and now she was playing chicken on Brayden's doorstep. Suddenly she wished she were home in bed, cuddling up with her pink Lambie.

Toughen up, she told herself, and pressed the bell, holding it a second longer than she had to because of nerves. She didn't know how Blackbeard reacted that fast, but she heard him charge the door, yapping like a maniac.

Brayden opened the door, scooping up Blackbeard, who promptly stopped his caterwauling. For some reason, he looked more baffled than happy to see her.

"Hi," Izzie said, feeling uncomfortable. "Am I early?"

Brayden had on a long-sleeved polo shirt and cords, but Izzie told herself to relax. Mira always said their Emerald Prep uniform could hold up in any formal situation. She'd had no time to go home and change.

"I... what are you doing here?" Brayden asked. She noticed his pale face and wondered if maybe he had fallen ill.

"You texted me to come over for dinner, and I brought cake." She showed him the Entenmann's box. The cake had a half-inch blanket of chocolate frosting on top. It was so bad and yet so good at the same time. "I know this isn't crème brûlée, but no one can resist Entenmann's. Grams and I used to be able to eat a whole cake in one sitting."

"Iz." Brayden's voice was strained. "I'm sorry I haven't called since I got back. I haven't stopped thinking about what happened, but...I know we need to talk. I just can't tonight." He hesitated. "Wait, what text?"

"Your text." Now she was confused. "The one you sent me." He stared at her blankly. "You mean you didn't send me a text?" He shook his head, and her stomach lurched. "Then who did?" she whispered.

That's when she heard the laugh. The pitch and tone were unmistakable. Savannah Ingram was in his house. Izzie didn't even have to ask to know she was right. Brayden's face said it all. "What kind of game are you playing?" She turned to go.

Blackbeard started barking again—apparently no one was allowed to enter or leave their house. "Iz, wait a sec! What text?" He ran down the steps after her and grabbed her by the shoulders. "I'm serious! I was going to call you— not text you—tomorrow so we could talk. I do want you to come for dinner. My mother can act like she's having a root canal all she wants—I don't care. I want her to know how important you are to me."

"That's what you said in the text!" Izzie yelled over the barking, and pulled out her phone for proof. She half wondered if the text was going to be there. Maybe it was a figment of her imagination. But no, there it was, and the two of them stared at the screen that showed the little text message bubbles to and from Brayden's cell on it.

"I didn't send those," Brayden said, and then his face hardened. "Dylan."

Izzie felt her anger from their fight return. "Of course. Blame her. It's easier than admitting you double-booked dinner." She was out of here.

"Brayden, who is here?" She heard Mrs. Townsend come to the open door. In a simple khaki dress with a thin belt around her tiny waist, Brayden's mom was dressed for a dinner party, only it was clear now that Izzie wasn't on their guest list. His mom spotted her in the diminishing evening light and pursed her lips. "Oh, Isabelle. So nice to see you again. Did you have a nice vacation?"

"Yes, thank you." Izzie's eyes turned downward even though she knew they shouldn't. Ms. Norberry was always stressing how important eye contact was.

"I'm afraid now isn't the right time for a visit, though, dear," Mrs. Townsend told her. "The Ingrams are here for dinner."

Like they are every week, Izzie wanted to say. She kept waiting for Brayden to speak up, but the problem was more clear now than ever. He couldn't stand up to his mother. Izzie couldn't imagine never being able to speak her mind. But Brayden looked so pained, she almost felt sorry for him.

Dylan appeared on the doorstep. "You should stay, Izzie,"

she said, and her mother looked at her. "Don't you agree, Mother? We never turn a guest away."

"Of course not." Mrs. Townsend maintained her cool. "I'll place another setting at the table. That is, if you don't mind joining us, Isabelle?"

"She doesn't mind," Dylan answered for her.

"Wonderful," she said, and Izzie could hear her heels retreating into the house.

Dylan pulled Izzie up the steps again, and Brayden almost got hit in the face trying to squeeze in the door after her. Dylan and Brayden were in each other's faces faster than Izzie could close the door behind her. They were nose to nose, looking ready for a cage fight. Izzie felt dizzy. *What exactly is going on here?*

"What is wrong with you?" Brayden seethed at Dylan. "First you send Mom and Dad home early when you knew I had something special planned for Izzie, and now you make our fight worse by texting her from my phone and telling her to come tonight? After all we talked about in the Caymans, I thought I could trust you again, and then you do this?" Dylan didn't say anything. "What are you trying to do here, Dylan?"

"Isn't it obvious? I'm trying to help you since no one helped me when I needed it most," Dylan said angrily. "But if you won't let me help you, then at least I can help her. She can see what this family is really like tonight and decide if you're worth the effort."

"You're so selfish," Brayden told her. "You don't want to help me or Izzie! You just want to get back at all of us for what happened to you last year."

Izzie was so confused. Were they talking about the car crash that got Dylan sent away to boarding school? She had never seen Brayden this angry. Dylan seemed to bring out the worst in him. Did that mean she would do the same?

"Maybe I am selfish, but I'm the only one in this house who cares." Dylan's blue-green eyes were full of determination. "You'll realize that someday. I'll meet you both at the table. Or, should I say, in the war zone."

Brayden's eyes seemed hollow when he looked at Izzie again. "You think she's on your side," he said quietly. "Everyone always does—but don't you see? Dylan only looks out for herself. That's what I was trying to tell you that night. She's not your friend. She's just using you to tick off my mother. That's what she does. She uses people."

Izzie's head felt like it was going to explode. Whom was she supposed to trust? Brayden, who had hurt her one too many times recently, or Dylan, who might not be who she said she was? "I don't know what to think," she said miserably. "If you can't stand Dylan, then why do you like me?" He looked at her. "I *am* Dylan."

"I told you. You're nothing like her," Brayden said.

"Yes, I am," Izzie insisted. "We have the same style, we

like the same books, and she feels the same way about EC that I do."

"Dylan feels that way about EC because she thinks this town turned its back on her." Brayden was clearly frustrated. "She could never fit in here, but you have! You've only been here a few months, and look at everything you've done with the Butterflies, cotillion, with your friends. I guarantee you that bothers Dylan. Maybe you like some of the same things, but you are nothing like her," he repeated. "You don't hurt people."

"I'm not so sure about that," Izzie said, thinking of her father. He was still trying to reach out, and she was still pushing him away. "All I do know is I wasn't raised like this." Her eyes caught sight of that scary, giant chandelier in the center hall above them. "I don't say the right things all the time. I don't dress the part like all these other girls do, and I don't care what these people think of me. If that's not the kind of girl you want, Brayden, then maybe you should go back to Savannah." Blackbeard was barking madly, and Izzie wasn't sure if he was cheering on her speech or wanted her to leave.

Brayden's expression was stony. "You know that's not what I want."

"Do I?" Izzie asked. "You have a hard time saying it out loud when it matters. You can't hide me away forever and expect me to still be there. One day, I won't be." She didn't give him a chance to answer her. She headed toward the dining room with Blackbeard at her feet and found the housekeeper dragging a dining room chair to the table. The Townsends, Dylan, and the Ingrams were waiting. Izzie put on her game face.

"Holden, Vivian, Savannah, I'm sure you know the Monroes'...daughter," Mrs. Townsend said tersely. "This is Isabelle. She's going to be joining us for dinner."

"Nice to see you again, Isabelle," said Savannah's mother coolly. Their last meet-and-greet in a department store dressing room had been cold, too. Whenever Izzie ran into the woman, she somehow screwed up. She didn't plan on doing that again tonight.

"How is your aunt, dear?" Mrs. Ingram asked. "She hasn't been to an Emerald Cove Cares meeting in ages." She glanced at Mrs. Townsend. "But, of course, it is such a *sensitive* time for Bill's campaign." Mrs. Townsend nodded knowingly.

Mr. Ingram, who reminded Izzie of a pudgy troll, dabbed at his mouth with his starched napkin. "Serves him right. If he had stuck with me on the coastal revitalization project, he might not have found himself in this sort of predicament." Izzie wanted to lash out at him for that comment, but she knew it wouldn't win her any favors in this room.

"Holden," Mrs. Townsend said pleasantly, "why don't we save the political discussions for after dinner? I know Chip

264

has some Cuban cigars he's been saving. You two can take them on the back veranda and discuss whatever nasty business is going on with our politicians."

"What my mother is trying to say is, don't bash Izzie's dad when Izzie is standing right in front of you." Dylan helped herself to a roll even though everyone's plates were still empty. Brayden had taught Izzie that you never served yourself till your hostess was seated with her napkin in her lap. She suspected Dylan knew that.

"Isabelle," Mrs. Townsend said, "why don't you take a seat next to me?"

"Mom, I'd like to sit next to Iz," Brayden said, surprising Izzie by opening his mouth, for once. "She is my guest."

"But, Brayden, you were already sitting next to Savannah. You can sit across from Isabelle instead." Izzie wasn't about to argue. She took a seat next to Mrs. Townsend and waited to see what Brayden would do next.

He stood there for a moment, as if the words were on the tip of his tongue, then sat down next to Savannah, who smiled at Izzie smugly.

"Smart move, Brayden," Dylan said as she buttered her roll. "Always do what Mommy says." Brayden's face flamed, but so did Izzie's. *Why does she have to make me feel so uncomfortable?* Blackbeard clearly wanted her to stay. He took a seat on Izzie's feet.

Brayden held up the Entenmann's box and passed it to

265

the housekeeper. By this point, Izzie had forgotten she had even brought it. "Iz brought this for dessert."

"Is that boxed cake?" Savannah asked. The hint of condescension in her voice was noticeable only to Izzie. "You're so sweet to bring dessert," she added with a smile that reminded Izzie of the cat from *Alice in Wonderland*. "We got Mrs. Townsend a custom Butter Me Up cake, since it's her birthday next week, but I hear the supermarket kind is good, too."

"Oh, God, Savannah," Dylan said, chewing her roll with her mouth open. "Don't act like you've never had boxed cake before."

Dylan was purposefully being over the top to get a rise out of her mom, and she was succeeding. Everyone at the table looked uncomfortable. Izzie might have had issues with people, but she tried to never take them public if she could help it. It made her wonder if she was as much like Dylan as she'd thought. She tried to make eye contact with Brayden, but he was too busy staring down his sister.

Mrs. Townsend motioned to her husband. "Would you talk to your daughter, please?"

Mr. Townsend shrugged, as if he were bored with the dinner already. He barely said a word about anything, Izzie noticed. Brayden said he couldn't be bothered with family matters, and Izzie couldn't help thinking of the differences between this man and Bill. Her dad showed up at his kids' games, meets, and school events. In the few months Izzie had been in Emerald Cove, she couldn't recall a single time she had seen Chip Townsend at anything.

"Dylan, I would like you to keep your comments to yourself." Mrs. Townsend's cheeks were pinched. Izzie stared at the bread to avoid the awkwardness. She was getting kind of hungry.

"Aww…am I embarrassing you? Too bad." Dylan's face was full of fury. "Why? Because I speak my mind? Or because I won't kiss the ground the Ingrams walk on so they don't talk about us behind our backs? That's what it's all about, isn't it, Mother? To make sure you're the one doing the back-stabbing rather than being stabbed yourself?"

"Dylan, stop," Brayden muttered.

Dylan glanced at the Ingrams. They seemed to be enjoying the family meltdown. "That's why you still have these people over for dinner. Not because you actually like them, but because you don't want them to dislike you even though your son dumped their daughter." Mrs. Ingram's arched eyebrows went higher if that were possible, and Savannah's face paled. "You do know that, right? That Brayden and Savannah broke up weeks ago?"

"But…" Mrs. Ingram apparently didn't. She looked from Brayden to Savannah, who wouldn't make eye contact with her mother. "Aren't you two going to cotillion together? Savannah, you said in Paris that…"

"Why don't we discuss this later," Mrs. Townsend said

267

quickly. "The dinner is getting cold." She picked up a bowl of collard greens and passed them to Izzie.

"I'm escorting Iz to cotillion," Brayden spoke up and stared across the table at Izzie. She froze with the collard greens in her hands. "She's the one I want to go with." He glanced at Savannah. "We broke up a while ago. You had to know I would want to go with Izzie." Savannah didn't answer him.

"Well, I didn't." Mrs. Ingram threw down her napkin and looked from Mrs. Townsend to Izzie, who sat quietly, afraid to put down the bowl in her hands. She had never seen anyone argue like this over dinner, and that said something, considering all the reality TV she'd watched. "This is embarrassing, Abigail. I thought you told me Brayden was escorting Savannah. We agreed he would." She pointed her finger at Izzie. "This girl is not even a real Monroe!"

"Excuse me?" Izzie felt the need to jump in now. The housekeeper rescued the collard greens before she dropped them.

"Oh, please," Mrs. Ingram told her, losing the dignified air Izzie usually saw her maintain. "We all know the truth. My husband told us today! You're not Bill Monroe's daughter. He faked the lab results to get ahead in the polls."

Izzie felt her hands go numb. "That's not true."

"The press is over at your house right now grilling him about it," Mrs. Ingram said smugly. "And I plan on hearing all about their discovery tonight on the news. At least at home, I can eat without rude interruptions or animalistic behavior." She glared at Dylan. "Let's go, Savannah. We're leaving. *Now.*" Mr. Ingram and Savannah quietly followed her out of the dining room. Savannah couldn't help throwing Izzie one last death glare on the way out.

"Vivian! Let me explain," Mrs. Townsend said desperately. "Would you do something?" she whispered heatedly to her husband before disappearing down the hall.

"Yes." Mr. Townsend stood up. "I'm going to get something to eat and take it on the patio. I didn't want to have them over in the first place."

"I'm going to leave, too," Izzie said, placing her napkin on the left side of her plate. She could hear ringing in her ears, and she felt queasy. Did her father really switch the lab results? Was she not actually Bill Monroe's daughter after all? Where did that leave her? The questions whirled in her mind.

"I'll go with you," Brayden said, but Izzie put her hands up to stop him. There were too many emotions in this room, and she was having a hard time figuring out which ones were her own. "I think I need to be alone."

"I hope you're happy," Mrs. Townsend said, flying into the dining room and surprising everyone but Dylan, who barely flinched. She stood up to face her. "The Ingrams are furious, and they have every right to be! You've ruined everything!"

"In my opinion, things are finally fixed," Dylan said. "Brayden is taking Izzie to cotillion, and I made the Ingrams feel as small as they made me feel when they told everyone at the club that I had flunked out of Vanderbilt already and was slumming it with some guy in Harborside."

Izzie looked up. Dylan was talking about Kylie's brother. But didn't she say she had left Vanderbilt, not failed out? Dylan glanced at Izzie quickly and looked away.

Dylan had used her. She thought she and Dylan were friends who had a lot in common, but apparently she was wrong. Dylan had cozied up to her to get under her family's skin. Brayden had been right about Dylan, but it didn't make Izzie feel any better.

"Why did you have to involve Iz?" Brayden shouted.

Izzie watched Dylan, Brayden, and Mrs. Townsend tear into one another again. All they did was fight and use one another. *They have no idea how lucky they are to have family,* she thought. Well, she wanted no part in their charades anymore. While they were distracted, she quietly walked out of the dining room. Ms. Norberry would be disappointed if she knew Izzie didn't thank her hostess for a lovely evening, but the truth was, it hadn't been one.

Nineteen

Since Izzie wouldn't be back till after dinner, Mira had persuaded Hayden and Connor to take a long walk around the
neighborhood after Kellen left. It was an unusually warm
night for late fall, and after everything that had happened,
Mira just wanted to get some fresh air. Izzie was waiting for
them when they got close to home, but strangely, she was
standing on a lawn a few houses away. Mira didn't know why
till she got closer.

"Who are all those people on our lawn?" Connor asked,
watching what Mira knew for certain was the kind of media
frenzy people usually saw on TV. "And why do they have
cameras and those long microphones on sticks?"

Photographers were swarming their front porch, the
driveway was packed with reporters setting up video cameras,

and vans had trampled their front lawn. Mira stepped in front of Connor, worried the sight of all this would scar him for life. "Maybe we should go for another walk."

"I'm tired," Connor complained.

"Why don't we call Mom and Dad and see what they want us to do?" Hayden suggested, and reached in his pocket for his cell phone.

Izzie laughed to herself. "Yes, let's call *Dad*. Darling Daddy." Her feet were tapping a mile a minute. It was close to nine at night, and Mira noticed Izzie was still in her uniform. Izzie hated the plaid skirt and itchy kneesocks and couldn't wait to tear them off every afternoon. So why did she still have them on today?

"Are you okay?" Mira had learned asking Izzie that question sometimes brought on more problems than it was worth.

"I'm fine," Izzie said, looking anything but. She ran a hand through her dark hair. "Considering I have no idea where I'm going to sleep tonight. Or the next night or ..."

But there was no time to decipher Izzie-speak, because the next thing she knew, the pack of news people was heading their way. The four of them grabbed for one another, not hearing the SUV screech to a halt in front of them on the sidewalk.

"Get in!" Callista yelled, throwing open a passenger door.

Before Connor was strapped into his booster seat, Callista took off around the block, weaving in and out of their winding development before heading back down Cliffside Drive and pulling into the garage. The few reporters who hadn't raced off after them stared in shock as the garage door went down in front of their faces. They were lucky the driveway was three cars wide. Callista didn't take out any of their camera equipment.

"Super maneuvers, Jeff Gordon," Hayden marveled. "You can drive my getaway car anytime."

"Hayden," Callista's voice was strained. She hopped out of the car. "No joking about getaway cars, love childs, or lab-tampering. We've had enough talk like that for one night." She glanced at Izzie. "Come inside. Your father needs to talk to you."

Izzie slammed the door extra hard. "No, thanks. I'm going upstairs to pack."

"What is she talking about?" Mira asked Callista. "Izzie, what is going on?"

"You're even freaking me out," Hayden said. "Can we do this inside? I'm getting a little nervous with all these heavy tools around for you girls to throw."

Izzie went through the garage door that led to the family room, but she didn't stop there. She kept walking and headed for the stairs. That's where their dad was waiting. Mira's mom hovered nearby.

"Thank God, you're home. Did the news crews stop you?" They shook their heads. "Good. I need to talk to all of you about why they're here," he started to say, but when he saw Izzie's expression, he stopped. He could tell she already knew what he wanted to talk about. "Isabelle, let me explain. Isabelle?" She tried to maneuver around him. "I know this sounds bad." His hair was a mess, and he had dark circles under his eyes. Suddenly, Mira felt scared.

"Please don't get upset," Mira's mom begged Izzie. She was disheveled, too. Her blond hair looked as if it hadn't been combed, and even though she was wearing her tennis whites, Mira had a feeling she had never left the house. "The story isn't true!"

"How am I supposed to believe you?" Izzie hurried upstairs. Halfway up, she changed her mind and whirled around, holding the banister. "I got ambushed by the Ingrams tonight! They knew the story about the mix-up at the lab before I did." Her lower lip quivered. "They said I wasn't really your daughter, and you knew."

"Mix-up at the lab? What are you talking about?" Mira was perplexed. "Do you mean the story about the other love child?" Now everyone looked confused. "No? What are you talking about, then?" Everyone looked at Dad.

"Did you say the Ingrams?" was all her dad could manage to say. Izzie headed upstairs again. Realizing his mistake, he ran up the stairs after her. "Neither story is true. It's all vicious lies." Mira realized Izzie was visibly shaking. "You *are* my daughter. There is no other child. There's just you." The two stared at each other. "You are my daughter," he whispered, trying to drill the truth into her.

"I am," she said more convincingly, and then she sank onto the stairs and shut her eyes like the whole thing was too much for her to handle.

Mira's mom looked at the others. "Connor, why don't you go watch *Phineas and Ferb*. I'll read you books in a bit."

"Even though it's late?" Connor asked hopefully.

"Even though it's late." She held her smile till he was around the corner, and then her face fell. "The papers are running a story about the lab that ran Isabelle's paternity test," she explained to Hayden and Mira. "They claim that we falsified the results."

"What?" Mira couldn't hide her surprise.

"The story is bogus, obviously," her mom said. "We've spoken to the lab, and they've given a statement testifying to the true results." She rubbed Izzie's back while she stared sadly at Mira. "Someone is trying to destroy us. I just wish I knew why."

"I'm sorry," their dad said, sounding defeated. "What happens in this family should stay in the family. You guys didn't sign up for this fight. Mira's painting shouldn't be front-page news."

Mira's head shot up. "My *what*?"

Callista glanced at Mira's dad. "Your self-portrait. Mira, I'm so sorry, but the *North Carolina Post* somehow got a hold of it. They're running it on the front page tomorrow."

"How?" Mira cried. Her dad and mom didn't say anything, but it was obvious they had seen the painting, too. "It was in my closet. How could anyone get their hands on it?"

"We don't know," Callista admitted. "That's what we wanted to ask you about. Who else knew about your painting?"

"Just you, Hayden, and Kellen," Mira said.

"Kellen?" Callista thought for a moment. "The boy who was here yesterday?"

"Yes, he's my date for cotillion," Mira said. "Why?"

"Nothing," Callista said hastily. "If he's your date, then you trust him, I'm sure."

"Does something concern you?" Mira's mom asked, and Callista side-eyed Mira.

"It's just..." She hesitated. "If we're the only ones who saw the painting, and you know Hayden and I would have no reason to take it, then the only other person who could have would be Kellen. I watched you hand him the painting."

"Kellen's a good guy," Hayden said. "He wouldn't do that to Mira."

"How much do you actually know about him?" Callista asked. She took off her glasses as if they were hurting her eyes. "I know you like him, Mira, but would he have any reason to do this?"

"No," Mira said right away.

Callista tried again, her voice softer this time. "Could he

276

have needed the money for anything? I know you go to an expensive school. Is his family well off?"

"He's on scholarship," Mira said, and glanced briefly at Hayden, "but that doesn't mean he'd—"

"The *Post* paid big money for your painting," Callista interrupted. "The holidays are coming. If he needed quick money, there'd be no easier place to get it than by selling a story—or a painting—to the papers."

Mira shook her head. "He wouldn't do that." But she felt confused as she tried to piece the story together. *Then who did?* a voice in her head asked. *He's the only other person who knew where my painting was, and he did say money was tight at home.* She felt the tears coming and couldn't stop them. "I'm so sorry, Dad."

"It's not your fault," he said, even though he clearly sounded frustrated. "I can't believe what we've let happen to us. When did we start hiding things from each other?"

"Like the community center?" Izzie asked, and he looked at her. "I saw you there a few weeks ago with the director." Their dad shifted awkwardly. "You never told me you were going. Why were you there?"

"I can't explain right now," their dad said. "I'm sorry."

"You seem to say that a lot," Izzie said bitterly. "You're really good at saying 'I'm sorry,' but you never follow through. Is that because you're just telling more lies?"

"Isabelle!" Mira's mom sounded surprised. "Don't talk to your father like that."

"I have a right to know." Her voice was rising. "Are you trying to save yourself by siding with the Ingrams on their plan for the community center?"

"I'm not—did you say before that the Ingrams knew about the story with the lab results?" he asked. "How could they if it hasn't run yet?"

"Who cares about the Ingrams?" Izzie cried. "What I care about is the truth. Why were you there?" Their dad didn't answer. "It doesn't matter. Everyone already knows what a joke I am. I just can't believe I fell for the joke, too. Well, not anymore. I shouldn't be doing cotillion and pretending to be someone I'm not."

"Cotillion!" Callista tried to change the subject. "Now that would be a super place to smooth things over."

"Not now, Callista," Mira's mom warned.

"You can forget about cotillion," Izzie told Callista. "I don't belong there." She stared at their dad. "And I don't belong here, either, if you can't be honest with me."

"Isabelle, please try to understand." His voice was strained. "If you would just give me a few days till this new feeding frenzy dies out, I can tell you why I was at the community center, but right now there is too much else going on to worry about Harborside!" Izzie was taken aback by his tone. "I need us to weather this new storm first. Then maybe if we can go

278

to cotillion together, this will all blow over," he said, lowering his voice. "You have to trust me."

Mira stared at her father as if she didn't even know him. "Trust you?" she asked. "Like we did with this campaign? Dad, ever since you decided to run for U.S. Senate, *our* lives have been turned upside down. We haven't even made it past the primaries, and every other day, there is a story in the papers about our family or someone is talking about us at school. When are you going to give it up, already, and put us first?" His face looked pained.

"Who cares how we look to the rest of Emerald Cove?" Izzie agreed. "We're miserable! We're barely talking to each other. Who are we trying to kid by showing up at cotillion? Half the room is going to be talking behind our backs, anyway."

"She's right," Mira said, the depressing reality dawning on her. "Want to know what's even sadder?" Her dad looked at her. "That you want us to go, after everything that has happened, just to save your stupid campaign. When you took us dress shopping, I thought maybe you were doing this for us." Her eyes welled with tears. "But you were just doing this for yourself. I'm not going, either." She hurried down the hall and flung open the sliding glass doors to the backyard. She had done enough talking for one day.

Mira heard someone run out behind her. It was Izzie. They stared at each other wordlessly.

When the back gate opened, Mira whirled around, ready

to tell off her parents or the first photographer who got in her face. She had so much anger that she didn't know what to do with it. But it wasn't the press. It was Kellen.

"Hey," he said, pulling off the parka hood that was obstructing his face. He smiled. "I almost didn't get in, but then I saw Hayden, and he said to head around back. It's a mob scene out there. Are you okay?"

He didn't seem to notice her tear-stained face in the dimming light or how angry she must have looked. But she was angry. How could he betray her like that? She wished she could hit him, but that wasn't her style.

Kellen put his arms around her, not noticing how she steeled herself against him. "I called and called when I saw the story on the news, but your cell kept going to voice mail. I got here as fast as I could." His face was full of worry, which made her almost laugh. He was a good liar.

Izzie's cell phone rang, and Mira was surprised to hear her pick up. "Hello," she said in a dead voice, and walked to the other side of the patio to talk.

"Is it true?" Kellen asked.

"Is what true?" Mira eased herself out of his arms. It was funny to hear Kellen use the word *true,* considering what he had done.

Kellen glanced at Izzie. "Is Izzie not actually your sister?"

"I have nothing to say to you, Brayden," Mira heard Izzie

say with a hint of emotion slipping into her voice. "I was wrong about you and me."

"You want the truth?" Mira said calmly. "Okay. The truth is, Izzie *is* my sister. The papers made the story up, and my parents have the sealed lab results to prove it." Kellen looked relieved, but she kept going. "But truth is a funny thing, don't you think? Because if we're talking about the truth, then maybe there is something you want to tell me, too."

"I don't belong in your world," she heard Izzie say to Brayden. Mira looked at her face, so strong despite how hard it had to be for her to say those words. "I can't pretend to be someone I'm not. Table settings, cotillion dresses, waltzes… it's not me. You let your family run your world. I'll never let my new family dictate mine."

"Mira?" Kellen tried to get her attention. "I asked you why you keep talking about the truth."

Mira heard Izzie arguing on the phone, but she blocked it out and forced herself to do the uncomfortable: Confront Kellen. "I'm bringing it up because you haven't been truthful with me. What happened to my painting? Did you sell it?"

"Sell it?" Kellen sounded flustered. "You told me to hide it in your closet. Remember?"

"I remember. I also remember telling you what was going on with my dad. How much Bill Monroe's daughter hates him is for me to know, not the *Post*. My painting is going to be on the front page tomorrow," she said bitterly. "How could you do that to me? I thought you liked me."

"I did, until you just accused me of selling you out," Kellen said. The words stung, but she tried not to let on. Instead, she lashed back.

"I know you said money was tight, but if you needed a loan that badly, you could have asked me," Mira told him. "You didn't have to make a quick buck selling my painting to a tabloid newspaper."

Kellen's face crumbled. "Is that what you really think of me?" His voice was eerily calm. "I didn't sell your painting, Mira. I'm not a thief. If it's out there, then maybe you should ask yourself who would want to hurt you like that. It's not me. I don't need your money. I don't need anybody's money," he said angrily. "But if you really knew me, you'd know that." Kellen turned and walked back to the gate he had entered only a few minutes before.

Despite willing herself not to, hot tears plopped down her face.

"Don't call me again, Brayden," she heard Izzie say in a steely voice.

It was hard for Mira to hear anything over her own crying. She'd lost her friends, her trust in her dad, and cotillion, and now she'd lost Kellen, too. She felt a tap on her shoulder and turned around. Izzie stood there, her cell phone hanging limply in her hand. Her lower lip was trembling, and one big, fat tear rolled down her cheek. It was the most upset Izzie had ever been in front of her. Mira wished she had a tissue so she could wipe her nose.

Izzie offered her the next best thing: her hand. Mira looked at it for half a second before taking it. She held on tight as they walked to the pool house.

Twenty

Izzie had never spent much time in the pool house. That might have explained why it took her a minute to figure out where she was when she woke up late the next day on top of a bunch of outdoor cushions. Then the night before came flooding back to her like a bad dream—the cringe-worthy dinner party at the Townsends, walking out on Brayden, fighting with Bill, wondering if he really was her dad, finding out he definitely was her dad but that he was still a big, fat disappointment, and telling everyone she wasn't going to cotillion.

She heard loud snoring and rolled over. Mira was asleep a few feet away, so many seat cushions and throw pillows stacked beneath her that she looked like she was auditioning for *The Princess and the Pea*. Her one arm was thrown across her eyes in a dramatic fashion befitting Mira even if the snoring was not. Izzie thought about taking out her phone and capturing the image on video but decided against it. Mira had been through enough of her own drama the night before, too.

Izzie threw off the pool towels she had used as blankets and tossed the pillow that had substituted for Lambie onto the couch. She couldn't figure out why this place was called a pool house when it was big enough to be someone's real house. It served as a shed for the outdoor furniture in the winter, but if the Monroes ever had guests, it could be a great guesthouse. There was a small kitchen, a changing area, a full bath, and a living room that had huge windows that overlooked the pool and the main house. Izzie could see movement through the den windows, but she wasn't worried about anyone spotting her. Earlier that morning, Hayden had brought out a tray of food Aunt Maureen had prepared. Both girls had told him they weren't ready to talk to anyone yet, which was code for "Keep Mom and Dad away." The pool house was eerily quiet. Maybe it was the exhaustion from the wave of fights they had both been through, but it was now almost one in the afternoon, and neither of them had gotten up yet.

There was a brief snort, followed by several more snorts, and then Mira shot up, seeming as confused about her whereabouts as Izzie had been. Her normally shiny, perfectly groomed hair was all frizz and flyaways, and she ran a hand across her mouth to stop the drool. But it was too late. Izzie had spotted it.

"Morning, sleeping beauty. Or should I say, good afternoon?"

Mira checked her watch, then fell back on the pillows, which made a squeaking noise—Izzie had forgotten Mira had a pool float under there, too. "Is it really one o'clock?" she moaned. "Why do I still feel so tired?"

"Mental exhaustion—at least that's what Dr. Oz would say." Izzie started stacking the cushions.

Mira sat up on her elbows. "You watch *Dr. Oz?*" She bit her lip to keep from laughing, which was a good thing, because Izzie glared at her.

"Maybe. When I lived with Grams. You can learn some good stuff on there."

"I'm sure." Mira glanced warily toward the windows. "If it's day already, does this mean we have to go back inside?"

Izzie sat down, as if the weight of that thought was too much for her. "Maybe they're so busy dealing with the campaign fallout, they've forgotten about us."

"My mom would never forget about us," Mira said wryly. "When I was little, my best friend, Joyce, lived three houses away, and we were always threatening to run away. We only made it as far as the bushes. By lunch, we were whining about food and sneaking in the house to use the bathroom. If I know my mom, she's biding her time till dinner, when she knows we'll cave."

"I would never cave for food. You can always scrounge up

something to eat," Izzie said, thinking back to her own runaway attempt. There was only one, right after her mom died. She spent a night in Kylie's cramped apartment and Grams got her the next morning. They never spoke of it. It was almost as if Grams knew Izzie needed space to figure things out for herself. Maybe Aunt Maureen was the same way.

"So what should we do, then?" Mira asked, arching her back and then turning into a yoga pose. "Hide out in here all day?"

Izzie shook her head, staring out at the crisp, almost wintry day. Christmas decorations had started going up all over town. Not at the Monroes, though—everyone was so preoccupied, they hadn't even bought a tree. Connor had been begging to get one.

Hayden stuck his head in the pool house door. "Everybody decent?"

"Don't you know how to knock?" Mira asked.

"You do know you're sleeping in our backyard, right? I don't have to knock."

Izzie could tell Hayden's voice wasn't its normally upbeat self. "What's going on in there?" she asked.

Hayden's face twisted slightly. "A big decision was made last night while you guys were out here. Dad is pulling out of the race." Izzie felt as if the air had been knocked out of her. "Callista pulled together a press conference for five PM today to announce it. He didn't want me to tell you guys—he wants to tell you himself afterward—but I thought you'd want to know."

Mira and Izzie looked at each other, and Izzie wondered if they were feeling the same thing: guilt. She didn't know why she thought her dad's failed campaign was her fault, but she did.

Izzie felt like the room was shaking. "I need to get out of here."

"Me, too," Mira agreed, smoothing her hair. "I need a latte."

Izzie tilted her head. "I was thinking more like a jog or swimming a few laps."

Mira frowned. "Where? It's freezing out. And besides, you're still wearing your EP uniform."

Izzie groaned. She'd forgotten that. She turned to Hayden. "Could you...?"

"Yeah," he said. "I'll be back in five minutes with clothes." Mira opened her mouth. "For both of you. But I make no promises your outfits will match."

Mira twisted one of her curls around her finger. "So you're really thinking about going for a jog? I hate jogging."

Izzie just looked at her. "You play field hockey!"

"But we don't jog. We just kind of glide down the field," Mira protested. "How about a walk through town instead? They had the tree-lighting ceremony last night, and I'm sure

Main Street looks festive. It will cheer us up!" she suggested. "And we can get hot cocoa instead of lattes. Please?"

Sometimes there was no fighting Mira. "Fine. We'll walk."

~

By the time Mira got moving—she didn't want to leave the pool house without makeup, which required Hayden to make another trip—it was almost two thirty.

"Our last cotillion initiation starts in a half hour," Mira realized as they neared Main Street. Her cheeks were pink, and Izzie couldn't tell if that was shame, blush and bronzer, or the cold air.

"I know." Izzie put her hands in her peacoat pockets to keep them warm.

"That is *not* why I suggested we walk into town, of course. I know we're not going." Izzie watched Mira's hands ball into fists. "We're not dressed for it. It's a shame, though," she said, and dropped a dollar into a bucket in front of a Salvation Army worker who was ringing his bell. "I was looking forward to finding out who our cotillion captain was. I wanted to thank her for giving Savannah such a hard time."

Izzie glanced at the sidewalk. Now did not seem like the right moment to admit she knew the answer to that question.

Izzie couldn't explain her relationship with Dylan to Mira. She wasn't sure Mira would understand. Izzie didn't understand it, either. Dylan had used her to make her own mom more miserable.

"It doesn't matter," Mira said. "We're not finishing our initiation, because we're not going to cotillion, and we can't go to cotillion unless we do our initiation." She side-eyed Izzie. "I didn't really want to go, anyway."

"Liar. You told me you thought about cotillion more than you've thought about your own wedding day. And you haven't stopped talking about your Amsale dress, even though you haven't let me see it."

"My dress," Mira said mournfully. "What am I going to do with it now?"

"Uh, save it for an actual wedding, which is what the dress was made for?"

Mira missed the point. "It won't be in style by the time I get married." She sighed. "Maybe I'll just wear it around the house. Even if I wasn't still mad at Dad, it's not like I have a date. I'm never talking to Kellen again." She covered her eyes, and Izzie noticed her nails had tiny flowers painted on them. "When I think about the paper running that picture of my painting, I'm so embarrassed. If the girls wouldn't talk to me before, imagine what they're going to say now!" Mira frowned. "And I feel bad Dad saw it."

"I still can't believe Kellen sold it. It doesn't sound like him." Izzie went over the details all night when she was tossing and turning on those uncomfortable chair cushions. "But then again, I don't get how the Ingrams knew the fake story about my lab results, either." Izzie scowled. "I don't know how you can stand that family."

"They weren't so bad," Mira said thoughtfully. "When Savannah liked me, they adored me and our family. But now that we're on the outs and you stole her boyfriend..."

"I did not steal," Izzie corrected her. "And he isn't mine anymore, either."

"What happened last night?" Mira asked softly.

Izzie's wavy hair whipped around her face like a mask. She could hear the wind howling against some of the windows of the stores they passed. "He didn't want me." She heard how hoarse her voice sounded. It had given out on her.

Mira was flabbergasted. "He said that?"

"No," Izzie had to admit. "But it's obvious, isn't it? If he wanted to be with me, he would have stood up for me with his mom and Dylan." She shook her head. "He was too busy arguing with them to even realize I'd left. Brayden belongs with someone like Savannah." She tried to convince herself of that by saying the words out loud. "He's better off escorting her to cotillion."

"He is *not!*" Mira hit her in the arm. "Please tell me that is not happening. Did he really let his mom pick his date?"

Izzie hesitated. The conversation came flooding back to

her. "Well…" She hesitated. "Not exactly. Maybe at first, but last night he told his mom in front of the Ingrams and Savannah that he was taking me to cotillion instead."

Mira stopped walking. "But then…wait. Why are you mad at him?"

"Because! This is about more than just cotillion," Izzie said. "He had so many chances to stick up for me, and he didn't do it till Dylan forced him to. And she only forced him to in order to make everyone in their house uncomfortable." She exhaled, the cold air visibly coming out of her mouth. "I told him last night on the phone. It's more obvious to me than ever that we don't belong together. Our worlds are too different. His mom makes me realize every day that I don't fit into his."

"Why do you let her make you feel like that?" Mira asked.

Izzie could still hear the soft jingle of the Salvation Army collector a block behind them. "I don't know. I guess people like her intimidate me." She looked at Mira wistfully. "Sometimes I wish I could be more like you." Mira seemed surprised to hear that, but thankfully she didn't gloat. "It doesn't matter who you're talking to—someone you like or someone who can't stand you—you always manage to know the right thing to say. You always sound so together."

"What's so great about that?" Mira asked. "I wish I had guts like you." Now it was Izzie's turn to be surprised. "You stand up for yourself no matter what the situation is. I could never tell someone off the way you do, and believe me, I wish I could. Savannah has deserved it so many times."

Izzie laughed. "Be happy you don't tell people off. That's a good thing in EC!"

"I'm serious," Mira said, staring at her with interest. "I think it's cool you're your own person." She clutched the emerald pendant around her neck. "But you can still be your own person and be with Brayden."

Izzie heard that and started to shut down, but this time Mira wouldn't let her.

"You keep saying, 'I don't belong in his world,' but don't you see? You already *are* in his world, whether you like it or not. You live here now, and that's not going to change. Emerald Cove is as much your world as it is Brayden's." Mira braced herself for Izzie's reaction, but she didn't need to worry.

Mira is…right, Izzie realized. Why was she always so worried about Brayden's family liking her? Look how screwed up they were! "I never thought of it that way before."

Mira hesitated. "While we're getting things off our chest, I have something I have to confess. I'm not sure you're going to like it."

The last thing Izzie needed was more lies. "What did you do?"

Mira wouldn't look at her. "You're going to find out anyway, but I promised Mrs. Fitz not to tell you till after cotillion." She glanced nervously at Izzie out of the corner of her eye. "I stepped down as Butterflies cochair." Izzie's jaw dropped. "I don't deserve the position," she said. "I'm not doing right by the group, and neither is Savannah. I couldn't get Mrs. Fitz to make Savannah step down, but I was able to get her to transfer my cochair title to you."

"What?" Izzie screeched. She sounded sort of like Mira. "Why?"

"Because you're the right person for the job," she told Izzie. "Mrs. Fitz agrees with me. You know how to get things done. I've seen you do it during initiation and in all the Butterflies meetings. Maybe some people don't like you yet, but they respect you. Even Savannah. Whether she steps down or not, I know you're going to get more done for the Butterflies than I ever could."

Izzie wanted to be mad. She wanted to tell Mira she was insane. But the truth was, this was the best news she had heard in a long time. She knew she could whip the Butterflies into shape, even with Savannah breathing down her neck. Ever since Mrs. Fitz mentioned she would make a good club cochair, she hadn't stopped thinking about it. Maybe she had wanted this job more than she even realized. "Thanks," she said shyly. "I won't let you down."

"I know you won't." Mira hugged her. "See? I know what you need better than you do. Dr. Oz has nothing on me." They both laughed.

"Well, if you're so smart, what are you going to do about Kellen?" Izzie asked.

Mira bit her lip. "Nothing. I can't forgive him for what he did."

"You've forgiven people for doing less," Izzie told her. "You put up with Taylor for forever, and he was a dud of a boyfriend, and look at everything you went through with Savannah." Mira looked away. "Neither of them cared about you the way Kellen seems to. Maybe you should try to work things out with him. You can find friends much better than the ones you had, but Kellen, he could be worth keeping around, if he can explain himself."

Mira gave her a look. "It would have been nice if you could have said this to me a few weeks ago, when I was a neurotic mess."

"And it would have been nice for you to give me the 'Emerald Cove is your home, too' speech before I showed up on the Townsends' doorstep last night." Izzie looked at her sister. "Are you sure Kellen was the one who took your painting?"

"I don't know," she admitted. "But who else could it have been?"

Something about the story with Kellen was eating at Izzie. She understood where he was coming from better than Mira. There were times she had needed money badly, too, but she never resorted to stealing, and she had a feeling

295

Kellen didn't, either. There had to be someone else they weren't thinking of.

Mira glanced down the street at the town square Christmas tree that rose in the distance. A group of girls in white tanks, knee-highs, and short shorts stood around it. "They've started initiation. I guess we're officially out of cotillion now."

Izzie glanced at her watch. "And Bill is two hours away from walking away from his senatorial run."

"Could this day be more depressing?" Mira asked.

"I can't believe Callista was able to put together a press conference so quickly," Izzie said. "Usually it takes her days to get a story out. She always complains the networks don't call her back right away." *Huh. That doesn't make any sense,* she thought. *Someone as scandalous as Bill Monroe seems like a story they would pounce on.* Something dawned on her. "Did anyone other than you and Kellen know where you hid your painting?"

Mira thought back. "Just Callista. She was there when I told Kellen where to hide it." They both looked at each other. "You don't think…?"

"She wouldn't," Izzie convinced herself. "What would she have to gain?" She hesitated. "But it is weird, isn't it?"

"Everything is weird lately," Mira said. "If another story comes out about how much I hate Dad, or how much you wish you lived back in Harborside, I am going to start thinking our house is bugged!" Mira laughed nervously. "Maybe you and I are the ones who leaked all this to the papers. We only talk to each other."

"Each other and Callista," Izzie realized. Mira's laughter petered out.

Could Callista be behind all this? Izzie wondered. She thought for a moment. Callista was always around when they needed her. She offered them rides, asked to hang out, tried to get Mira a modeling gig. Maybe she was bribing them for information without their knowing it. Izzie suddenly felt sick. She opened herself up to so few people. How could she not have seen how Callista was manipulating her and Mira?

"This doesn't make any sense!" Mira cried. "Callista was our friend. She said we could confide in her about anything."

"Of course she did." Izzie started tapping her foot. "She made us think we were friends. Meanwhile she was selling stories to the press. But what does she have against us?"

"I don't know, but what I do know is that Dad is getting ready to hold a press conference," Mira said. "And if we're right about any of this, then he needs to know. Now."

Izzie felt adrenaline running through her chest. She turned Mira toward the direction of home. "You know that gliding you do in field hockey? Today, you're going to make it a full-fledged run."

Twenty-One

Mira flew through the front door with Izzie on her heels, and for a split second, she felt a zing of satisfaction—she had reached the house first! Then reality set in, and she started yelling. "Mom? Dad?"

"Aunt Maureen? Dad?" she heard Izzie say, and they both looked at each other.

Izzie had used the word *dad*, and she hadn't burst into flames.

Hayden came flying down the stairs with a finger over his lips. "Keep it down! Dad is in a huge meeting. You'd know that if either of you turned on your phones."

The girls looked at each other guiltily.

"I was avoiding Kellen," Mira confessed.

"Brayden," Izzie admitted.

"Instead, you avoided me," Hayden said, "and that was a mistake because you two are not going to believe what is going on."

Izzie cut him off. "Is Callista with him?"

Hayden nodded. "Yeah, and so is..."

"Did he pull out of the race yet?" Mira blurted out. "Because we have to talk to him first."

"He's not pulling out," Hayden told them. "He doesn't have to. Holden Ingram is in Dad's office right now striking a deal."

"Deal?" Izzie repeated darkly. "What for? We think Callista is the one who..."

The door to Dad's office opened. Their dad walked out with two lawyers and Mr. Ingram in tow. Mr. Ingram's jaw was set squarely, and his lawyer followed close behind him. "Mira, Isabelle, Hayden," he said and then continued down the hall, shutting the front door quietly behind him.

"Mirabelle and Isabelle, can I see you both for a moment?" Mira detected a note of triumph in their dad's voice as she followed Izzie into his study. "I'm sure you're wondering why Mr. Ingram and both of our lawyers were here."

Mira spent a lot of time in her dad's office when she was little. He'd be on the phone with some political powerhouse, and she'd be on the other side of his desk with crayons and paper, making her own bills and laws. Her dad's walls were filled with memorabilia from his days as a ballplayer and in

299

his second career as a state senator. He was beaming in all of the photos, which was a sharp contrast to how beaten down he had looked these past few weeks.

"Mr. Ingram just confessed to hiring someone to plant false stories about our family in the papers," their dad said. "Well, some were false." His right eyebrow rose. "The ones Grayson Reynolds got his hands on just weren't meant for public consumption."

"So you're not dropping out of the race?" Izzie asked. Their dad nodded.

Mira felt relief wash over her. "Savannah's dad did all this?" she asked. "Because we thought Callista—"

Their dad cut off Mira abruptly. "Callista has been fired. Mr. Ingram hired her to dig up dirt on me, my campaign, and our family. He apparently found out who I hired through Lucas Hale, and he sought her out and offered to pay her double what I was paying her."

Hearing they were right about Callista, Mira and Izzie exchanged looks of slight triumph.

"Wow. I knew Savannah hated me, but I can't believe the whole family would go after us that hard core," Mira said.

"I don't know if Savannah knew what her father was up to," her dad pointed out, "but he certainly didn't want anyone else to know. Hence the lawyers and our deal." He picked up a crystal paperweight on his desk. "Callista is taking the fall and making a statement, I am getting what I need from Holden, and the rest will stay quiet." He exhaled. "Remind me why I went into politics again?"

"Because you're good at it," Mira said. He smiled wearily.

"How did you find out the truth?" Izzie asked.

He took a seat in the leather swivel chair Mira used to spin around in like she was on the teacup ride at Disney World. "After our blowup last night, your aunt kept thinking about all the things that had been written about us since I announced I was running. We pulled up some stories on the Web, and started rereading them, and it was eerie. It felt like we had been bugged," he said incredulously. "Some stories were things we joked about in private, like 'What is the press going to come up with next? A story on mixed-up lab results and a love child?' And then there the stories were in the paper!" He glanced apologetically at Izzie. "We were just trying to blow off steam when we said those things, but they weren't funny. These last few months have been so frustrating. It has felt like the papers and Grayson Reynolds knew our moves as soon as we did, and there were only a few people in that category. You guys and Callista." He looked at Izzie again. "When you mentioned what the Ingrams said at the Townsends, I knew Holden had to be involved. He denied it at first, but when I threatened a lawsuit for defamation of character, he was here within the hour."

"You said you got what you needed from Mr. Ingram." Mira was still piecing the story together. "What was that?"

Their dad leaned back in his chair and looked pretty pleased with himself. "His coastal revitalization project is dead. The thing is off the table as part of our agreement."

"Are you serious?" Izzie's butt left the chair. "The community center is no longer in danger of being torn down?"

"Not by Holden Ingram," he told her. "But that doesn't solve your funding issues—even with the money raised from the Falling into You Fest, the center doesn't have enough money for heat, programs, repairs."

"I'll find a way to get more," Izzie said resolutely.

He slid something across his desk toward her. "I'm proud of you for trying, but this will make life a little easier. This will explain why I couldn't tell you about the center last night. The details weren't finalized till today, but I already called the center to share the good news."

Mira leaned over to read along with Izzie. A giant Java Joe coffee logo was on the top of the page with *Java Joe Gives Back* written on its classic coffee mug.

"Harborside Community Center has just won a Java Joe, a yearly community-center revitalization grant," he explained. "It's going to receive fifty thousand dollars in funding to fix up the building, and it's going to learn ways to bring in more revenue. I don't think we're going to have to worry about your center going anywhere for quite some time."

Izzie walked around the desk uncertainly and gave him a quick squeeze around the neck. "Thank you." Her voice cracked.

"You're welcome." He choked up.

"Why didn't you tell me?" Izzie asked. "When I asked you why you were at the center, you let me lay into you about lying to me. Now I feel terrible."

"I didn't want to tell you till I knew it was definitely happening," he explained. "It seemed safer to wait till the deal was done and to not get your hopes up." He grabbed her hand and looked from Izzie to Mira. "I feel like all I've done since we blended this family is let you down. That's going to change." He reached across the desk for Mira's hand, too. "I know I can't take back what I did, Isabelle, but I really do want to be a father to you like I am to Pea." He smiled sadly at Mira. "I love her whether she feels a part of this family or thinks it's a figment of her imagination."

"You understood my painting! Everyone else thought the me in the window was a ghost."

He let go of their hands and opened his bottom desk drawer. There was the painting.

"How'd you get it back?" Mira asked.

"I have my ways." He took down one of his World Series photos and taped her painting in its place. "I know it still needs a frame, but if you don't mind, Pea, this is going to hang in my office to remind me what happens when I lose sight of what's important: my family."

303

Now Mira wanted a hug. "I'm so sorry about all this, Dad."

"*I'm* sorry," he corrected her. "Nothing like this will ever happen again. *If* I stay in this race, things are going to change. I won't let anyone hurt you guys again."

"Where is Callista now?" Izzie asked.

"She's packing up her things in the pool house," he told them.

"I didn't know she used the pool house," Mira said.

"Only on occasion. Probably when she needed to make covert calls. Your mom is out there with her to make sure she doesn't take anything." He gave them a look.

"Do you mind if we go out and see her?" Mira asked tentatively, glancing in Izzie's direction. "There's something I want to say to her."

He nodded. "Go ahead."

~

Callista was carrying a box to her car by the time they reached her. Mira's mom was standing watch from her post at the pool house door. When Callista saw the girls, her face hardened. "I guess you two have come to tell me off, too."

Mira was surprisingly calm. "I thought you liked us," she said, knowing how naive she sounded.

304

"I do like you," Callista said. She glanced over her shoulder at Mira's mom. She was out of earshot, but she still looked pretty mad. "You're super. This was just business. Do you know how much someone in PR makes outside of Manhattan?" she asked. "It's not pretty. I got a better offer, and I took it."

"That's what this was about? Money?" Izzie was not happy. "You didn't care who you hurt?"

Callista hiked her box up to maintain her grip. Mira couldn't believe how aloof she seemed for someone who had practically caused a whole family to crumble. "That's politics. For my next job, maybe I'll do PR for a cosmetics company." She smiled somewhat. "Less cutthroat." Neither girl laughed. "I'm sorry you two got caught up in this, though," Callista said. "You guys were always great to me." She balanced the box with one hand and pulled a small slip of paper out of her messenger bag. "This is for you, Mira. To make up for the painting fiasco."

"What is it?" Mira looked at the scribbled name and phone number.

"That is an editor at *Justine*," Callista explained, and Mira looked up in surprise. "Even without your dad, they want you for a shoot. I sent them some pictures of you. They think you'd make a great model."

"They do?" Mira began twisting one of her curls around

her finger. "To model? I mean, I never thought about modeling before, but that could be...what did they say about me, exactly?" Izzie nudged her. "I'll think about calling them."

Callista glanced at Izzie. "They're interested in you, too, you know."

"No, thanks," Izzie said bluntly.

"Well, I guess this is good-bye, girls." Callista headed to the gate. "Sorry it had to end like this."

Mira's mom followed her out, as if she couldn't be quite sure they were really rid of Callista until she drove off in her Prius. Once she was gone, Izzie, Mira, and her mom stood quietly on the front porch. Mira couldn't help but wonder what the last month would have been like if her dad had hired a different PR person, or hadn't hired anyone at all. Maybe the truth was they needed something like this to happen so they could figure out how to be a family again.

But she wasn't going to say that out loud.

A few seconds later, a minivan with the Emerald Cove Dry Cleaners logo pulled into their long driveway. Their dry cleaner delivered even though most people lived only ten minutes away from the store. A young guy jumped out and ran several items in plastic and on hangers to the front door. Mira's dad and Hayden appeared in time to tip him. Mira noticed their dad's tuxedo was one of the items delivered.

"I guess you won't be needing that next Saturday," Mira said.

"Why not?" He spun the tux toward him. "If you girls still want to go, I will be there." They looked at each other. "I'm sorry I made you think cotillion was more about me than you. This night has always been yours. You should go. We bought a whole table for the event. We should use it." He looked at them oddly. "You didn't officially bow out of cotillion, did you?"

Mira eyed Izzie. Neither could tell him about the initiation. Even though they could technically still make their debut, it would be social suicide to show up. "We haven't, but after everything, I think we're better off sitting it out." The words tasted bitter coming out of her mouth.

"If you don't want me to present you..." their dad began, trailing off.

"It's not that." Mira had to think quickly. "I don't have an escort."

"Make that two of us," Izzie said, and a smile spread across her lips. "I stand corrected. *One* of us doesn't have an escort. If an escort is the only thing stopping you, I think you could get yours back." Mira gave her a questioning look.

Kellen. She had forgotten how he fit into this whole twisted puzzle. She didn't even want to think about what she'd said to him. She hadn't even given him a chance to defend himself. The things she said were so humiliating, she wanted to erase them from memory. How could she accuse him of taking her painting for the money? He might never forgive her, but she still owed him an apology. "I am not sure I can make that happen, but I'll try," she told Izzie.

"What about Brayden? He isn't up to escort snuff anymore?" Hayden asked. Izzie didn't seem to have an answer for that one. "Well, if he doesn't work out, I have been told I'm an excellent escort."

Izzie sighed. "I guess it's either go with you or ask Kylie, but she'd look pretty strange in a tux."

"Kylie is coming?" Hayden asked.

Izzie looked at him strangely. "I was kidding. She wouldn't go to the Winter White Ball if you paid her."

"And we can't go, either," Mira reminded Izzie. "We, uh, didn't finish our training." Mira had finally turned her cell phone back on, and it rang to make its presence known. She didn't recognize the number. Hopeful it was Kellen calling from home, she picked up. "Hello," she said, and stepped off the porch for some privacy.

"Hi, Mira. It's Dylan Townsend."

Her stomach gave a small lurch. "Hi."

"We missed you at the final initiation today."

She knew she'd been cut for not showing up, but was she about to face worse? "Sorry. We had a lot going on."

"I heard. Everything okay now?"

"Yeah," Mira said curiously. "But how did you…"

"Let's just say an old friend of yours explained why there was no way you and Izzie could have made it this afternoon.

So you get a free pass. Although you might want to look at the pictures we posted of the others on Facebook."

They were getting a free pass? She instantly felt lighter. "Are you sure the cotillion captain doesn't mind?"

"Mira, I'm the cotillion captain," Dylan said. "I would have told you that if you'd been there today, and I also would have given you your final assignment."

"Final assignment? But I thought..."

"We like to give everyone a personal task at the end," she said cryptically. "Or more like a reward. Yours is going to be speaking at cotillion."

Her heart was at full throttle now. "I thought that was usually done by the deb at the top of her class. I didn't even do today's initiation."

"When you stuck up for Savannah like that during the scavenger hunt, it showed real guts. It was impressive, especially when that girl has, from what I've heard, treated you like larva. That's why we picked you to give this year's speech."

"Thanks," Mira said in awe. But cotillion was just a few days away! What would she say? How long did her speech have to be? Could she use cue cards? She didn't want to bother Dylan with the questions.

"You're welcome." Dylan hesitated. "There is one more thing. You have to promise me you'll get Izzie to cotillion so she can finish her assignment, too. Promise?"

She wasn't sure Izzie ever wanted to see Dylan again, but if it meant they could all make their debuts, she'd get her there. "I promise. Thanks, Dylan." She hung up and joined the others on the porch again. Connor had finally left his LEGO table and made it outside, too.

Izzie stared at Mira. "So? Who was...that?"

Mira couldn't look at her. "Dad, I think you're right about cotillion. We should go. All of us."

"But..." Izzie started to say, her expression strained.

Mira smiled. There was so much to do in so little time, but she would get it done. She always did. "No buts," she told Izzie as much as she was telling herself. She took her hand. "We're going, and it's going to be spectacular."

Twenty-Two

"Ladies!" Ms. Norberry clapped her hands loudly. "Your formal presentation to Emerald Cove society begins in fifteen minutes!"

Izzie wasn't sure anyone heard her.

The group of girls making their debut had taken over one of the suites in Emerald Cove Castle on the Cliff, where the debutante ball was being held, and the room was sheer madness. Garment bags from pricey bridal boutiques were scattered all over the floor next to ripped stockings and shoe boxes. Makeup for touch-ups covered the bathroom counters, where private makeup artists hogged the mirror space. The rooms smelled overwhelmingly of hair spray, and everywhere Izzie turned, girls were screaming things like "Does anyone have an extra bobby pin?" and "Does this blush make my face look ruddy?"

Izzie surveyed the scene with amusement. She had never seen Lauren cry before, but she was practically bawling over a jammed zipper on her couture gown from Paris. That outrageously pricey dress had to be jerry-rigged with safety pins, which would have to be covered with a shawl.

An ethereal Savannah, an annoying vision in the only lilac dress in the room, passed by Izzie with a team of helpers on her trail—make that chiffon train, which everyone was tripping over. Izzie noticed the glance Savannah threw her way. "I think we need to see how my hair and makeup looks in real lighting just to be sure it doesn't clash with the hydrangea in my hair," Savannah was saying. "When Brayden sees me at the bottom of those stairs, I want him to remember why he's lucky to be my escort."

Izzie wasn't surprised to hear Savannah gloat. When Izzie turned Brayden down, she was sure Mrs. Townsend would find a way to put herself back in the Ingrams' good graces. And since Brayden always did what his mother wanted, she was sure he agreed to escort Savannah. She tried not to picture the two of them entering the ballroom together. Even though she knew she had done the right thing by cutting Brayden off, it still stung.

A bronzing brush came insanely close to Izzie's face, and she jumped back. "Dude, I told you, I don't want that stuff."

Her aunt's personal makeup artist, whom she used for

all their important events, turned to Aunt Maureen and held up his makeup brushes in surrender. "She won't let me touch her," he complained. "If you don't want her looking like a pasty doughnut, maybe you can talk some sense into her."

Aunt Maureen approached Izzie with a worried glance. "Isabelle? Sweetheart? Won't you let Jacques put a little bronzer on your cheeks?"

"Seriously, Aunt Maureen, some of these girls look orange." Izzie glanced at Lea, who was a shade away from being mistaken for Ernie on *Sesame Street*. "I feel strange enough in this white dress as it is."

Aunt Maureen studied Izzie's face. Izzie had agreed to wear a flower in her hair for the ceremony. It was a compromise she made for not letting the hair salon pull her short hair back into some tacky updo. Instead, Izzie's wavy hair was styled into pretty curls that were kept out of her eyes with the gardenia. She didn't want to admit it to anyone—especially not the weary hairstylist she had fought with for an hour—but the flower looked pretty. Not that she'd ever be caught wearing one again. If Kylie saw her dressed up and superaccessorized like this, a picture would be up on Facebook in two minutes. This was a one-night-only glamified Izzie. At least that's what she told herself.

"How about a darker shade of lipstick, then?" Aunt Maureen suggested. "Or more eye shadow to make the hazel in your eyes pop? Like Jacques did with Mira."

"Izzie, are you really still fighting the eye shadow?"

That night, a swishing sound followed Mira everywhere she went. Izzie could hear her coming without turning around. Her normally curly hair had been tamed into a tiny knot at the back of her head, and she was wearing the tiara Aunt Maureen had worn at her own debutante ball way back when. Mira viewed Izzie with a skeptical eye.

"Your hair looks beautiful," Mira said with one white-gloved hand on her hip, "but if you don't let Jacques put just a little eye makeup on you, you are going to look completely washed out in pictures."

"That's fine by me," Izzie said, adjusting her long, itchy white gloves.

Mira made a face. "You have on this gorgeous dress, but your pictures are going to turn out so white and pasty."

Izzie's dress really was spectacular, if she did say so herself. If she had to wear a bridal gown—and she did not plan on wearing one again for a very long time, if ever—then this was definitely the one to have. Simple. No accessories, except for the flower holding the gown together at one shoulder. Aunt Maureen called it classic. It might have been the first time anyone had ever said that about something she had worn. She stared at her reflection in the mirrors that had been brought in to cover every available inch of space (at Ms. Norberry's request—"We don't want any of our debs getting a surprise as they are presented, do we?"). She frowned. Her summer tan was officially gone, and maybe the white dress did make her look a *tad* washed out.

"Ten minutes, ladies!" someone announced, and the calls of "Who has another safety pin?" and "Does anyone have an extra pair of stockings?" rose to a fever pitch. Izzie was glad she had brought her iPod.

"Okay, fine," she said, and a giddy Aunt Maureen waved Jacques back over. He appeared skeptical, not that Izzie could blame him. "If we're going to do this thing, then let's do it," Izzie told him. She popped in her earbuds, turned on her iPod to drown out the desperation around her, and closed her eyes. "I'm all yours, Yoda."

~

Before she knew it, Ms. Norberry was giving the girls their final instructions. They had been herded into another room that was close to the long, scrolling staircase where they would be making their grand entrance. All the mothers had disappeared to take their places at the five-hundred-dollar-a-seat tables they purchased, and now it was just a sea of big white dresses.

"It has been an honor watching most of you grow and evolve over the last few years," Ms. Norberry told them with misty eyes. She herself was wearing a floor-length deep purple gown that accented the hydrangeas that covered the staircase and floral arrangements throughout the grand ballroom. "In a few moments, we will be moving into the hall, where your fathers are waiting. Mrs. Townsend will begin making her opening remarks from the top of the staircase, and then she will begin calling your names." Someone sneezed. The room smelled like so many different perfumes, she was starting to get nauseated herself. "You will proceed down the stairs in time to 'Thank Heaven for Little Girls,' which will be playing over the speakers...."

"'Thank Heaven for Little Girls'?" Izzie gave Mira a look. "Is she serious?"

"It's tradition," Mira sniffed. "Stop with your snide comments. You're going to ruin this for me."

"You're really okay with doing this without an escort?" Kellen hadn't forgiven Mira for doubting him, and Mira had spent all day yesterday upset about it, staying in her room and listening to sad Taylor Swift songs. This morning she had emerged with a new attitude.

"I'm not going to let a silly boy ruin my cotillion." Mira sounded much more confident than she looked. At least she was trying. "Ms. Norberry has an escort understudy I can use."

"An escort understudy?" Izzie deadpanned. "Is that where escorts who aren't good enough go to die?"

"There is that sarcasm again," Mira warned her. "It's

unbecoming of someone about to be presented to Emerald Cove society."

"Society? Please." Izzie wasn't a fool. "We're walking out in front of the same people we see at every event. Tonight they just paid five hundred dollars each to see us." She felt a tap on her shoulder and froze, thinking it was Mrs. Townsend.

But it wasn't. It was Dylan. She looked incredible in a knee-length black gown that was both sophisticated yet trendy at the same time. She tried to break the ice with a small smile. "Hey." She held out a blue envelope. "I have your final assignment."

"It's a little late for that, don't you think? We're seconds from starting." Izzie's voice was hard, and she wished Mira would tell Dylan to scram. She looked over. Mira was gone. If Mira had abandoned her to put on another coat of lip gloss, she was going to kill her.

"…and then after you walk with your father, you will be greeted by your escort at the bottom of the staircase," Ms. Norberry continued. "He will lead you onto the dance floor for your first dance." The girls were buzzing with nervous chatter, and Ms. Norberry was straining her voice to be heard.

Dylan tried to give her the envelope again. "You have time to get this done. You don't have to open it in front of me. I know I'm the last person you want to talk to."

Izzie would rather stare at the back of Savannah's egg-shaped head than look at Dylan. "I guess you finally got one thing right."

"Look, I know I got carried away. My mother makes me crazy," Dylan said. "But I shouldn't have dragged you into our family dystopia. Despite what you might think, I really do like you, Izzie. We're a lot alike."

"No, we're not," Izzie said sharply. "I would never use someone the way you used me or your brother."

"I know," Dylan said. "You're a better person than I am, and that's why you're so good for Brayden." She glanced at Izzie's dress. "I guess I was jealous of your relationship with him. He stood up for you in a way he never did with me. You see, I once had an 'Izzie,' too, so to speak." She smiled. "Andy. I called him Andrew in front of my mom, but she knew the minute she met him that he wasn't from around here, and she never let me forget it. She did everything she could to keep us apart, and no one tried to stop her. Brayden didn't have it in himself to fight for me yet. He could barely fight for himself." Dylan wrung her hands at the memory. "When Andy and I got in that accident together, there was no turning back. My mom blamed it all on him, even though I was driving, and she shipped me off to boarding school without even giving me a chance to explain." Her eyes seemed sad. "I haven't talked to Andy since."

Izzie wasn't sure what to say. What Dylan had done to her and Brayden was still wrong, but she felt bad for her suddenly.

Dylan shook her head as if to push the memory away. "I've moved on, but when I saw you that day at Scoops with my brother, it felt like I was watching the whole thing play out all over again. I couldn't let it. I knew I had to get him to fight for himself, or get you to fight for you." She shrugged. "I guess I failed at both. All I did was make everyone around me miserable."

Izzie folded her arms. "That's for sure."

Dylan grimaced. "The difference between you and me is that you keep Brayden real and he needs someone like that to keep him from turning into those soulless droids in my house. Don't give up on him, okay?"

It was too late for that, but she didn't tell Dylan. "I'll try."

"Read my note. I know you're going to have a great time tonight if you let yourself," Dylan told her. "Me, I'll be ducking out of here pretty soon. Doing it once was enough." She raised her eyebrows. "But you'll like it more than you want to. Trust me. Especially the food." Dylan stepped back into the crowd, nudging her way through the future debutantes. "The lamb chops are outrageous. Don't tell my mom I said that," she added. "They're her favorite, and I do not want her to think I like anything she likes."

Izzie shook her head. When Dylan was gone, she turned the envelope over in her hand.

Ms. Norberry tried to get their attention again. "Ladies, if you could put on your white muffs, being careful not to crush the delicate hydrangeas on the top, we will proceed down the hall to the left, where your fathers are waiting."

Excited gasps were heard around the room. Izzie couldn't stop thinking about Brayden. He had wanted to go to cotillion with her, but she had said no. Was she wrong to blame everything that happened on him? She thought about that as she walked over to where former debs were handing out their muffs. Izzie stuffed hers under her arm (to the gasp of one girl) and opened up her note from Dylan. How was she supposed to have time to complete an assignment when she was about to be presented?

Izzie, if you're reading this, then you must care just a little about this whole cotillion business, and that shows you're better equipped to survive EC than I ever was. Your final assignment is simple: Make your debut into this crazy, self-absorbed world. No matter what happens on that staircase tonight, keep going. Avoid making the scenes I'm so famous for. And smile. You have such a pretty one, and I hope I'll get to see it from where I'm watching. If I

don't, maybe I will the next time I swing
through town. I owe you dinner-make that ten
dinners-for all the trouble I caused. Enjoy
tonight! XO, Dylan

What could Dylan be up to now? And what did she mean
by telling her to keep going when she reached the bottom of
the stairs? Why wouldn't she keep going? At that point, the
only thing that would stop her is if the entire ballroom
turned into zombies. Hmm...some of the people in Emerald Cove kind of already were.

"There's a welcome smile," she heard her dad say when
she found him lined up with the other fathers. "You look
beautiful, Isabelle."

"Thanks," she said, and stuffed the note inside her muff.

He held out a small box. "I brought you a corsage."

She opened the box. The wristlet was made up of hydrangeas and baby's breath. It looked similar to the one he
had given her at her first event in Emerald Cove. That felt
so long ago. "It's beautiful," Izzie said. She slid it over her
white-gloved hand and admired the blooms. "Have you seen
Mira?"

He shook his head. "Ms. Norberry told me that you will
make your debut third, and Mira will make hers last, since
she is the cotillion speaker. That will give me time to get back
upstairs." He had another floral box under his arm. "I have a

corsage for her, too, if she'll wear it. Pea hasn't worn one since the sixth grade, but maybe she'll make an exception tonight."

"I have a feeling she will," Izzie said.

"We're starting!" Ms. Norberry ran down the line, yelling in a whisper. "We're starting! Mrs. Townsend is starting!"

"Good evening," Mrs. Townsend's velvety voice crackled from a speaker above them. "I'd like to welcome you to the Winter White Cotillion Ball, presented by the Emerald Cove Junior League. Tonight's cotillion will benefit the Emerald Cove Charity League." There was polite applause from the bottom of the staircase. That's when Izzie got nervous.

Her mind was full of questions. Was she really allowing herself to be presented to society like a made-up Barbie doll? In front of so many people who couldn't stand her? Was she going to stand by and watch Savannah do the fox-trot with Brayden? Hadn't she been hurt enough?

Izzie glanced at her father. He had taken her elbow and was leading her to the stairs. Savannah was a few girls behind her, but neither Izzie nor her dad turned around. Izzie suspected it would be a while before Mr. Ingram had the nerve to speak to her dad again.

She thought about everything the Monroes had done for her since she came to Emerald Cove. They had given her so much to be thankful for. They weren't perfect, but neither was she. She owed them this, escort or no escort. No guts, no glory, as her mom would say.

"I am pleased to present to you this year's cotillion class, the debutante daughters of Emerald Cove." More applause.

What if she tripped?

"Lauren Salbrook, daughter of Beatrice and Parker Salbrook the fourth, escorted by Teagan Adams the third..."

What if she couldn't curtsy in this slim-fitting gown?

"Lea Price, daughter of Vera and Elton Jonathan Price the second, escorted by Teddy Darcy..."

What if this stupid flower fell out of her hair during her first dance with Hayden? What if Hayden wasn't waiting at the bottom of the stairs?

"Ready?" Her dad's hazel eyes were warm.

Izzie took a deep breath. "As ready as I'll ever be." She just hoped this stupid green eye shadow didn't melt off.

"Isabelle Scott, daughter of Chloe Scott and Bill Monroe..."

For a moment, her feet felt like Jell-O. They had said her mom's name, here in Emerald Cove. *Of course they would*, she thought, feeling stupid. And yet hearing Mrs. Townsend mention her mom among all these strangers, haters, and a few new friends somehow comforted her. As they descended the steps, her thoughts were no longer on the beautiful scene below. They were on her mom. It was as if her mom was watching over her right then, letting her know it was okay to do something she wouldn't have done in a million years. Izzie was so wrapped up in her emotions, she almost missed the rest of Mrs. Townsend's introduction.

"…escorted by." There was the slightest of pauses, but Izzie heard it. What was wrong? Was Mrs. Townsend about to nix her whole debut over some glitch in her debutante training? She had done everything they asked of her! She'd fox-trotted, curtsied, given all her free time to a nursing home, practiced conversational techniques, and learned how to work a toilet in Japan. What more could this woman want?

"…escorted by Brayden Townsend," Mrs. Townsend said in a strange voice.

Brayden?

Izzie stopped short in disbelief, but there he was, waiting at the bottom of the stairs. He was wearing a black tuxedo, and his blue-green eyes were locked on her.

"Isabelle, are you okay?" her dad whispered.

Whether Brayden's mother was freaking out internally or Savannah was having a coronary at the top of the staircase externally, she didn't know. What she did know was that Brayden was finally there for her the way she wanted him to be. He had chosen her.

The question was, did she choose him back?

Dylan's note went through her head. *No matter what happens on that staircase tonight, keep going. Avoid making the scenes I'm so famous for. And smile.*

Dylan knew Brayden would be there for her tonight. She

also was smart enough to make sure Izzie didn't get stubborn and muck it up. There were things to say, but when all of Emerald Cove was watching was not that moment.

"I'm fine," Izzie said surely to her dad. "Let's keep going."

When they reached the bottom step, Brayden slowly extended his hand. Her fingers were trembling, but she took his arm. She looked back at her father once and then let Brayden lead her into the ballroom.

The Emerald Cove Castle on the Cliff ballroom took her breath away. The twinkling lights and Christmas trees shone brightly in the low-lit room that was filled with dozens of large tables where guests wore wedding attire and tuxes. The girls had been instructed to walk into the ballroom and then stand on the side of the dance floor and wait for the rest of them to make their entrance.

"You look beautiful," Brayden whispered.

"You think compliments are going to get you anywhere?" Izzie said with a big smile. Aunt Maureen was already snapping pictures, and Hayden, that sly dog, was standing next to her, taking video. How many people were in on this?

"You got Dylan's note, obviously," he said.

"Obviously," Izzie said, and they took their place in line with the other couples. Ms. Norberry told them to line up and watch each couple enter, and then when everyone was there, they'd have their first dance.

"Before you bite my head off, let me say something,"

Brayden said. "I know the past few weeks have been a disaster between the Ingrams, my mom, Dylan...."

"Disaster doesn't even begin to describe it," Izzie whispered. "You never called me to apologize that night your parents came home early. You just let me stand there while you went off to have dinner with Savannah's family, and then the next time I see you, you're having dinner with them again, and you still don't apologize!"

"I know I let things go too far," he agreed. "I should have apologized, but I was mad. You really made me think about my family," he said, sounding flustered. "I know my family is messed up. Why do you think I try to escape to the beach so much?" he asked. "Anyway, Dylan and I had a long talk the other night after you left. It was way overdue. I think deep down my mom thinks she's doing what's best for us." He straightened the bow tie on his tux. "Dylan isn't so sure of that, but she knows she has to back off a bit. She made a mess of things, but I didn't help, either. I've always done what my mom wanted, but not anymore. What my mom thinks is best for her isn't necessarily best for me."

Izzie hadn't thought about it that way before.

"Dylan's answer is to rebel. Mine is to go surf. Whose plan has worked out better so far?" Brayden's eyes searched hers. "Just because I don't come back at them all the time doesn't mean I won't fight them for what I really want. It doesn't mean I won't fight for you, Iz, if you let me."

For some reason, hearing him say that made the hair on her arms stand up. "But how do I know you will fight for me this time?" she asked, trying to keep the fear out of her voice. "The last few times we've been together, you did nothing—"

"Last time I saw you, I didn't even know you were coming," he reminded her. "But I already knew what I was going to say that night at dinner with the Ingrams. I had planned on telling everyone there that the only person I was going to cotillion with was you." He smiled at her. "Our families are friends, so we're still going to cross paths, but I told my mom I'm not going for dinner at the Ingrams anymore. I'd rather have dinner with you and the Monroes, if you'll have me."

"Dinner, huh?" Izzie said, because she had to say something to keep up the attitude. Inside, though, all she could think was, *he chose me.* In front of his mother, his family, Savannah, and the rest of Emerald Cove, he had picked her. She wasn't ready to let him off the hook just yet, though. "I'm not sure I'm ready to commit to dinner," she said, and he looked a little disappointed. "Why don't we start with lunch, and then we'll go from there?"

He thought about it for a second and grinned. "I like lunch."

"Me, too." Why was she being so jokey? This wasn't funny. He had to know how much her heart had hurt the last few weeks. "Just don't screw up again, because you are running out of chances," she said fiercely. "Fight for me like you said you would."

Brayden looked at her intently. "I will." And this time, she believed him.

From the corner of her eye, Izzie saw Savannah make her entrance. Her face was beet-red, and she wouldn't hold her escort understudy's arm. She glared at Brayden and Izzie as she passed, but Izzie didn't care. She had finished Dylan's assignment, become an official debutante, and won the boy. (She just wasn't entirely sure she was ready to let him know that yet.) She belonged there as much as Savannah did, and Izzie promised herself she wouldn't forget it.

Twenty-Three

When Mira saw Dylan walking over to Izzie, she bolted from the dressing area. Unfortunately, she didn't know where to hide.

"Mira?" Charlotte walked over. "Wow, nice dress."

"Thanks." Mira swished the skirt proudly. "It's Amsale."

"Cool," Charlotte said appraisingly. "Mine's a Charlotte Richards." Mira blinked, confused. "That's my name. I made it myself."

"You made that?" Charlotte's dress was incredible. It looked like a modern, upscale trench coat. Her white dress had V-neck lapels, a belted waist, and a slit up the middle of the gorgeous brushed satin hoop skirt. Crinoline peeked out from underneath.

"My parents were all for buying me one, but I figured if I

could make something as difficult as a bridal gown, a career in fashion isn't as much of a pipe dream as I think."

"I would say it's definitely not a pipe dream." Mira admired Charlotte's handy work. "It looks like something Stella McCartney would make."

"That's exactly the look I was going for," said Charlotte, her eyes lighting up. "I had to change it up a little. I didn't want to copy the master. Are you a Stella fan, too?"

"Who isn't?" Mira said. "Although I can't say I own too many pieces. My mom may like clothes, but even she draws the line at six-hundred-dollar shirts that are only in style for one season."

"Mine, too," Charlotte said with a sigh. "Although I once found a shirt marked down for next to nothing at Barneys in New York City."

"I was just there for Thankgiving," Mira said. "I loved that store! I would have slept in one of the dressing rooms if they let me."

"Me, too." Charlotte pushed her reddish hair out of her eyes. "I love New York."

Mira wondered why she and Charlotte had never really talked before. They were in the same grade at EP. They took some of the same classes. How could a potential friend have been right in front of her the whole time and Mira not realize it?

"Listen, I'd love to talk fashion all night, but the real reason I'm out here is to send you on a mission," Charlotte said discreetly, and her red hair fell in tiny ringlets around her heart-shaped face. "I was told to tell you that someone is waiting for you in suite fourteen."

Emerald Cove Castle on the Cliff was so exclusive that the place had only twenty-eight hotel rooms. They had been reserved for cotillion years in advance.

"Who?" Mira asked.

"I can't say." Charlotte's lips pursed slightly. "But it's a good surprise—I swear."

"I'm going to hold you to that," Mira told her before heading off. "Hey, do you want to hang out sometime?" Mira's voice was so tentative, it surprised her. For some reason, she really hoped Charlotte would say yes.

"Sure," Charlotte said. "I'd give you my number right now, but as you can see, this dress barely has enough room for my bra."

Mira laughed. "I'll look you up in the EP directory." Mira would be the last one to make her cotillion entrance because she was giving the debutante speech, but she still didn't have a lot of time to just hang around. She was one door away from suite fourteen when she saw Savannah.

Mira's heart sank. "What are you doing here?"

Savannah held up a small pencil. "My parents are staying here tonight, and I left my lip liner in their suite. I can't be without my MAC on a night like this." Mira had a feeling no one would be looking at her lips. Her dress was the real showstopper. The top half was covered in an almost lilac chiffon and the bottom fitted with a small train. Mira thought that part should be bustled, but fashion was never Savannah's strong suit. She'd always relied on Mira for that.

Tonight, Mira had no problem saying what was really on her mind. "I can't believe you have the nerve to talk to me after what your dad did."

"I was hoping I'd run into you," she said, sounding remorseful. "I had no idea what he was up to. I swear." She gracefully lifted the bottom of her dress so it wouldn't drag and walked over to Mira. "What my dad did is so humiliating. Can you imagine if our friends found out?"

Mira bit her lip. *Humiliating.* Of course that's what Savannah was worried about. Not how wrong her father was for faking stories about Mira's family. "They're not my friends anymore, remember?"

"Right." Savannah touched her smooth updo. "Still, I wanted you to know the truth. I've been mad at you, sure, but I wouldn't try to destroy your whole life. Even if you have been cocky lately." Savannah's brown eyes got even darker when she was angry, which she appeared to be at the moment. "Just because your dad is running for the U.S. Senate, you seem to think that makes you better than me."

Mira couldn't believe what she was hearing.

"Parading around with your sister, getting in *Teen Vogue*

magazine, shining at all the cotillion initiations while I got the grunt work, and then getting picked to be lead debutante tonight? That was the icing on the cake."

Savannah ticked off the indiscretions in an almost patronizing voice, and that's when Mira realized she hadn't imagined it—Savannah was jealous of *her*.

"But I'm not a petty person," Savannah added, and Mira bit her tongue. "I don't forget when people have my back." Her eyes softened. "You were decent to me that day at the scavenger hunt. I don't know what I would have done if you hadn't helped me out with the tiara."

Mira wanted to keel over. "You're welcome."

"I knew I couldn't let you miss tonight." Savannah stood unsurely, shifting from one stiletto-clad foot to the other. "That's why I went to Dylan and explained why you weren't at the final initiation."

"*You're* the one who talked to Dylan?" Mira couldn't believe it.

Savannah played with the pearl bracelet she wore over one of her white gloves. "When you didn't show up at the final initiation because of what happened with our dads, I had to tell her what was going on. I know how much you wanted to be here tonight." Savannah looked at the marble floor. "I remember how you used to talk about wearing a bride's dress all the time when you were little. It didn't seem fair that you would miss cotillion because of something my dad did."

She couldn't believe Savannah remembered the bride's dress story. "Thank you." She looked around the stone hallway that had been built so long ago. "I really did want to be here."

"I know," Savannah said, and started to walk away. "Have fun tonight." She held up the lip liner. "I have to finish getting ready. I'll be walking down those stairs to meet Brayden in just fifteen minutes."

Mira still couldn't believe Savannah, not Izzie, would be making her entrance with Brayden. She pushed that thought out of her mind and looked for suite fourteen. She wasn't sure who to expect on the other side of that door. Maybe that's why she sucked in her breath and closed her eyes when she found the suite and opened the door.

Kellen was the last person she'd expected to find waiting for her, but there he was in a tuxedo, holding a red rose. The whole thing felt like a scene out of one of those romantic comedies Hayden thought were so cheesy but she adored. If Taylor Swift music started playing right then, she would have to pinch herself.

"It's you," Mira said. She was surprised, but not as surprised as she thought she should be. She had told Izzie she didn't need an escort, but in the back of her mind, she still hoped Kellen might be waiting at the bottom of the stairs for her.

"It's me, but the rented tux is due back at four PM tomorrow."

Mira swished toward him. She pointed to the rose. "Is that for me?"

"No, it's for the maid," Kellen said drily. "To thank her for making the room smell so pretty."

"Oh, so we're back to joking now?" Mira asked, her heart beating wildly.

He let the tip of the rose touch Mira's nose. "I think so. Your groveling messages and the desperate painted plea were hard to ignore."

"It was the painting that got to you, wasn't it?" Mira asked.

When Kellen wouldn't return any of her phone calls, and even a last-ditch bus ride to Peterson didn't get Kellen to talk to her, she had walked to Sup to get a latte before taking the bus back to Emerald Cove. She had been so pleased with herself for taking the bus without asking anyone for help (well, except that nice girl at the bus stop who explained what route she was looking for). But Kellen still wouldn't speak to her, and she was out of playing cards until she saw Sup's new contest.

SAY IT, DON'T SPRAY IT!
FORGET GRAFFITI. TELL THE PERSON YOU ADORE WHAT'S ON YOUR MIND THROUGH A PAINTING. FIRST PRIZE GETS A PRIME SPOT ABOVE THE CONDIMENT STATION AND A SLOT IN NEXT MONTH'S GALLERY EXHIBIT.

Mira didn't have to think hard about what she was going to draw. She headed home that night, spent all evening painting, and took the bus back to Sup the next day. Even though the contest wasn't officially over for a week, she persuaded the barista to hang her work up by the cash register so Kellen would see it. The barista had just been through a nasty breakup herself, and she felt Mira's pain. Apparently, so did a lot of other people. It had only been there for a few hours when the barista called Mira to say how many people were talking about her painting. The picture was of a sad girl who had cut out her own heart with scissors and was offering it in her outstretched hand. It was a little graphic, even for her, but she kept the blood to a minimum and focused on her small, neat dedication at the bottom.

For Kellen, because I was an idiot. Mira.

"The idiot part was my favorite," Kellen said, his mouth twitching. "I look forward to taking your picture in front of that painting at Sup."

"I'll do it proudly," she said, and bit her lip. "Anything to make up for accusing you like I did." She couldn't believe she'd thought Kellen would sell her out for a few bucks. "I feel like a real jerk for thinking that."

"Your family had a lot going on. You weren't thinking

straight," Kellen said. "I forgive you. I just hope you know that I would never do anything that would hurt you, Mira."

"I know that now." Mira grabbed his hand. "I should have known that then. I'm so sorry."

"It's hard to stay mad at you, you know that?" Kellen played with her hair. "Besides, I didn't want you to have to brave cotillion alone tonight." He rolled his eyes. "I know, I know, you're like, 'Kellen, ugh! Why would you want to go to cotillion? It's so pompous and inflated,' but I have to go." He held out the rose again. He was so close that Mira thought the flower might prick her chin. "You see, the girl I'm into has always wanted to go to cotillion, and I'm a sucker for making her happy." He leaned down and kissed her softly on the lips before she could respond. And that's just the way she wanted it anyway.

~

"Presenting Mirabelle Beatrice Monroe, daughter of Maureen and Bill Monroe, escorted by Kellen Harper."

Mrs. Townsend's announcement was Mira's cue to take her father's arm and descend the staircase covered in hydrangeas and twinkle lights. *Town & Country* did not do it justice. Time seemed to slow down, and she tried to remember every moment she had waited so long for by taking mental pictures in her mind. Her dad sliding the corsage over her white glove (and Mira letting him because even though corsages were juvenile, it was really pretty). Her name being called by Mrs. Townsend. Walking down that gorgeous staircase with everyone's eyes on her incredible dress. And seeing Kellen waiting for her at the bottom of the staircase.

She took careful steps so she wouldn't trip as she smiled for the cameras and made her entrance into a society she had wanted to join since she'd seen her mom's debutante pictures as a kid. When she reached the bottom of the stairs, Kellen bowed and she curtsied. The whole exchange felt very royal.

She was the final debutante of the evening and, she suspected, possibly the happiest, although when she spotted Izzie standing next to Brayden, she couldn't tell which girl's smile was bigger. She didn't have time to decide. She let Kellen lead her to the center of the dance floor, where they led the other debutantes in a waltz. As Frank Sinatra's "The Way You Look Tonight" played softly in the background, she breathed in the scent of the fresh blossoms and Christmas trees and gazed happily around her. She could see her parents and Hayden watching as Kellen twirled her around. Charlotte gave her a little wave as she danced nearby. Izzie was dancing, too, but she only had eyes for Brayden. Savannah had eyes for Brayden, too. Or more like daggers. But those could have been reserved for Izzie. Before Mira knew it, the first song was over, which meant it was time to give her speech.

Frank started to fade away as Mrs. Townsend took to the hydrangea-covered podium in the center of the room. That's when Mira started to feel ill.

"You nervous?" Kellen asked. Mira had told him all about Dylan naming her lead deb and asking her to give the welcome speech.

"Just a tad." Mira eyed the crowd. Every important and influential person in Emerald Cove was there to watch her choke. She could put together a killer ensemble in five minutes and put on her eye makeup blindfolded, but she had not inherited her dad's natural gift of gab. Mrs. Townsend said to keep it short and sweet. She could do that. Right? Was she really going up there? Would Dylan notice if she didn't? Mira hadn't seen her since she made her debut, but did she really want to take that chance?

Kellen twirled her one last time. "Do like I do in speech class—picture everyone in their underwear."

Mira laughed. "There is no way that works. It's just an expression."

Kellen grinned. "Maybe. But it's fun to try."

"Ladies and gentlemen, I'd like to present this year's cotillion class speaker, Mirabelle Monroe."

Kellen led Mira to the podium. "Good luck," he whispered in her ear.

Mira needed it. She gripped the sides of the podium to keep from clenching her hands into tiny balls and stared at the audience. She prayed that her voice wouldn't quiver.

"Good evening, and welcome to the annual Emerald Cove Junior League cotillion." There was a round of applause, and she paused before she continued, which gave her a good chance to catch her breath. "I'm pleased to be your lead debutante, and I know all of this evening's cotillion participants join me in thanking you for your generous donation to the Emerald Cove Charity League." More applause. That was the easy part. "I've wanted to take part in our town's cotillion tradition ever since I was a little girl. Back then, it was all about the dress." She smiled at the memory. "I could not wait to make my communion just so I'd have a white dress! I actually made my mom buy me a communion dress a year early so I could get in some early cotillion practice." The crowd laughed.

"When I got older, my mom signed me up for the junior cotillion league, and I learned there was more to this tradition than just white gloves and a dress. Cotillion is etiquette lessons and dance classes with boys, but more important, it's about giving back to your community and the ones beyond our gates." She knew Izzie might find this next part cheesy, but it was true. "The service I did through the Junior League taught me to care about more than just a new pair of shoes or getting the must-have phone. Giving back taught me what a true sense of self was, and a true sense of self doesn't require money. All you need is your mind, your heart, and your family."

It was hard to spot Mira's own family through the spotlight, but she knew they were listening, and what she said next was the most important part of her whole speech. "I wouldn't be who I am without my parents, my brothers... or my sister," she said. "I'm so lucky to have them, and I hope they know how important they are to me."

Her speech was met with applause. She shook Mrs. Townsend's hand and accepted congratulations from several people standing around her, but the only people whose opinions really mattered to her were her family's. Thankfully she didn't have to wait long to know what they thought. They had gathered around the podium and were waiting to envelop her in a big hug.

Twenty-Four

Izzie's dad leaned precariously close to the gutters and hollered down to her from the roof. "Isabelle, give me some more slack on those Christmas lights!"

His dangling was starting to make her nervous, but she did as she was told and unwound her fourth set of lights. She couldn't believe how many lights they were putting up. She and Grams had stopped hanging holiday lights when it became just the two of them, and Izzie hadn't realized how much she'd missed the tradition till she saw them on the Monroes' house.

My house, she corrected herself. She lived here now, too.

"Just seeing him up there makes me nervous," Aunt Maureen said. She looked ill as she stared at the roofline in a bulky hooded parka. "Every year I tell him we should hire a company to hang our lights, like the Townsends or the Prices do, but nooooo, he won't listen. That man is stubborn."

Paying someone to hang lights sounded wasteful till Hayden's foot fell into the gutter two seconds later, and he struggled to pull his boot out. Suddenly, watching her dad and Hayden on the roof was making Izzie nervous, too.

Aunt Maureen took a sip of the homemade hot cocoa she had made for the occasion and shook her head. "Bill hung Christmas lights with his dad when he was little, and now he wants to do the same with all of you. That means I have a heart attack every year watching him do this."

"The lawn stuff is done," Connor reported, jumping up and down because he was so proud. "I finished setting up the snow people and the reindeer. I did a good job, right?"

The decorations on the lawn were placed so close together they looked like a group of carolers. Izzie suspected they were supposed to be spaced out across the lawn, but neither of them had the heart to tell Connor that. The poor kid had been begging for holiday decorations for weeks—normally Aunt Maureen put them up the day after Thanksgiving—but between the changes in the campaign team *again*, the press scandals, the family fighting, and finally their reconciliation before cotillion, everyone had been preoccupied. Now it was a few days before Christmas, and they were scrambling to get every holiday decoration in its rightful place in time for the fat guy's landing. Thankfully, the outside of the house was almost done.

"Great job, sweetheart," Aunt Maureen told Connor, and winked at Izzie. "Why don't you head inside and start working on the Christmas tree next?"

"I thought you said I couldn't put the decorations on the tree without you because you like to tell me where they go," Connor reminded her. "My Star Wars and Transformers decorations go on the bottom, right?"

Izzie side-eyed her aunt. "Yes, I'm that type A with everything I do," her aunt admitted, and Izzie laughed. "Where do you think Mira gets it?"

～

Mira was in the kitchen showing Kellen how to make her favorite Christmas cookie in the world, the Hershey's Kisses cookie, which was basically peanut butter cookie dough rolled into a ball with a Hershey's Kiss smushed into the top. The house was beginning to smell the way it should in December, full of baked goods and melted chocolate mixed in with fresh pine from the live tree. Wreaths and evergreens covered every chandelier and banister. Everything felt like it was finally coming together, just like the ingredients in her recipe.

Mira lifted the handle on the KitchenAid mixer and slowly dropped in large plops of peanut butter and butter. "So now we'll mix this till it's smooth," she told Kellen, "and then add in the sugar and beat it till it's fluffy."

"We're going to beat the sugar? That's cruel." Kellen stuck his finger in the bowl and took a lick.

"You're not supposed to stick your fingers in the bowl," Mira scolded. "Now the batter has your germs!" Whenever Connor did this, she started the recipe over. She was a notorious germophobe in the kitchen, but being with Kellen relaxed her somewhat. They had been inseparable in the last week since cotillion. If they weren't at the art studio together, they were at Corky's or Sup. The kissing was amazing, and so was the conversation. She had no idea Kellen knew so much about, well, everything. The only area he seemed to be lacking in knowledge was baking. Today was their first lesson. Mira was making a double batch of cookies so Kellen could take half home for Christmas Eve.

"Baking is no fun if you don't taste along the way," Kellen told her. "Besides, isn't that what they say to do on all the cooking shows?"

Yes, but using a spoon, she thought. She stared down at the mixing bowl as it continued to slowly whirl around, lifting and folding the dough. She needed to learn to relax. Maybe now that she'd stepped down from running the Butterflies, she finally would. "Okay, I guess one lick won't kill us," she told Kellen, rubbing her eyes with the back of her hand. "Next step. I already put some flour on the counter, so we can roll the balls and they won't stick." She gestured to the pile of white powder scattered about in front of them.

"Sometimes I add some granulated sugar to the dough, so I put some of that on the counter, too."

"For someone who is a neat freak in the art studio, you are a disaster in the kitchen." Kellen looked at the huge mess Mira had created. Flour, sugar, Hershey's Kisses, and kitchen tools were everywhere. Some of the flour had even fallen onto the floor.

"I don't like to look for anything once I've started," Mira said. Mira's mom would kill her if she saw this, but thankfully her mom never left the front yard when her dad was hanging Christmas lights. Her mom always worried that he would fall off the roof. "I like to be prepared when I bake," Mira went on, trying not to grin. "I'm not the type of person who runs around the room saying, does anyone have a fine-point brush?" She imitated Kellen's voice. "I can't find mine!"

"Hey, I always have my supplies with me. I just don't always remember where they are." Kellen picked up some of the loose flour and tossed it in her direction.

Mira gasped. "You're making a mess!"

"You've already made a mess." Kellen tossed more flour at her.

Mira started laughing. She picked up some flour and tossed it back. Soon, flour was flying everywhere, and a haze had settled in the air between them, making Mira want to sneeze. "You'd better help me clean this up, or I won't ask you to the club for our holiday get-together," she threatened, even as she threw more flour at him.

Kellen started throwing Hershey's Kisses now. "Oh no! Anything but that! I just live to wear those penguin suits." He picked up an egg and gave her a mischievous grin.

Mira threatened to clock him on the head with a wooden spoon. "Don't. You. Dare." Kellen put the egg back in its carton. "Good boy. Now you can come with me. Or if you want, you can join us there on New Year's Eve instead," she suggested. "They do a countdown, and we have a DJ and..." At the words *New Year's*, Kellen's face darkened. "What? You can skip the countdown if you want." Something about the expression on his face made her anxious.

Kellen looked down. "I have been putting off telling you this."

"You hate New Year's, don't you?" Mira guessed. "A lot of people do. That's okay. If you don't want to go out, we can stay in." Did she just offer to leave her new black velvet dress in the closet and sit on a boy's couch? She must like Kellen more than she'd realized.

He gave her a small smile. "That's not it, although your offer is pretty cute." He wiped a smudge of flour from her cheek. "The truth is, my dad was on the phone with work all morning. Remember how I told you his job situation wasn't good?" Mira nodded. "Well, it looks like if he wants to keep his job, then we have to move to Detroit."

"Detroit?" Mira said breathlessly. *That is far.*

"His company is moving their headquarters there in

347

January," Kellen explained. "It looked like they were going to keep some departments here, but now I don't think that's happening." Kellen's face was strained. "He said he's going to look for a new job here, but it's still pretty bad out there, so I'm not getting my hopes up."

"But that would mean you have to move," Mira said even though it was obvious.

"Yeah." Kellen looked down at their hands. "Sometime in the next two months if it happens. I'm not sure where that leaves us."

Mira wasn't sure how to react. She could feel her chest rising and falling in time to the mixer she had forgotten to turn off before their flour fight. Her cookie dough was probably soup now.

Connor walked in and gasped. "Mom is going to kill you when she sees this!"

Mom can yell all she wants, Mira thought miserably. The boy she had fallen for was moving thousands of miles away, and this problem was one Mira couldn't fix.

~

Aunt Maureen's color slowly returned to her face as Izzie's dad and Hayden descended the ladder. When they reached the ground, they stared at their handiwork.

"All we need now is to test the lights, and then you can call everyone outside for the ceremony," Izzie's dad said.

"The ceremony?" Izzie repeated.

"Yes," he said cheerfully. "I like the whole family to be here when I light the Christmas lights for the first time."

"He pumps Christmas music in from his iPod and everything," Hayden said. "The whole production gets cheesier every year. One of these days, we're going to get written up in the papers for having the most Christmas lights in Emerald Cove."

"I'd rather get written up in the papers for that than any of the other stuff Grayson Reynolds has been writing," Aunt Maureen mumbled.

Izzie's dad put his arm around her. "Hopefully that is all behind us now. I'm putting a new campaign manager in place who is going to crunch my numbers and see if we can get back in this thing in time for the primaries. If not, then we bow out. Either way we'll be okay."

Ever since Izzie became part of this family, politics had played a part and cost them a price. She didn't know what their lives would be like without a campaign going on. Then again, she worried darkly, what was going to happen if her dad did become a U.S. senator? It was too much to wrap her brain around.

"I'll go inside and get Mira and Connor," Aunt Maureen said.

"Did I miss the annual Monroe Christmas light ceremony?"

Izzie turned around and grinned. Brayden was walking up their front path.

"You know about the Christmas lighting, too?" she asked.

"The whole town knows," Brayden said.

"See?" Izzie's dad said proudly. "People really like our holiday display. Come on, Hayden, let's get ready to fire it up." Hayden shook his head and walked off to test the circuit breakers in the garage.

"Your family's lights are famous for their power surge," Brayden whispered. "Once the Monroes light up, I can barely power my laptop."

"Cute," Izzie said. "Very cute."

Brayden shrugged. "I know I am. People tell me that all the time."

Izzie punched him in the arm. His orange parka took the hit for him. "How did you get here, anyway? I don't see your Jeep."

"My mom dropped me off," Brayden said. "She said to tell you hello." Izzie gave him a look. "Seriously. She is anything but impolite."

"True. Still, I can't believe she dropped you off."

Brayden wrapped his arms around her, and instantly she felt warmer. "We're together now, and she knows that is not going to change."

"Is that an official statement?" Izzie asked. "Because maybe I should call the press and..." Brayden drowned her out by kissing her softly. She could get used to that. "That will work, too."

"Good." He started to kiss her again, and she closed her eyes, thinking about his warm lips.

"Is it safe to come out?" Connor interrupted. Izzie and Brayden pulled apart. "Mom said to wait till you stopped kissing."

Aunt Maureen was standing in the front doorway with a tray of hot chocolate and cookies. She smiled apologetically. "I didn't say that....Okay, yes, I did. I always tell Hayden and Mira not to, um, you know, in front of him." She coughed. "Cookie, Brayden, dear?"

"Thanks, Mrs. Monroe." Brayden took one from the tray and side-eyed Izzie. "These look great."

She needed permission to kiss? Izzie wasn't used to having so many people have an opinion on her dating life. The rules of dating that came along with family seemed to be very different from the rules that came with living with her grandmother.

"Bill! We're all here!" Aunt Maureen yelled. "Come get your hot cocoa!"

Kellen and Mira appeared on the porch behind Aunt Maureen. They were both holding hot chocolate, but they were staring hollowly into their marshmallows. They looked like they were in a trance. Something seemed off between them. Brayden walked over to talk to Kellen, but Mira still just stood there.

"You okay?" Izzie asked her, appearing at her side.

Mira nodded. "Fine."

"Are you sure?" Izzie asked again.

"I don't want to talk about it," Mira said, her voice cracking, "if you don't mind."

"Okay." Izzie grabbed her sister's arm and squeezed it through the down coat she was wearing.

Mira smiled at her sadly and squeezed Izzie's arm, too. They stood there quietly, holding on to each other, as they watched Hayden walk over with a large extension cord.

"Everyone ready?" He looked like a little kid with a very expensive toy.

"Yes, please! I'd like to go inside, already," Aunt Maureen said, rubbing her arms.

"Okay, here we go," their dad announced. He plugged the extension cord into an outlet on the house, and the darkening late afternoon sky instantly lit up like a giant firecracker. The whole family cheered. Mira was the quietist, Izzie noticed.

"Whoa, that really is a lot of lights," Izzie said to Brayden.

"You ain't kidding. See what I mean about my laptop losing power?"

"What do you think, Isabelle?" her dad asked. He looked so pleased with himself.

"The house looks great," Izzie told him.

He put an arm around her shoulder. "Good. I bought several new strands of lights, and I added that giant Santa sleigh on the lawn over there, and a lighted tree on the back porch that you can see from the family room." He hesitated. "I wanted everything to be perfect this year."

"Why is that?" Izzie asked.

He smiled at her. "This is your first Christmas with the family, and I want you to always remember it."

Izzie didn't want to get choked up in front of all of them. "I'm sure I will."

"Excuse me? Is this the Monroe residence?" Izzie heard from behind her.

Her dad looked up, and Izzie felt him stiffen. She turned to see who was there.

Mom?

Her heart felt like it was in her throat as she stared at what had to be a ghost. A woman in jean leggings and a brown leather jacket was walking toward them. She looked exactly like Izzie remembered her mother to look, with her long brown hair and her bright green eyes. *But it can't be my mom,* Izzie told herself rationally, even if the resemblance was uncanny.

"Zoe." Bill said the name so softly that Izzie thought

she'd imagined it. *Zoe? That's the name Grams called me that day in the nursing home.* She felt ringing in her ears.

"Hi, Bill," the woman said. Her eyes focused on Izzie. Her smile was so warm, Izzie could swear she'd seen it before.

"You can't just show up here, Zoe," Bill said, sounding short. "You should have called."

The woman sort of laughed. "Called? After all these years? This couldn't wait. I'm here to see Isabelle."

Zoe smiled softly, and Izzie felt chills. That smile was her mother's.

"Isabelle, I'm your mother's younger sister," she explained, and Izzie felt as if her heart stopped completely, if that were possible.

My mom didn't have a sister, Izzie thought. *Did she?*

Acknowledgments

Winter White wouldn't be what it is without Pam Gruber, who guided me through this next chapter and beyond, and helped make Izzie and Mira the belles of the ball. To the one and only Cindy Eagan: You will be sorely missed, but we will save you a seat at Tortilla Flats, okay? To everyone in the Poppy and Little, Brown family, including designer extraordinaire Tracy Shaw, Ames O'Neill, Andrew Smith, Mara Lander, Christine Ma, and Jodie Lowe: Thank you for all you do.

Much gratitude goes to my agent, Laura Dail. I wouldn't survive a day without you! Thank you also to Tamar Rydzinski for helping me navigate the world.

Rory Cory made me sound smart in the area of politics (any errors are clearly my own), Christie Greff continues to help me be a great swimmer, and Miana Delucia's knowledge of scavenger hunts, pranks, and sorority rules have all been shared while she's riding a bike (quite a feat). Thanks to Alexa DeMartino for zinging the mean-girl comebacks in a way only she could.

Thank you to everyone who is in my corner, including my incredible parents, Nick and Lynn Calonita; Mara Reinstein; Sara Shepard; Elizabeth Eulberg; Sarah Mylnowski; Kieran

Scott; Courtney Sheinmel; Joanna Philbin; Julia DeVillers; and my Beach Bag Book Club cohorts: Larissa Simonovski, Jess Tymecki, Kelly Rechsteiner, and Pat Gleiberman.

And to my family, Mike, Tyler, and Dylan (and let's not forget Jack), for making this whole experience worthwhile.

Turn the page for a sneak peek of
The Grass Is Always Greener

How many secrets can one family keep?

THE GRASS IS
ALWAYS GREENER

a BELLES novel by Jen Calonita

Their shared sweet sixteen party is right around the corner, and half sisters Isabelle Scott and Mirabelle Monroe are ready to cut loose, despite being the daughters of a prominent public figure. When Izzie's estranged aunt, Zoe, breezes into town unannounced, it just might be the change the family needs—or not, depending on who you ask. . . .

An irresistible conclusion to the Belles series.
Available now.

Was Emerald Prep always this big?

That's what Izzie wondered the first day back after her "extended" winter break.

It turned out the most torturous part of being back was not dealing with the clique of girls who thought the universe worshipped them. It was the major upper- and lower-body workout she got racing from building to building. She felt like a Ping-Pong ball as she bounced from her final class to the Bill Monroe Sports Complex to talk to Coach Greff, and then to the administration building for a Social Butterflies meeting. And she had only a half hour to do it all. Thankfully Brayden was up for a jog.

"What did Coach Greff say?" Brayden asked as they took off again. He had been waiting for her outside the sports complex with a bottle of raspberry iced tea and a giant black-and-white cookie. She thought it was sweet that he had brought her favorite snacks to lessen the blow in case her coach didn't forgive her for missing almost a month of swim meets.

But it turned out that Izzie didn't need a pick-me-up. "I'm not suspended," she said with a grin, and Brayden hugged her. "I have to swim in the first heat till I prove myself again, but other than that, I'm still on the team." The first heat was the slowest, but Izzie was just happy she hadn't been benched.

"It seems fair to say you survived your first day back," Brayden said, turning up the corners of his fleece to block the light wind. Gardeners were planting bulbs and cleaning up flower beds along the path students took to the administration building. Spring was coming early in North Carolina, which meant summer weather was right behind it, and being on the beach meant Izzie had something to look forward to.

"I'm not sure if that makes me feel any better," she said, and Brayden looked at her strangely. "Look at them." Izzie pointed out students walking past on their way to club meetings or practices. "Their lives are exactly the same as they were a month ago, while mine's... How am I supposed to act as if nothing in my life has changed when everything has?" Izzie felt like there was a void left inside her by Grams's death and she wasn't sure it would ever be filled.

"You just need some time," Brayden said.

Izzie pulled her phone out of her pocket. She had felt it

vibrate. She didn't recognize the number, and she frowned when she read the text.

ZOE'S CELL: Hi Isabelle! This is Zoe. Sorry for the text, but didn't know if I should call. Would love to see you and talk. Want to meet me for dinner?

No. Izzie hit Delete and put the phone back in her jacket. "Zoe."

"What did she want?" Brayden's voice was full of concern. She loved how protective he could be.

"To have dinner. Like that would happen." Her face was dark. "Did you know Grams asked her to be my guardian before we knew about my dad and she said *no?*"

"Mira mentioned it." Brayden looked uncomfortable. "Did she have a reason?"

"Whatever her reason is, it was wrong." Izzie took a giant bite of cookie. She could feel the anger bubbling up inside her. "She didn't want to help me, and that's all I need to know."

They stopped in front of the administration building. She'd already told her club adviser, Mrs. Fitz, that she would be a little late. Brayden pulled her toward him, his muscular arms enveloping her in a tight hug. "Forget her, then. You have me."

Izzie prayed crumbs weren't all over her lips as he leaned in to kiss her. When he did, all thoughts of Zoe went out the window. "Thanks for that. And the cookie."

"Any time." He turned back to the sports complex for his baseball practice, which started right after the period for club meetings and extra help. She couldn't believe he was doing that walk twice just to spend time with her. "Play nice with the Butterflies," he teased.

Izzie gave him a wry grin. "All but one in particular." She didn't expect the meeting to be in full swing when she got to the classroom, but there was Savannah at the whiteboard, her blond hair so long that it covered her plaid uniform skirt. (Savannah wouldn't be caught dead wearing the optional khaki pants that Izzie had chosen that morning.) Izzie slipped into the back row near Violet and Nicole before Savannah noticed her.

"The Founders Day celebration is coming up," Savannah reminded the group in her thick Southern drawl, "so we really need to put our best Butterflies' foot…er…wing forward. There is lots to do between the parade float and the booth at the street fair, and this is not the time for us to slack off," she practically threatened with a smile on her porcelain face. "That's why I think we need to—"

"Look who's back, everyone!" Violet interrupted. "Izzie's here!"

People stopped paying attention to Savannah and immediately rushed to see Izzie, which really surprised her. Maybe she wasn't the only one who hated lectures from Savannah.

Mrs. Fitz muscled her way over. "It's wonderful to see you, Isabelle," their adviser said, oblivious to the strained smile on Savannah's face. "I was so sorry to hear about your grandmother, dear."

"Thanks." Izzie quickly looked around for a distraction. Savannah's whiteboard presentation, which used green swirly fonts and lots of flowers, was hard to miss. "It's good to be back to help with Founders Day."

"It's a lot of work and it's coming up pretty quickly," Savannah said. She was still standing at the front of the room. "Do you think you can handle it after all you've been through?" She glanced at Mrs. Fitz worriedly. "If Izzie is too distraught, I think I've proven I can manage this event on my own."

Savannah did her best stab at fake modesty, but Izzie wasn't buying it. She was back and there was no way she was letting EC's self-professed princess push her out of the castle that easily. "It's nice of you to be concerned, but I'm ready to be cochair again," Izzie told Mrs. Fitz and Savannah.

Mrs. Fitz actually looked relieved as she dabbed at her brow with a hankie. The only other person Izzie'd ever seen use a hankie was her grandmother. "Wonderful! We're so happy to have you on board again."

"Definitely!" Savannah said with a tad too much enthusiasm. "I was worried about you, but, of course, I could use the help. Lord knows there is enough to do between the parade and the street fair and the annual costume ball."

"Right." Izzie nodded. "Because how would EC survive without another over-the-top ball?" Unfortunately, no one laughed. *They take these things seriously*, she thought.

"You shouldn't joke about the Crystal Ball." Savannah sounded ruffled. She glanced at her yes-men—Lea Price, Millie Lennon, and Lauren Salbrook—for backup.

"It's the highlight of Founders Day," explained Lauren as she played with her hair. "We celebrate with reenactments, historical readings and tours, a parade, and a street fair reminiscent of the ones they had in the eighteen hundreds."

"But none of those things compare to the ball," Savannah added. "The Junior League plans a lot, but the Butterflies are a very important part of the fair and the parade. We cannot mess this up. Founders Day is the most important event of the year."

"I'll let Christmas know it's been pushed to second place," Izzie said. Again, no one laughed, and Izzie started to suspect they all had lost their sense of humor.

"How can Izzie be trusted to help us when all she does is make jokes?" Lea snapped.

Violet rolled her eyes. "Spare us the drama, Lea. How hard can it be to glue glitter on a parade float?"

"Who cares if she knows how to handle a glue gun?" Lauren snapped. "Savannah's been coming up with Founders Day ideas for weeks, and now *she* shows up and acts like Founders Day is a laughing matter." She narrowed her eyes at Izzie.

Everyone started bickering, which was as much a club tradition as saying the Butterflies' pledge. Violet came back at Lauren, and Nicole at Lea, while Savannah moaned to anyone who would listen and poor Mrs. Fitz tried in vain to gain order.

Izzie tried not to smirk. How twisted did a person have to be to enjoy this? Somehow she did. Being back on the swim team, walking across the ginormous quad with Brayden, wearing those oppressive uniforms, and tangoing with Savannah was getting her blood flowing again. Izzie placed two fingers in her mouth and whistled as loud as she could. Savannah jumped.

"Let's all just calm down!" Izzie shouted, and they looked at her. "Savannah and Lauren are right. We have a lot of planning to do, and I've been out of the loop. I shouldn't make jokes when Savannah is trying so hard." Izzie took out a notebook and a pen and motioned to Savannah. "I'd like to hear what she's come up with." It killed her to say some of this stuff, but when in EC, act like an ECer.

Savannah's mouth was open so wide it could have doubled as a fly trap. "Okay, then." She turned to the whiteboard and looked like she'd forgotten how to work it. Finally she clicked the remote, and pictures of Savannah and her friends on elaborate floats filled the screen. Mira was in all of them. "We all know the highlight of Founders Day is the Crystal Ball because the Emerald Cove community reenacts the sounds and styles of 1888, the year Emerald Cove was founded. What you guys don't know is that this year, the Junior League has decided we can attend as guests instead of as volunteers." An excitement Izzie didn't understand rippled through the room. The girls were acting as if they'd never been to a dance before, which was funny considering most of them had just gotten their cotillion gowns back from the dry cleaner's.

"And since this is a year of change, I thought it would be nice if we retired our usual float and fair booth ideas and came up with new ones." The girls mumbled in agreement as Savannah jumped to a new page on the screen that had the word *suggestions* written in pink. "The festival parade and fair need to speak to the time and place of the first Founders Day. So how do you think we should do that?" She looked from one girl to the next.

Izzie leaned over to Mira as Savannah continued to question the group. "*This* is the toiling work she's done while I've been gone?" she whispered in Mira's ear, almost choking on the scent of her flowery perfume.

"Be nice," Mira warned. "You stole her boyfriend and her date to cotillion, and she hasn't killed you yet. Go with it."

Izzie sighed.

"Maybe we could have a bake sale and sell green bagels," Izzie heard Millie suggest as Savannah's smile turned into a frown. "You know, green, like emeralds?"

Lame. What could they do for Founders Day that was exciting but also had to do with EC traditions? Izzie didn't know many traditions yet, but she did remember the ones she had with Grams. Always wear a football jersey on a game day, keep salt in the freezer for luck…. "What if we did something that had to do with our club mission?" Izzie said, out of turn. "Whatever we come up with benefits the same charity that the Junior League picks for Founders Day." Everyone looked stumped. "Founders Day does benefit a charity, right? Every event this town has benefits a charity." Mrs. Fitz blushed.

"Not Founders Day," Lauren told her. "Admission to everything is free, except for the gala."

How is this town not poor? Izzie wondered. "But I thought the Butterflies only took on missions that helped others."

Lea pulled a strand of her too-glossy-to-be-true hair in front of her mouth to avoid anyone seeing her lips moving. "Here she goes again."

"Guys, this is a no-brainer." This was one point Izzie was not willing to negotiate. "We aren't Butterflies if we don't turn a profit to help a charity close to the town's heart."

"How about the EC Children's Hospital?" Charlotte suggested from the back of the room, where she was doodling skirt sketches in her notebook. She was an even newer

Butterfly than Izzie. She'd signed up after cotillion. Maybe that was why she didn't fear Savannah's wrath.

"That is an excellent idea," Mrs. Fitz said, jotting it down in her planner. "What do you think, girls?"

"I like it," Mira said. "We could even do a kids' theme for our booth to tie into the hospital. Like a craft or spin art."

"Spin art?" Savannah sounded less than enthused. A picture of her and Mira in happier days shone bright on the whiteboard behind her head. "How does that have anything to do with our history? If we're going to do this, then it has to tie in with the theme." Even Izzie had to agree with that. "What is EC known for?"

Millie raised her hand like they were in class. "The bay."

"Money!" said Lauren.

"Main Street shopping!" offered Nicole.

"Mining," Violet said with a shrug.

Mining. That gave Izzie an idea. "Have you guys ever seen those carnival mining booths? The ones where you dig through sand to find jewels? The kids love that booth on the boardwalk," she told the group. "I know the guy who runs it, and he charges six bucks for them to fill up a bag with colored rocks." She looked at Savannah. "We could ask for donations to dig for emeralds. Fake ones, but you get the idea."

"My family did that at the state fair!" said Millie. "My brother loved it."

"We could easily make a mining booth," Charlotte seconded.

"I bet Mira could paint a cave on a tent and we could have the mining station set up inside and…"

The room was buzzing with ideas. Everyone had suggestions on how to build a wooden mining station, where to buy fake jewels, and how to find kids' mining hats.

"Girls, this is fantastic!" Mrs. Fitz marveled. "We've made more progress in fifteen minutes than we have in weeks." Savannah smiled weakly, then almost blanched when Mrs. Fitz pulled her and Izzie into a group hug. "With the two of you in charge, the Butterflies are going to have their finest appearance at the Founders Day celebrations yet! Wait till I tell Headmaster Heller," she added. "The children's hospital. Genius."

"Make sure you tell him it was a group idea," Savannah called after Mrs. Fitz as she walked away. "I'm the one who called this meeting!"

"Good idea!" Izzie said drily. "Maybe the headmaster will give you extra credit." Savannah obviously didn't appreciate her comment. When no one was looking, she yanked Izzie out of the classroom. "Hey!" Izzie shouted.

Savannah dragged Izzie around the corner using what could only be described as sudden superhuman strength. When she turned around, she looked like she was going to pull a giant clump of brown hair out of Izzie's head. "And here I was trying to be nice to you because of your grandmother!" she snapped, sounding more like her old self.

Izzie was unfazed. "If that was nice, I'd hate to see you on a bad day."

That comment only ticked Savannah off more. "You and I both know we can't stand being in the same room together," she said, sounding shrill, "especially after all that happened, so why—*why*—do you insist on torturing me by being a Butterfly?"

Izzie shrugged. "I like it. The fact that you hate me being there is a bonus."

Savannah became unhinged in a way Izzie had never seen her. "This is not funny. You stole my boyfriend and turned my best friend against me, and you have half of my town smitten with you." Her voice didn't have its fake sweetness or even its perfected biting venom. "You are *not* taking the Butterflies, too!" Izzie opened her mouth to protest. "I won't let you ruin Founders Day with your ridiculous ideas. We're stuck with the children's hospital," she said as if helping sick kids was the worst idea in the world, "but I know what EC needs, so we'll go with *my* suggestions, because if you don't…"

Izzie didn't do well with being threatened, especially when it was by a girl who had tried to take so much from her already. "If I don't, you'll what? Steal my boyfriend back? You tried that and it didn't work." Savannah looked ready to breathe fire. "You may scare most of the girls in that room, but you don't scare me. I like the Butterflies and I'm staying, whether you like it or not. I have as much of a say as you do."

An eerie calmness suddenly came over Savannah (possibly because others had started to trickle out of the room and she didn't want to cause a scene). She smiled, but the gesture was anything but sincere. "You want a say?" she said. "Fine. You got one. See you at our first tête-à-tête." She started to walk away.

"When is that going to be?" Izzie asked.

Savannah didn't look back. "When I feel like e-mailing you."

Izzie watched as Savannah sashayed down the hall as if it were a catwalk and she owned it.

TWO SOUTHERN BELLES
AND ONE LIFE-CHANGING SECRET.

How many secrets can one family keep?

THE GRASS IS ALWAYS GREENER

novel by Jen C

Two Southern girls. One life-changing secret.

BELLES

Jen Calonita

The secret is out, but the drama is far from over.

WINTER WHITE

a BELLES novel by Jen Calonita

Don't miss **Jen Calonita's BELLES** series!

More juicy novels by
Jen Calonita

Secrets of My Hollywood Life

The fabulous (and not-so-fabulous) sides of being a hot teen star in Hollywood.

Sleepaway Girls

Turns out you can't hide from high school drama—even in the wilderness!

Reality Check

A TV exec picks four normal girls as THE next big thing in reality TV. Can their friendship withstand the spotlight?

Belles

A brand-new series about two very different girls sharing one roof . . . and a secret that will change their lives forever.